There were rules in the cash-for-beauty game. The money held the power. The beauty followed the rules and jumped through the hoops.

THE BRIDE
I knew what everyone would think if they knew the truth about my marriage.
They'd be shocked and appalled. And rightly so.
I was a young, modern, independent woman, and I'd done the unthinkable.
I'd sold my virginity to a spoiled, rich boy. To a stranger who didn't love me.
And yes, I'd done it all for money.

THE GROOM
My bride was as gorgeous as she was unwelcome.
As desirable as she was unwanted.
I wanted nothing to do with her, but that didn't seem to matter exactly the second she got close enough to touch.
I wanted her to hate me more than she loved the millions she'd sold herself for.
I wanted to spurn her, but unfortunately, I wanted to fuck her more.

ARRANGED is a standalone erotic romance.

ARRANGED

by

R.K. LILLEY

ARRANGED

ISBN-13: 978-1-62878-051-2
ISBN-10: 1-62878-051-7

Cover photo by Sara Eirew
Cover design by Okay Creations
Edited by The Word Maid
Interior design by Warkitty Formatting

www.rklilley.com

Give feedback on the book at:
authorrklilley@gmail.com

Twitter: @authorrklilley

Instagram: @Authorrklilley

www.facebook.com/RkLilley

First Edition

Printed in the U.S.A

This one's dedicated to all the people who didn't take the opportunity to kick me while I was down and are still here after all this time. I am unspeakably grateful for your support. Especially you, Chris. Always. I'm positive I wouldn't have finished another book without your inexplicable encouragement of my every random whim, and your willingness to go with me absolutely anywhere at the drop of a hat.

CHAPTER 1

NOURA

I'd memorized exhaustive details about the man standing beside me at the altar, and yet I didn't know him at all.

My groom was a stranger.

His name was Calder Banks Castelo. He was a beautiful spoiled, rich boy, and I'd just handed him the unmitigated power to make my life hell.

I stole a glance at him. He cut an imposing figure in his black tux. He was tall, slim hipped, broad shouldered, and he held himself with a stiff, proud posture. He was carelessly handsome, and he struck me as just the kind of man who was cruel and calculated enough to use that very thing against me.

Our gazes clashed with a direct hit. His eyes were a striking, stormy gray and remarkably dispassionate.

I hadn't had much time to judge him face to face, but so far he was beyond hard to read. He was utterly stoic. Unemotional. Cold. And if I had to guess at reading him just then, I'd say he was disinterested to the point of bored.

I wished I was bored. I wished my lips and the tips of my fingers would stop trembling.

I looked away first.

This is worth it, I told myself firmly. *This is what I want. Wealth beyond my wildest dreams.*

I made myself repeat the words in my head all throughout our stilted ceremony.

I knew what everyone would think if they knew the truth about this marriage.

They'd be shocked and appalled. And rightly so.

I was a young, modern, independent woman, and I'd done the unthinkable.

I'd sold my virginity to a spoiled rich boy.

And yes, I'd done it all for money.

Because let's be real. Money is no small thing. It's a lot of things. Comfort. Stability. Security.

And the amount of wealth I'd just tied myself to was a whole hell of a lot more than a paltry bit of cash. It was—potentially, if I lasted long enough—the keys to an empire.

I was deep in my thoughts, but I didn't miss a beat when I heard my cue. "I do." The words left my lips with no hesitation. Not so much as a catch in my breath. Nerves of steel. Or at least the right kind of nerves to fake it all, and by that point, what was the difference?

I'd been modeling full-time since I was fourteen, which gave me just the right skillset for something like this. I could pose. I could act. I could smile on command. I could fake just about any damn thing.

My hands never stopped trembling but I didn't hesitate, and my voice was strong and steady as I sealed my fate.

His *I do* was indolent to the point of defiant.

I stole a glance at his face. He was looking at me. His eyelids were at half-mast over his stormy eyes. As I watched, the boredom on his face turned to belligerence.

I looked away.

Even now, when our lives were being bound together—till death do us part—I felt like I couldn't stare. Every glimpse I got today was as furtive as all of the past ones I'd stolen during our two neat, obligatory, sterile ten minute meetings.

Roughly twenty minutes together before we met at an altar in front of seven hundred and fifty wedding guests, but I'd gathered plenty of intel during those meetings; none of it good.

To say my groom was not happy about this

wedding was a bit of an understatement. He had to hide it from our wedding guests and the world, but I doubted he'd ever bother to hide it from me. Somehow or someway, his father was forcing him into his.

I wasn't sure what leverage was being used against him, but I had a few ideas, all of them involving his potential inheritance or the lack thereof.

Knowing all this, I didn't assume he'd be any kind of a decent husband to me, and I'd already made my peace with it.

I, on the other hand, had agreed via prenup to be an exemplary trophy wife.

You can get away with more weird shit in a prenup than in any other legally binding contract. Ah, marriage. What a stellar institution. They had slipped some real fun stuff into ours. Including six months of training.

Yes. Training. I'd been remade for this man. Groomed, tutored. Schooled and instructed. I was well aware of what I should expect and how I should perform.

My duties consisted of:

1. Maintaining an impeccable appearance as the perfect trophy wife at all times—I was not allowed to miss a gym or grooming appointment without a very convincing and pressing excuse.

2.   Keeping a team of my father-in-law's choosing on hand for purposes of security, tutoring, training, and general behavioral policing. They were there to keep me in check and keep on polishing me until I shined.

3.   Making intelligent and appropriate conversation with his friends and business associates—I'd become well versed in social niceties and business talk.   I spoke three languages conversationally, and I was to use this skill whenever it was necessary or requested.

4. Attending any functions: galas, balls, parties, soirees, *anything* he required me to. What good was a trophy wife if you couldn't show her off?

5. Spreading my legs and/or sucking my husband's cock whenever he needed a release— I'd been advised that this could happen multiple times a day when he was at home or if/when I was traveling with him.

I was informed (quite firmly) not to ask or speculate about where he put that dick when it wasn't being shoved somewhere inside of me.

There were rules in the cash-for-beauty game. The money held the power. The beauty followed the rules and jumped through the hoops.

I'd been vetted in every imaginable way. IQ and personality tests. Physical exams. Psych eval upon psych eval.

Over the past six months I'd been forged into the perfect combination of untouched and knowledgeable. Chaste but polished.

I'd been made into a jaded, skilled virgin, and from today forward, I existed for my husband's pleasure.

I was jolted out of my fatalistic musings when the officiator pronounced us man and wife.

I turned to kiss my groom. I had to tilt my head back to look at his face. He was very tall.

He bent to me, the corner of his mouth twisting down just the tiniest bit. His lips looked soft and lush, but his eyes were *hard*.

I closed mine, tilting my head up to seal the deal with my very first kiss.

It was the briefest moment, the barest press of lips, but it signaled the beginning of my new life.

I was his now. I belonged to Calder Banks Castelo.

He owned me but he didn't love me.

He never would.

I blinked my eyes open, seeking his indifferent gaze, but he didn't look at me again. His eyes were on the cheering crowd. For them he smiled. They were all his. No one had come for me. Everyone I knew I'd left out of this.

He held out his arm, and I took it dutifully, bestowing my own practiced, demure smile on the crowd of *his* friends, family, and business associates. He walked me out of the church with a confident stride. I had to hustle with my elaborate train and needle point stilettos to keep up.

Hours of photo ops followed. It was one of the more comfortable parts of the long day. Just the kind of thing I'd been doing for years. Modeling. Today I was selling the perfect wedding day of a pretty, rich boy and his innocent eighteen-year-old bride.

It wasn't much different than a day at the job except for my trembling hands and what was to occur *after*.

Still, I sold it like it was an average day at work, and I was getting paid *top* dollar.

It was simple if I looked at it like that. Fake smiles, staged touches, choreographed embraces, and counterfeit laughs.

It was a particularly warm March this year in Portugal. It was a sunny, idyllic day for a beautiful wedding. If it was happening to someone else, someone who wasn't living a lie, I'd have found it charming.

I made a big show of pretending that I was close with his parents, which had been planned beforehand. They were in on the act. In fact, his father had written the play. And both of my new in-laws were good at playing this game. They were used to being spectacles. Used to playing happy for the cameras. They had decades of experience.

His mother, Diana Castelo, was somewhere in her fifties, but no one would have ever guessed it. Science and good genes had her aging like the supermodel she was. She was dark-haired and gray-eyed like her son. She had an ageless beauty and a smile so warm I almost believed it.

She'd been a model, who'd had a brief career in film, which was where she'd caught his father's eye. Their courtship had been high profile and was widely considered to be a romantic fairytale.

His father, Pasco Castelo, had been a lone son born into a billion dollar empire. Looks-wise, he was much like his son. Large, austere, formal, intimidating, and quite handsome. He had black hair, black eyes, and a swarthy complexion. I didn't think he liked me, but I wouldn't be marrying his son if he didn't approve. I'd been told by my handlers that he was quite conservative and traditional, and the fact that I was a virgin and had attended Catholic school had gone a long way toward earning that approval.

Next was the receiving line. It was beyond tedious and seemingly endless. It felt like a test.

I passed. I appeared happy and remembered all of the pertinent names.

The reception itself was less tedious than what preceded it, mostly because of my first taste of champagne.

"Drink up," my groom told me quietly. "You're going to need it."

I'd been ordered by my handlers to drink as little alcohol as possible, and *never* to overindulge, but it was my husband that handed me the flutes of champagne, and his wishes overruled all of my instructions, *always*, so I wound up consuming more than was perhaps wise.

"How's the champagne?" my husband asked me, his cold eyes watching me as I tried my first taste.

I wasn't sure what to think of it, but I told him I liked it because it seemed the appropriate thing to say.

"Have you had it before?" he asked, his eyes becoming more intent.

"No."

"Have you tried *any* alcohol before?"

"No."

He was clearly annoyed. "Well, that's not helpful. You'll be expected to drink at most social gatherings. You have to build up at least a token tolerance."

"I'm too young to drink in the states," I pointed out. We were at his family's estates in Portugal for the wedding, but we'd be living in New York.

His eyes on me were disdainful. "We aren't in the states now, and the types of functions you'll be attending will not require you to show proof of age, so there's no need for you to point it out."

"I apologize," I said, and finished off the glass.

He went from looking annoyed to stiff and almost angry. "Slowly. Don't choke on it."

I hated that I almost apologized for apologizing, but held the words back. Barely.

In spite of that less than encouraging interaction, he nabbed me another flute almost immediately and told me to drink it.

I wasn't sure who'd planned our wedding or reception, but it was obviously someone with luxurious, expensive tastes. The ceremony had been beautiful, as was the gathering that accompanied it. The theme of the day seemed to be white flowers of every kind, threaded through grand crystal chandeliers, strewn across tables, even decorating the walls until it felt like the large room was boxed in with tall hedges of pure blossoms. It must have cost a fortune. Someone had wanted our wedding to impress.

I complimented my husband on his choices.

"You worked with the wedding planner

to pick everything out," he said tersely, voice pitched low. "You've been tirelessly planning this for six months. It's all your doing. Your taste is impeccable." It was impossible to mistake the biting sarcasm in his words.

"Of course. Thank you," I said, following along with the charade. That was what my life was going to be, after all. One big, pretty, elaborate lie.

Dinner was a lavish seven course meal, and I made a point to take a few neat bites of every dish. I was sure it was all up to snuff, of course it was, but I didn't taste anything except the champagne, which became more crisp and delicious with each sip.

My husband handed me another glass after I drained the second one.

My head already felt a bit fuzzy, but in a pleasant way, like the day suddenly had a softer filter on it.

"Do you like to dance?" my husband asked.

I glanced at him. He wasn't looking at me, his eyes trained straight ahead.

Instead of answering the question, which was irrelevant, I listed off all of the dance training I'd been through. It was extensive. I was a well-trained bride, and I wouldn't embarrass myself on the dance floor.

He sighed, knocking back another glass of the dark amber liquid he'd been consuming since we sat down. It was immediately replaced with a new one by a diligent server. I didn't know what he was drinking and I didn't ask. *Do not ask him questions or pry in any way, no matter how innocuous the subject.* That rule was clearly imprinted in my brain.

"I'll take that as a no," he finally remarked, his voice deep with something I couldn't name. "So if you don't care to dance, are you ready to retire?" He met my eyes squarely with that question, and I felt a jolt of something move through me.

I couldn't take his eyes.

I looked away. "Whatever you prefer."

He thrust his glass at me suddenly.

I shook my head, taking the glass because it seemed to be what he wanted.

"It's bourbon. Go ahead. Have a taste."

I took a sip and nearly choked on the burning liquid.

One corner of his mouth quirked up. I'd amused him.

"Not a bourbon girl," he remarked. "It's not for everyone. More champagne?"

"Yes, please," I said instantly. I should have been worried about overindulging, but just then

I'd have done anything to soften the edges of the day.

He sighed heavily. "Well, if you're not dying to go to bed early, we should probably commit to a few rounds of dancing."

He stood, holding his hand out to me. I let him pull me to the dance floor and take me in his arms.

My belly felt warm from the champagne, and his proximity. Being close to him, his hands on my back, mine on his broad, hard shoulders, made it much warmer.

The shaking in my hands and the trembling in my lips had eased. Yay alcohol.

His mouth was near my ear, his voice, oh that voice, was a deep rumble that resonated through my whole body when he spoke. "You might want to smile. These pictures will likely end up in the local paper and, if I know my mother, *People*."

I obeyed, eyes running over his tan throat, his thick, attractively stubbled jaw, his lips. I had to tilt my head back to meet his eyes. He was *very* tall, I noted pleasantly.

I didn't even have to pretend to get lost in his stormy gray eyes. He was just as intent on mine, and he looked different suddenly. Hungry.

My whole body felt heated. My knees went a little weaker, but his arms were holding me so securely that it didn't even slow us down.

I let him guide the dance, following his lead easily. Too easily. The strength and demand of his will issued an almost tangible command over my movements. He was clearly his father's son; a man who was built to command, and I was sure that my body was a paltry conquest for him.

Perhaps this wouldn't be as miserable as I thought. We moved well together. Naturally.

This was a sham marriage, but at least we wouldn't have to fake the chemistry.

"What should I call you?" I asked him. I'd heard family and friends calling him Banks throughout the day, and I knew he went by that, his middle name, more often than not.

It took him a long time to answer, and I realized as I waited for him to speak that my question had somehow shattered the moment, whatever it had been. "Calder," he said stiffly, his jaw setting stubbornly.

Despite mentioning multiple rounds of dancing, Calder deserted me to his brothers after just one.

The doom of my groom's life was that he had too many male siblings. Too many other inheritors to his family's vast fortune. From what I understood, they kept each other relatively honest, for spoiled rich kids. Poor little rich boy

Calder had too many brothers and had to dance to his billionaire father's tune if he wanted a slice of that thick cash pie.

I was Calder's act of good faith.

My husband's five brothers were in attendance. They ranged in age from fifteen to twenty-nine, and I danced with each one.

All five were far more pleasant than my husband. Wasn't that just my luck?

CHAPTER
2

It was a solid hour before I dealt with Calder again. I was sitting back in my seat, and he took his beside me again without a word.

I accepted another glass of champagne. He knocked back another drink then turned, speaking to the server, his voice so low I couldn't catch the words.

The server returned promptly with two tiny glasses filled with dark liquid.

My husband handed me one, clinking them together when I accepted. "It's port. Bottoms up," he said, then polished his off, eyes unblinking on me.

I blushed and looked away.

With a trembling breath, I took a drink of the port. I nearly had to choke it down. It was strong and bitter compared to the champagne, and I felt the effects within moments after finishing the tiny glass.

"It does not go well with champagne," he noted, "you'll have to try it again sometime when you've learned to drink properly."

I didn't know what to say to that, so I just nodded. If drinking port was part of this arrangement, then it went without saying that I would do it and just about anything else that was required of me. Worse than this was undoubtedly coming. I'd suck it up and deal with whatever I had to.

I'd been working nonstop for years, and with the cost of living in New York, combined with my fair share of misfortunes, I'd never managed to do much more than keep myself afloat.

After today, that was all going to change. I'd traded my body for wealth beyond my wildest dreams.

It's a small price to pay, I told myself, yet again.

The wealthy of the world did what they liked. Their money made the world go round and solved all of their problems, while the little people took what life gave them, weathering whatever punches fate decided to lay on them with no anesthetic to soften the blows or means of protecting themselves. I knew that firsthand.

I had a chance to switch from the latter to the

former, and I was taking it with both hands and eyes wide open.

Yes, I had sold myself. Yes, it was my choice. The price: my freedom. The benefit: I'd just been upgraded from lowly peasant to one of the elite of society.

Now I was set for life. Untouchable.

Except for my husband. He'd get to touch me however he liked.

"What a joke, huh?" Calder said suddenly.

"Pardon?" I asked, looking around for what he might be talking about.

"All of this." He waved his drink around at the room. I realized that he, like myself, was feeling the alcohol. "My father thinks that if I spend even a little bit of time with you I'll grow to *like* you and then he'll feel justified for this whole mess. He thinks I'll get *attached*." His words were crisp with a bite, his eyes square on me and *contemptuous*. "To someone like *you*. He's delusional. As if I could ever care about a gold digger. Let me be crystal clear with you. I'll never be reconciled with this marriage. I'm never going to care about you. I'll perform when I have to, but never forget that while you chose this, I did not."

I felt my temper flaring but didn't respond. It was a hard thing to do, but if there was anything

I needed to get used to in this arrangement it was holding my tongue.

Shut your mouth and cash the check, I told myself.

My husband seemed done with his tirade. We engaged in a minor stare down that was only halted when a heavy hand settled on both of our shoulders.

"You need some air," my father-in-law's voice spoke from behind and above. "A stroll through the garden will help. Son, take your bride for a walk."

We both rose like puppets on strings.

"Of course, Father," Calder said tersely.

He took my arm and led me out of the room. "Meanwhile a photographer will follow behind to capture candids of us," he muttered, but only after we'd left his father's earshot.

I glanced at him. His father's words had been an order, of course, not a suggestion, and I wondered what was going through his head. I'd done nothing but learn his habits and preferences for the last six months, but I wondered what leverage his father had over him, and how it could have led to him saying yes to a marriage that so clearly disagreed with him. It struck me just then that I really was married to an *absolute* stranger.

It was beautiful out, the night lit with stars. I made myself look past my nerve-wracking day and take in the sight.

He stopped suddenly, his hand at my elbow halting me with him. He pulled me around until we were facing each other, his tall form bowed over me.

Standing that close to him was a strange assault on my senses. It was disconcerting. A shock to my system. His proximity had a keen, visceral effect on my body. It wasn't necessarily pleasant, but it wasn't unpleasant either. It was stimulating. His powerful frame radiated a heat and intensity that I felt down to my bones. I'd never experienced anything like it. His hands held my hips firmly and the contact branded itself through me. I wondered how long I'd feel his hands there after he let go.

"Let's get this over with," he drawled, his head angling and lowering.

I raised my face and he sealed his mouth over mine.

I was shocked at how soft his lips were.

It took a belated second for my reaction to hit me, but when it did, it was surprising. I liked the taste of him, the feel of his mouth. I wanted more.

I didn't even realize I was moving as my hands

buried themselves in his silky black hair, gripping him to me as his tongue stroked lushly against mine.

One of his hands stayed at my hip, gripping me closer, and the other rubbed up and down my back, petting me like a cat.

I heard a soft moan, and realized in some distant part of my brain that it was my own.

His mouth didn't stop, eating at mine as he tugged my body inexorably closer to his, until we were plastered together. I felt his hardness digging into me, and instinctively it made me tense up and shrink away.

A low rumble vibrated in his chest a beat before he tore his mouth away.

I couldn't quite catch my breath.

He cursed under his breath, his head falling back, eyes aimed up at the sky.

I didn't know what to do or say, so I just stood there, catching my breath.

Eventually he spoke. "Let's go back inside. I could use another drink."

So could I.

"You may head to your quarters," he said from his spot beside me at our table. It was sometime later, but my mind was still back on that kiss. It had been brief, but I felt it still. My lips were tingling. "I'll join you soon."

My heart tried to pound its way out of my chest, but I hid it well.

I looked at the woman mentioned, my expression deceptively bland. I'd taught my face to lie first and best.

I hadn't seen Asha since she'd overseen my preparations before the wedding. It had been nice to spend a few hours without having to set eyes on her face. Without being directly under her thumb. I'd tried my best to forget that she even existed. She was my *handler*, and she relished the duty as much as I despised it.

"Of course," I said pleasantly, rising.

I followed Asha on unsteady legs to my quarters.

Bits of lingerie were laid out on the large bed. It was all a filmy white lace that didn't look like it would cover anything essential.

The perfect wedding night ensemble for a bought and paid for virgin.

"Put it on," Asha ordered brusquely. "You know what to do. Do *not* make him wait."

I faced her. She was a petite, spare woman, with curly black hair that she perpetually tamed back into a severe chignon. Her features were harsh but even, her skin pale. Her eyes were big, dark, and mean.

"Okay . . . You can go," I told her blandly. "I don't need you anymore."

She gave me quite the look for that bit of impertinence. "You think those vows changed anything? You think when he fucks you that you'll have more power? You don't know him at all. He'll get bored with you in one night. You're a pretty bauble that he'll forget about the moment you're out of his sight. You're a possession to him. You'll always be just as much of an employee to this family as I am. In fact, you're more expendable. I outrank you. Never forget it."

I knew she wasn't wrong. I *knew* it. That didn't mean I didn't *hate* it. I vowed, not for the first time, to gain at least enough favor with my husband to get her fired. "Do you want to lecture me, or do you want me to get ready for my husband? I'm not changing until you leave." It had been a long day and I was not in the mood for her shit.

She gave me one last murderous look and left.

I knew I'd be paying for that bit of sass later. Asha always gave as good as she got with interest.

It was worth it.

CHAPTER
3

I'd been told repeatedly that my new husband was good in bed. During my training, it had been repeated so often and with such unquestioning authority that I'd come to resent the knowledge, but by no means did I doubt it.

Even amidst all of that certainty, though, I was too nervous to be optimistic enough to think that would mean that my wedding night could be good for *me*.

It wasn't good. Not even a little bit.

He came into the dark room and started undressing without a word. He was holding a drink, the dark liquid sloshed out of it as he set the tumbler less than gently onto the nightstand.

I'd put on the beautiful lingerie that'd been lain out for me and gotten into bed, beneath the covers, hoping he wouldn't turn on any lights.

More to hide my vulnerable expression even than my body.

I got half my wish. He turned on the light in the attached bathroom, but not in the room. It was still too much. I could make out his face in the dim light, so that meant he could see mine.

One mercy, though. He barely spared a glance at my *face*.

He undressed with swift, angry movements. I fixed my eyes on the canopy above the bed.

He pulled back the covers and paused for a long time, never saying a word. I could feel his eyes on my body.

I was trembling, and I knew that he had to see it. My fingers and lips always trembled the most. I bit my lips and clenched my fists.

"So I suppose we're doing this," he said coldly.

"I suppose so," I replied, infusing all the calm I could shove into the words. "They would probably know if we didn't."

I stole a glance at his face. His heavily lashed, stormy eyes flashed at me with all kinds of hostility. "Of course they will," he drawled. "Didn't they tell you? They're planning to check the sheets in the morning, and if that weren't enough, they're sending a doctor to examine you, to make sure I've properly fucked you."

I hadn't known that. They'd examined

me beforehand—you didn't pay millions for something like that on word alone—but I hadn't known about the checkup after.

"I've never had to fuck on command before," he added bitterly.

"Me neither," I replied.

"I would hope not. I hear my father paid a small fortune for a virgin bride."

I swallowed hard, my face turning red. This was even more humiliating than I'd envisioned. His antipathy, or at least this level of it, was unexpected. My voice was measured and composed as I replied, "He did."

"Well, let's see if you're worth it," he said, something ugly growing in his voice.

I tried to keep my breaths even and measured, but a few ragged puffs escaped in spite of me.

"Spread your legs," he ordered gruffly.

Awkwardly, I did it. He cursed. My lips trembled. I dug my nails into my palms harder. The lingerie that had been laid out was an intricate white lace teddy that just happened to be missing a crotch. He wouldn't even have to undress me to consummate our union. How terribly convenient was that?

"My God, they didn't miss a trick, did they?" His question was incredulous and rhetorical, and there was an unmistakable bite to it.

They were the team that had transformed me into the perfect fake wife, and no, they hadn't missed a trick.

"They did not," I agreed.

Without another word he climbed on top of me, his elbows braced on either side of me, his hips slipping between my thighs.

My eyes fixed on his throat as he lined his hardness up against my softness.

"Are you absolutely sure this is what you want?" he asked, voice harsh. "It's not too late to back out. You can still walk away without a scratch."

I nodded.

It wasn't enough.

"I want to hear you say it," he gritted out, his breath hot on my face. "Tell me that you are absolutely sure that this is what you want."

"I'm absolutely sure that this is what I want," I replied, enunciating every syllable clearly. I was proud that my voice held barely a quiver.

I was so dry and tense, he had to spit on his hand and rub it on himself to ease inside. He looked so angry and put upon while he did this that I shut my eyes and kept them that way. I bit my lip until it bled as he made his way in. It hurt much more than I'd imagined, a sort of pointed, raw pain that just felt *wrong*.

He reached the barrier inside of me, jarring against it. He didn't stop, not at all. He didn't so much as pause as he hit the barrier he'd paid so dearly for. Swearing roughly, he tore straight through it. The pain was sharp and sudden, a mean pinch deep inside.

Without hesitation, he drove in to the root. It was too much to take. Too hard, too big, too deep. I was stretched to the limit. Beyond it. I squeezed my eyes shut, biting my lip as I worked through my discomfort.

"Jesus fucking Christ," he gritted through his teeth. "I'm not going to last a minute."

Then he started fucking, pounding into me with relentless, focused precision.

At least he was right. He didn't last a minute. He cursed as he started to come. I opened my eyes and our startled, raw, vulnerable gazes clashed.

I wished then that I could've known him just a *bit* better before the wedding. Not that any amount of superficial pain would make me regret the whole arrangement, but I just wished we could have warmed up a bit more first. Enough that I could've perhaps felt comfortable enough to ask him—not to stop, of course—but perhaps to slow down.

It was mortifying to even think about, but I'd

hoped he would in some way seduce me first. I hated myself for looking at it so emotionally, for even *thinking* something so pathetic, but I couldn't push the thought away.

Even at the height of the discomfort though, I didn't consider actually asking for anything like that. That added humiliation would have been far worse to me than the pain. Pain came and went in life. Shame *lasted*.

One blessing was that it was mercifully quick. He'd been right. He didn't last a minute. About thirty seconds (I counted) after he fit himself inside me and begun to move with *thick*, heavy thrusts, he started coming, jerking in and out roughly, his breath hitting my ear with soft, energetic little puffs that quickly devolved into low, rough curses.

I wasn't at all sure if the curses were directed at me or himself. Neither seemed like a good sign.

He didn't linger, dragging himself out of and off of me like I'd burned him, or he was afraid that I would trap him in if he hesitated. I sucked in a breath at the brutal rawness of that swift, long, slick pull.

I kept my eyes shut, but I felt him staring at me after, looming over me and watching.

I don't know if it was the unaccustomed

liquor, the hostility I felt from him, or the nerve-wracking debacle of the day all coming to a head, but I suddenly and horrifyingly became quite ill.

Oh shit, I thought in horror as my body turned on me completely.

I almost threw up right there on the bed. It was a very close thing.

I used my last ounce of energy to drag my limp form off the mattress, stumble across the room, stagger into the bathroom, and dive for the toilet.

I didn't even close the door behind me. I vaguely realized that I was having the most mortifying, graceless moment of my life in front of my new husband as my body started heaving, bile rising up.

This wasn't what he or his father had paid for, but I had no control over my body as I started retching, emptying out the contents of my stomach.

My marriage had been consummated, and my wedding night couldn't have gone worse.

I tried to hold my hair back from my face, clear of the vomit, but I quickly gave up even on that. All of my energy reserves were being used to stay upright, aiming the deluge, and holding myself directly over the toilet bowl.

I threw up until there was nothing left, and

then I dry heaved for a good long while after that.

When I felt reasonably confident that my stomach was done rebelling, I grabbed my toothbrush, dabbed toothpaste on it, and started brushing. I shrugged and contorted my way out of my delicate teddy with one hand, tearing it to pieces in the process. When I was finally free of it, I walked directly into the shower.

I turned the water to scorching and stood under it. It was burning my skin, but I barely felt it. Somewhere along the course of the night I'd gone a bit numb.

I kept brushing my teeth until I'd gotten the bad taste out of my mouth, and then started in on my hair. I shampooed it three times before it felt clean.

I'd never been so wrung-out-tired in my life, but I stayed under the spray of water and washed every inch of myself, over and over. Each time I thought, *this time I'll feel clean*, but it never happened.

Eventually I just sat down on the tile until the water ran cold.

A long time later I shut off the faucet and dragged myself out of the shower.

I wrapped my hair in one towel, and my body in another. I desperately wanted to avoid the bedroom, but I *needed* sleep, and the bathroom floor just wouldn't do.

I was relieved to find that at some point he'd at least closed the bathroom door for me.

Hopefully it had been before I'd started throwing up.

I opened the door with dread, not wanting to face him.

I was unutterably relieved to find him gone. I walked on shaky legs over to the huge bed.

I winced when I saw the blood and other fluids staining the spot where we'd lain on the mattress, but I quickly moved on. I wrapped myself in every blanket I could find and curled up on the clean side of the bed.

I don't even remember trying to fall asleep. My head just touched the pillow, and I was out for the count.

I had no romantic illusions when it came to my husband. Yes, he was handsome and rich, but he was no prince charming. He would never love me. He would never care about me at all.

He owned me. I was property that was expected to behave in a certain way, and if I somehow showed I was not worth what he'd paid, I was positive that he'd promptly cut his losses and walk away.

Even so, I was surprised when I woke up completely alone after our wedding night.

It didn't register at first what that meant. I

assumed he'd just slept in his own room, which had been a relief after such a stressful day.

But he hadn't just left my room. Or even the property.

He'd left the country. I didn't see him again for a month.

CHAPTER
4

It was a busy month, which was for the best. When I *wasn't* busy, my mind went back to *him*, and our disaster of a wedding night. I'd relived, rehashed, obsessed over every moment of it.

It was a completely useless line of thought. A waste of energy. He'd done his duty—swiftly, badly—I'd humiliated myself and he'd left without a word.

I hated that I thought about him at all, because I knew that he sure as hell wasn't thinking about me.

He hated me on principle, and he fascinated me in spite of myself.

So I tried to keep myself active, and my mind occupied with other things. That wasn't too hard.

Two days after the wedding I was moved into

a luxurious apartment in midtown Manhattan and began modeling again.

I loved that apartment. I loved that it felt like *mine*.

I'm possessive. I like to feel like the things I covet belong to me. Everybody does to some extent, I think. Everyone goes *I have this little café I love* or *you have to try my yoga studio* or *check out my apartment*. Those phrases are a lie in cities like New York. Nothing belongs to anyone who isn't filthy rich. Not even a little bit. Everything is shared, but now I was one of the elite few who got to share *less*. It was great.

Even better—my six month marriage-training hiatus didn't seem to have done any harm to my career.

Just the opposite, in fact.

I now had more callbacks than hours in the day. My high profile wedding to the handsome son of a famous billionaire had drawn the hungry attention of the fashion world. Everyone wanted to work with the gorgeous, rich boy's fresh new bride.

One thing surprised me, though. How hard it was to swallow the pill of going from hunger to gluttony practically overnight.

I'd wanted this kind of success for so long. I'd been working my ass off for it for *years*. Achieving it—especially the reason I was achieving it—was not nearly as satisfying as I'd always pictured. Sure, there was some gratification to be had from my newfound success, but more than anything I found contentment in the fact that it was keeping me very, very busy.

Life was all about perspective, and I was trying my damnedest to appreciate my new position in spite of the things I'd done to reach it. To appreciate the fruits of my labor with all of the enthusiasm my cynical young heart could muster up. Thanks to my new status, modeling now came with a sense of security. All of my extravagant living expenses were taken care of by my absent husband, so every cent I earned went into *my* bank account, which was already very well padded due to the details of our prenup.

I told myself that was a good thing. Just what I'd been going for. The relief of that took a lot the stress out of the job, that and the fact that I was instantly treated with more deference now that I was Mrs. Castelo.

I'd always loved fashion, enjoyed dressing up, and for the first time I enjoyed the photo shoots, had fun with landing ad campaigns, and walked new runways like I didn't have a care in the world. See? Untouchable.

Well, I did have a few cares. One of which was

that it felt strange to be a married woman and not feel married at all. Even when I attended events that I was invited to as Mrs. Calder Castelo, I went sans husband.

I obediently went to Mass every Sunday with the Castelo family minus one very significant presence. I sat every week in the pews amongst his charming brothers, but his charmless self never bothered to come.

I'd also agreed to attend many designated galas in our contract, and I even liked that part of our arrangement, but I'd always assumed I'd be attending on his arm.

I was used to being alone. I'd been completely independent since I was sixteen, and had taken care of myself from a young age, but it still felt strange to be doing everything as a newly made Mrs. *by myself.*

Well, that wasn't precisely accurate. I never actually went *anywhere* alone. Two men escorted me. Their names were Chester and Vincent.

Vincent was my driver. He was a short, small-framed bald man with a trim gray beard. I never asked but I guessed that he was in his fifties. He was quiet but polite to a fault. He had a rare but kind smile.

Chester was my bodyguard. He was built like a bear, massive from his head to his size fourteen feet. I was far from short, and I almost always wore heels, and still he towered over me. He had to be at least a few inches taller even than my tall husband, though I'd never seen them standing side by side, due to the fact that I never saw my husband at all.

He had a generous mane of fiery orange hair threaded through with streaks of gray. He usually wore it in a man bun though he refused to call it that. It matched his perfect beard and handlebar mustache. He wore thick framed glasses that complemented his sweet brown eyes. If he was a little younger, I'd have pegged him as a hipster.

I knew that Chester was forty-six because he mentioned it often, usually when he was lamenting about his various aches and pains.

It was Chester that went with me everywhere. He was good company, so I never minded. He was a hell of an upgrade from Asha the Dour.

Though Asha hadn't gone far. She didn't escort me around as diligently as Chester, but I still had to wake up to her presence in my life every single day.

It was almost a month in and my routine was down pat.

I woke up at six a.m. sharp. My alarm went off and I was up and in the shower within one minute.

God forbid I'd hit the snooze button and have Asha in my face calling me a sloth.

From the shower, I slipped into a robe and padded to my extravagant, sunken living room. I contemplated my view of the bustling, sleepless city while I awaited my team meeting.

Yes, I had a team. My husband was absent, of course, but I never lacked for company.

Chester brought me coffee, and I accepted it with a grateful, "Thank you."

For convenience as well as protection, Chester and Vincent were housed in the apartment directly next door to mine.

When we were home, however, they could more often be found hanging out in my living room.

"You're welcome, Duchess. Good morning."

"Good morning, Chester," I returned with a smile. His nickname for me had appeared early on in our acquaintance, and it never failed to amuse me. I hadn't married into any kind of title aside from *rich man's wife*, but I was apparently close enough to nobility for Chester. It didn't hurt that he always infused warm affection into the word, making it an endearment.

I liked Chester. A lot. He made it almost bearable to deal with Asha.

Think of the devil. At just that moment Asha's

dour form swept into the room. I turned from the view to meet her severe gaze.

"A robe is hardly decent attire to be wearing in front of men who aren't your husband," she opined harshly, her mean eyes raking over me.

"It's the crack of dawn, and I'm standing in my own living room," I returned coldly. "I'll wear whatever the hell I like. Just get started with today's schedule, please."

I was well aware that Asha saw me as nothing but an insignificant eighteen-year-old piece of fluff who'd married for money. I'd made the mistake of deferring to her early on, as I'd been told that her job was, in essence, to manage me, and that I should listen to her. After the wedding I'd changed my strategy with her. I stopped putting up with all of her shit in silence. I didn't have the power to fire her, but I also didn't have to bear her insults quietly.

So far, standing up for myself and speaking my mind had given me no consequences from her higher ups, which was fortunate, because I had no plans to stop.

"Before we get to the schedule," Asha began imperiously, completely ignoring our rude exchange, which was typical, "let me go over yourcall backs and bookings. You got the Stuart Weitzman job. Congratulations." She said every word with utter disdain. "That will be very high profile. They tell me this will be an extensive amount of work for you starting as early as next week. You also received an offer to do the YSL fragrance campaign, but I'm still working with them on the schedule for that. It consists of a long video which shoots in Paris, and they want you for an entire week. That will be tricky but it's being worked out."

I didn't see why it mattered if I was gone for a week, since I never saw my husband anyway, but I didn't say anything. This was the arrangement I'd agreed to.

"You booked four more runway shows," Asha continued, "and the offers are already coming in for fashion week, and let me tell you, that's going to be a messy affair. I'll clear it all with Mr. Castelo. What else? Oh yes. About the lingerie campaign you were offered. Your husband and the VS people finally came to an agreement. A limited one. You can take the job, but he sees each garment before you model it. They agreed to let him give the thumbs up or down, which was unexpected, but there you are."

Vincent, my driver, walked into the room just then, nodded his head at me and sat down without a word.

"As for today," Asha continued searching

through her notes, not so much as sparing him a glance, "at noon sharp you have a luncheon with your mother-in-law and the board for the Castelo Foundation. That will last several hours. Next on the list is a photo shoot at four. You'll have to go there directly from lunch. You'll need to come home and change for a gala tonight. Your in-laws will be attending. Try not to embarrass them."

"Is that everything?" I asked. I already knew that all of the free time left after that schedule would be spent either eating or working with my personal trainer.

"Since you don't have anything until noon, I've scheduled you for two hours with your trainer starting at six forty-five. I see you already showered, but you'll just have to shower again when you're done. Hair and makeup will be here at nine thirty to prep you for the luncheon."

I just nodded. I'd expected as much as soon as I'd seen that I'd been allotted significant windows of free time.

I left to get dressed, hoping that was the end of my morning interaction with Asha.

No such luck. She followed me into my closet. "The paparazzi will be at your gym, so make sure you're presentable."

I'd assumed as much. My workout was a very

public affair. If you had a shiny new wife that worked her ass off at the gym on a daily basis, why not make the best of it and show her off?

Paparazzi set up camp at the entrance to my swanky health club, taking pictures of me coming and going.

Sometimes that was the extent of it, and other times they were allowed to take shots of my actual workout through the window, as though I was an unaware subject and they were my voyeurs.

I treated it as any modeling job, using my best angles to make sure the photos would at least be flattering.

"I don't know if you saw the . . . rather distasteful photos they published of you two days ago. The ones featuring your . . . derriere."

I rolled my eyes. Of course I'd seen them. They'd caught me in the middle of a grueling round of dirty dogs and taken full advantage. I'd assumed the whole thing was staged, as everything in my life was.

"Your husband was rather . . . agitated by those, so he would prefer it if you could refrain from doing that specific exercise in front of the ground level windows."

"Do you think that was *my* idea? Reggie tells me how and where to train, and I do it. Take this up with him and whoever keeps calling the paparazzi every time I leave the house."

"I believe your husband has already done so, but in case he missed any details, you should have a mind toward displaying yourself in a more ladylike fashion at all times."

Asha relaying my husband's messages to me was nothing new. We never communicated directly.

It was almost laughable. I didn't even have his phone number. Our *people* communicated for us.

"You want me to work out in a ladylike fashion?" I asked, an edge to my tone. "That's not a thing, Asha."

She turned bright red with temper. "I don't understand," she spit out furiously, "how he could have found someone without one *ounce* of decorum or *class*. What he saw that made him choose a low-born *slut* like you I'll *never* understand." She was nearly foaming at the mouth by the end of her tirade.

Ah. There she was. She tried her best to stay frostily composed, but this was the hateful bitch who'd trained me to be the perfect, soulless, mail-order bride. "You should know better than anyone that I'm not a slut," I told her calmly. "You were in the room when I was examined for a hymen."

"A hymen that you *sold* like a common *slut*."

"I doubt common sluts get paid as much as I did," I told her deadpan, purely for the purpose of riling her further. She wasn't going anywhere, and neither was I, so I figured I may as well make the best of it and give as good as I got.

I made a shooing motion with my hand. "Now move along. This *expensive* slut would like some privacy while she gets dressed."

"As if you care," she shot back as she moved away. "I've seen you at those *vulgar* modeling jobs of yours, changing like common *riffraff* for anyone to see."

I rolled my eyes as I walked to the large dresser that was designated for my workout gear.

There was a binder on top, and it was open to a page spotlighting a blush pink workout ensemble that my personal dresser had designated for today's exercise session. I carried the notebook across the closet.

Closet was an understatement in every way. The room that held my rich wife wardrobe was twice the size of my last apartment.

My stylist was organized to a fault, which made getting dressed simple but in the most complicated way.

I had to follow the numbers she'd typed next to each piece of clothing to its matching rack.

The top was a tiny, strappy pale pink sports bra that was numbered with a 67. I went to the bra section of the room and nabbed it off a hanger.

I set the binder down on the nearest surface, slipped off my robe, and pulled the skimpy top over my head.

When it was fastened I moved on to don nude thong panties, then skintight, stretchy burgundy leggings.

Even my shoes and socks matched. I thought about complaining when I saw that the maroon running shoes that'd been picked out for me had a hidden wedge in them, (because who worked out in heels?) but I decided it wasn't worth it. If I was going to throw a fit about something, it wasn't going to be shoes.

A trip to the gym took minimum prep, even for me, but I still took care with my appearance, treating it like another type of photo shoot. Just another part of the job.

I arranged my thick, streaky blonde hair into a practiced messy topknot, then moved onto makeup. I applied it lightly, going for natural with a rosy glow.

I had just finished applying nude lip-gloss when I heard my name being called.

"Yes?" I called back.

"Ready, Duchess?" Chester asked, voice

pitched to be heard across the apartment.

"Always," I replied, grabbing my workout bag and heading for the door.

CHAPTER
5

Just a few days after the wedding I'd seen the wedding photos.

I found them in magazines. Several spreads had been set up in advance across varying publications.

No one had bothered to show them to me. I had to troll the internet for them just like everyone else.

They were breathtaking. The photographer was talented, the setting was sublime, and we were very convincing—the gorgeous billionaire madly in love with his fresh, barely legal model bride.

Snapshots of what must have been a perfect day; it had all been immortalized for the world to see.

Us kissing at the altar. That brief, obligatory

pressing of lips looked like so much more. Our romantic stroll out of the church and through the gardens, the sun on our smiling faces. His mother kissing my cheek with affection. His father putting his arm around me, welcoming me to the family.

Me huddled with four bridesmaids I only knew on paper.

Him laughing with his groomsmen like it was the happiest day of his life.

Another kiss set amongst white flowers, another brief, perfunctory contact frozen into a hopelessly romantic moment in time.

So many flawless snapshots of a spectacularly gorgeous lie. And God were they convincing.

I spent hours looking at them all. Days probably.

The photographer even captured the moment when Calder had me try my first taste of champagne and bourbon, my new husband smiling at me fondly. Oh how charming it all looked.

The shots of our first dance did indeed end up in the paper. I looked flushed and nervous and like I couldn't take my adoring eyes off him. He looked like he wanted to devour me whole.

The photographer had even caught our 'private' kiss in the garden under the stars. I stared at that picture the longest.

That kiss had stayed with me. I'd thought

about it way more than I wanted to. Just thinking of it made my lips tingle. I'd forgotten it was even a photo op.

What a fool.

Well, it'd worked out. Looking at that passionate embrace, even I felt myself starting to wonder if we felt something for each other. Or at the very least question what I felt for him.

I shook off the foolish thought. That just went to show the power of sexual chemistry and fantastic photography.

"We're here, Duchess," Chester called from the front seat of the Benz. He switched between riding shotgun and keeping me company in the backseat, depending on whether or not we expected to be photographed when we exited the vehicle. When we were being photographed, he rode up front because he thought it appeared more professional and intimidating to anyone who might so much as think about messing with me.

He'd very considerately explained all of that to me the very first time we'd met. He tended to do that; to explain all of the reasons for his methods. It was one of his most stellar qualities, and he had quite a few.

The car stopped, and Chester got out. He opened my door for me and handed me out of the car, took my gym bag, then put himself between me and the half dozen photographers that were waiting to pounce.

I wasn't remotely annoyed with the paparazzi (of course I wasn't—they'd been called there by someone on my team), but I didn't answer any of the questions they flung at me on my short walk from the car to the glass doors of my gym.

My personal trainer, Reggie, was there waiting, letting me in before Chester or I could reach for the handle. We greeted each other briefly and got to work.

He set me up on a treadmill facing the front windows. On display. The entire front room had been cleared out just for me. I was getting used to it. Again, I treated it all like a modeling gig. It made my life feel more productive that way, as opposed to feeling like I was constantly being hounded and overexposed.

It was all about attitude, I told myself.

I walked and jogged for forty-five minutes. It was one of the most pleasant parts of my day. Chatting with Chester and even Reggie had a lot to do with that. Endorphins helped, as well.

I could forget for a moment that I'd made some drastic life choices. I could forget that I'd traded my freedom for financial security. I could forget that I hadn't spoken to my stranger husband in nearly a month.

My wedge tennis shoes were surprisingly functional for a workout. Not comfortable, perish the thought, but not excruciating either.

"Asha told me you were retaining water, but I don't see it," Reggie was telling me. "Regardless, I sent some recipes along to your chef that should help. They don't taste great, but it's always worth it to stop the bloat, right?"

I tried not to grind my teeth. This was how Asha got her digs in. Of course I wasn't retaining water, and my diet was already down to eleven hundred calories a day. Now it would also be unsalted and bland for two weeks, at least.

I didn't correct him, though. And I wouldn't react to the shitty, flavorless food. Reactions were what Asha wanted, and I'd become very adept at depriving her of the more satisfying ones.

Reggie had clearly gotten the message about me doing dirty dogs in front of the windows loud and clear. After my cardio he made a point of taking me to a different room when I did all of the ground work strength training that might be taken in a suggestive way.

I finished my workout with laps in the gym's large lap pool. I still couldn't get used to the fact that they emptied the large room out just for my use, but I did appreciate it. There was something so serene about having that large, echoing room all to myself. It was the most peaceful part of my day. I always drew it out as long as I could.

I showered again, then headed back to the apartment, where I surrendered myself to my beauty team.

I was well turned out in a lightweight Helmut Lang white shirtdress that showed off most of my legs. Some creative cutouts at the arms gave a modern twist to the cold shoulder trend. A tan Burberry belt added structure to the silhouette of the dress, and nude Stuart Weitzman stilettos kept the overall look understated and classic.

I buttoned the shirt down low enough to show a fair amount of cleavage, and left my collar bare of jewelry. In fact the only jewelry I wore were a pair of thin gold hoop earrings, and my wedding ring.

Bernice, my makeup artist, gave me a fresh faced fine tuning.

Gretchen, my hair stylist, smoothed my thick golden hair into loose, tousled waves.

When my luncheon prep was finished, I headed out the door again, Chester in tow, or vice versa.

Lunch was pleasant enough, if a tad boring. My mother-in-law was actually a pleasure to deal with. She was a friendly, somewhat familiar face in a crowd of strangers. I was always relieved when I found out she'd be at an event.

She was a lovely woman, a former model and actress who kept herself in fighting shape to this day. Her thick dark hair was pulled back into a complicated chignon that might have aged another woman, but only brought out her impeccable bone structure and pale gray eyes. God, what a beautiful family.

She wore a fitted cream dress that made it look like we'd coordinated our wardrobes.

For all I knew, we had.

We embraced, kissed cheeks, and sat down to pretend to eat for three hours. What we did while we pretended to eat was plan out a star-studded auction benefitting the Castelo Foundation, a charity my mother-in-law herself had started twenty-five years prior. It was a multi-functional charity, but it focused largely on funding cancer research.

"I'd love to see a runway show attached to this," she told the board. "Now that we have two supermodels in the family, why not use that? Having us walk a runway together for our family charity would surely get the event more press. Are you game, Noura?"

"Of course," I responded instantly.

I actually valued this part of my fake new life. While I doubted my presence did anything to add to the already well-established charity, it at least *felt* like I was contributing something. It felt purposeful, and I needed purpose.

From the luncheon I went directly to a photo shoot. I modeled thigh high tan suede boots and a cream cashmere sweater for several hours, went home, prepped for a gala, and was off again.

Rinse, repeat.

Busy, busy, busy. Just how I liked it.

I ran into my husband's parents at the gala. We were photographed together, and I wondered when the headlines would start focusing on the fact that Calder Castelo's fresh new wife was never, ever with her husband.

"You look lovely, as always," my father-in-law told me after our photo op was finished.

He always looked so severe that even when he was being complimentary it came off coldly. Still, I thought I sensed a change in him. I wasn't sure if it was wishful thinking, but I thought he was warming to me a little more with each meeting.

"You flatter me," I told him shyly.

"Not at all," he remarked back, his deep complexion turning a tad darker as he flushed. "It's me that's flattered to be escorting the two loveliest ladies at the ball.

If I didn't know better, I'd think my father-in-law was starting to like me. It didn't necessarily run in the family.

CHAPTER
6

I was backstage at a runway show. It was the following afternoon. I was mid-prep, scrolling through the blasted fake wedding pictures yet again—I'd saved them on my phone—when my cell screen flashed a message at me.

Asha: Your husband is taking you out to dinner right after your show. Change quickly. Don't keep him waiting.

I just stared at the words for a beat, trying to work through my shock.

I hadn't even known he was in New York. Last I'd seen (from tabloids) he was working hard and probably playing harder in London.

And.

Could he not have messaged me himself? Did

he even *have* my cell number?

I texted Asha back.

Me: Got it. Is he attending the show?

Asha: How should I know? Just be ready.

I modeled two looks—both white, which seemed to be a theme in my jobs since the wedding. I suspected my husband or his family was behind that. A reminder to the world that I was his shiny new bride.

I walked the catwalk, but didn't have the nerve to search the crowd for him. I knew it would throw me off, and what did it matter? If he was there, it was only for appearances.

After the show I left my hair and makeup as is (why waste it?) and slipped into a paper thin, cream, silk frock with a short hem and a plunging neckline that accentuated my cleavage and left little to the imagination.

I assumed by my outfit that my stylist had known about my dinner plans before *I'd* been informed.

It was a distracting dress for a distracting evening. I wondered if it would do its job.

I was just stepping into a pair of soft pink,

feathered Jimmy Choo mules when I felt a shift to the air in the room.

I knew what had done it, I'd felt that energy before, but instead of looking for Calder, I stole a glance at the other models, all in various stages of changing.

It was comical how they all just froze, as though they'd scented fresh blood in the water.

I wondered how many of them my husband had fucked. He had a reputation for one night stands with leggy models.

Finally, I looked. It didn't take me long to find him. His large, masculine presence dominated the room.

Our gazes clashed. My heart stuttered in my chest, and he smiled like he was happy to see me.

It was a disarming sight, to say the least.

I heard the quick shutter of multiple professional cameras going off.

Ah, there it was. There was no reason to set a stage without an audience.

I smiled back.

He started toward me, and I wondered if I was supposed to meet him halfway. I was too disarmed and he moved too quickly, so the decision was taken out of my hands.

It was all I could do to devour as many details of him as I could before he was on me.

I hadn't seen anything but pictures of him since the wedding. I'd almost forgotten he was even better looking in person. More gorgeous than my biased memories had allowed me to hold onto. More refined and polished than any model in the room.

More memorable and overwhelming. He was dressed in a dark three-piece suit and he was bigger than I remembered. Even in a room full of tall divas his stature demanded every eye.

His dark hair was pulled back from his face. It brought out his stark, perfect bone structure. Gorgeous like his mama's. Works of art, that family. And his eyes. God, his eyes. Pale gray set against his deep olive skin, with enough intensity in them to make my knees go weak.

He had something in his hand, but I barely had time to note it before he'd wrapped his free arm around my shoulder to pull me in for a hug.

"Hello, Mrs. Castelo," he said gruffly.

I looked up at him. "Hello, Mr. Castelo."

I barely got the words out before he bent, putting his lips to mine. He laid one on me.

I knew it was a perfunctory, for the cameras kiss. A kiss from the movies.

I fell for it anyway.

One of his arms was lightly wrapped around my back, his hand gripping my waist. His other hand reached up to lightly cup the back of my head. He dipped me a little. His lips were every bit as soft as I remembered. It lasted only a minute, but I was gripping his lapels and forgetting where we were long before that.

He pulled away faster than I wanted him to, straightening, his calm eyes studying my face.

He didn't look like he'd been up to anything at all.

I had to school my face back into composure, make my slack mouth shut, and blink my eyes out of their daze. It took some effort.

"I see you're doing quite well," he said with utter composure. "I brought you something." He placed a large velvet box into my hands.

I didn't respond for a long moment, just staring at the gift that was obviously jewelry. "What's this?" I asked.

"A gift for my beautiful bride. Open it."

"Open it *here*?" I asked, and instantly wanted to snatch the words back. Of course here. He was clearly staging a moment for the tabloids.

"Yes." His smile didn't reach his eyes, but I was sure it would photograph just fine all the same. He knew what he was doing. He'd been raised in a beautiful, rich, famous family. Photogenic didn't begin to cover it. Live-action-video-genic more like.

I turned my attention to my gift. I had to mentally brace myself to give the right reaction for the cameras.

This is just another modeling job, I told myself as I opened the box. *Just gush like you're doing an ad for Tiffany's.* Hell, maybe I'd land something with them next. This could be my audition.

Laid out inside was a dazzling diamond and yellow stone-studded choker, earrings, and bracelet.

I knew this jewelry. It was his mother's topaz collection. It was worth a small fortune to the tune of one point two million dollars.

It was not a gift but a loan. I knew this because our prenup was quite detailed about such things. If or when we divorced, I would not be keeping any of the family jewelry, regardless of how publicly he gifted it to me.

I took all of this in in mere seconds, and then let out the appropriate response, gasping loudly, my free hand flying to my throat. My excited eyes flew up to his, and I smiled with as much fake joy as I could muster. "Oh my God, Calder! They're beautiful. You shouldn't have."

"Of course I should have," he said with a charming smile. His eyes were on me, but I knew our audience had his full attention. I was a less significant accessory to him than this jewelry, though at least I could reassure myself that after our wedding night I was worth considerably more. "It's our one month anniversary. Didn't you realize?"

I had not. Was that why he was taking me out? It must've been, but I couldn't imagine him flying into town just for that. Not after a month of no contact.

I recovered from my surprise quickly. "Of course!" I said with loud enthusiasm. "How could I ever forget such a monumental milestone?"

He smiled, and it was a bit crooked, only one corner of his mouth quirking up. It was less perfect than his usual straight, polished, fraudulent smile.

I'd genuinely amused him with that over the top bit of nonsense, I realized.

Why did that make my chest warm with pleasure?

"On every one month anniversary I'm going to drape you in new jewels, wife."

"You spoil me, husband."

"Happily."

When it came to backstage model antics, I'd always been one of the quiet ones. I didn't cause a lot of drama, or make a lot of waves. I tended to keep to myself. I saw it as a job that I wanted to retain, so I tried to be professional, always. I was friendly with the girls who weren't terrible, though I'd never made any close friends in the business. I had too hard of a time opening up and being vulnerable to let anyone close, so I tended to come across a touch distant or even cold. It was a defense mechanism, but it had never won me any popularity contests.

Becoming Mrs. Castelo had shifted all of that in a subtle way. I received more attention now in general, both good and bad. Opportunism battled with jealousy for what I ran into more often. There was a different winner from one day to the next.

Jealousy was definitely going to win this day, I saw as my eyes swept over the crowd on my way out of the large, crowded room.

Calder had me pulled close against him, his arm around my waist possessively.

I smiled in as friendly a way as I could muster at every single pair of eyes that met mine.

Who could guess how long this sham of a marriage would last? I didn't know any of the other women well, but I didn't want to be a social pariah when all was said and done.

I was ushered swiftly from the backstage to a car. It was my usual Benz, Vincent driving, Chester working security.

Silence reigned on the way to dinner. It wasn't

a comfortable silence. It was awkward with the knowledge that I didn't know the first thing about so much as attempting to interact even casually with my husband.

And he didn't touch me once we were closed inside of the vehicle. In fact he sat as far away from me as the backseat would allow.

Why did I feel a sharp pang of disappointment about that? The feeling was followed swiftly by irritation with myself. Foolish girl.

"When did you arrive in New York?" I asked him, my tone polite and impersonal.

He didn't spare me a glance, his gaze trained out the window.

"Not important," he said, his tone steeped in finality.

Chester glanced back briefly from the passenger seat to give me a sympathetic frown.

That was my first and last attempt at conversation in the car.

We arrived at Beautique in Midtown. I'd never been there, but I'd heard of it. It was a notorious hotspot for celeb sightings. I wasn't surprised. Our entire evening together was obviously for publicity.

Calder dismissed my driver and bodyguard casually as we exited the vehicle. "We no longer need your services for the evening, gentlemen."

"But what about security for . . ." Chester said, caught off guard. Keeping me safe had been his sole purpose for the past month. "Should we at least wait to take you home?"

Calder eyed him. It wasn't friendly. "I think we'll muddle through. You're dismissed."

Chester got back in the car, his reluctance unmistakable in every line of his body.

"He likes you," my husband remarked dispassionately as we made our way inside. He was leading with a hand on my arm. We walked side by side with me stealing glances at his face.

I shrugged, self-conscious of his eyes studying me closely. "We spend every second together, and he's good at his job, so of course we're friendly."

His mouth twisted into an ugly smile. I looked away and didn't look back even when he spoke, his voice harsh.

"I suppose it's second nature to you, wrapping poor schmucks around your little finger. I hope you know I'm impervious to that. To you."

That stung enough that I couldn't hide one gasping shocked breath. God, he was mean. "I'm aware," I managed to volley back at him in a smooth tone.

"Good."

We were seen to a booth the instant we walked in the door. It was early so the restaurant was quiet enough that we could speak quietly to each other and still be heard.

We sat side by side, hip to hip.

A glass of white wine was immediately placed in front of me.

I thanked the waiter, taking a deep swallow of the cold, refreshing liquid.

I'd gotten somewhat better at drinking since our wedding night. Not great, but much improved.

"Used to wine now?" my husband asked me.

I didn't look at him, but he sounded amused. "Yes. At least, I think so. I try to have exactly two glasses at galas, no more, no less. It seems to work well."

"Sounds wise."

I watched his large hand as he lifted his own glass of bourbon on the rocks to his lips.

"How was London? Are you finished with your business there?" I asked him, trying to keep the conversation going. Trying to create a conversation in the first place. Also, I was curious.

"Forget about me," he said coldly. "Tell me about you. How are you settling in? Do you like the apartment?"

"Of course," I said automatically. "It's very nice, thank you for asking."

What else could I even say?

It's perfect but also too extravagant. A lot for one person. It has the biggest, loneliest bed I've ever slept in.

Nope. I wouldn't be saying any of that.

"And you have everything you need?" he asked.

"Yes, thank you," I replied.

"If that changes, please don't hesitate to inform Asha. She'll make sure it's taken care of."

I almost laughed. I almost rolled my eyes.

Of course he didn't tell me to inform him directly. God forbid I'd be able to communicate with my own husband.

Keep it together, I told myself. *This is what you signed up for. This is what a marriage of convenience means.*

It couldn't have worked out better, I reminded myself. *You don't want to spend time with him either. Just smile, take it, and count the money.*

Honestly, when I'd decided to put myself into the infamous Bride Catalogue, a husband who ignored me had been the best-case scenario. I needed to remember that.

It was such a simple plan, so why did it become so much harder to execute cleanly as soon as my husband came anywhere near me?

My mother used to say that it was good to have conflict inside you. I'd never fully understood what she meant, but apparently I'd taken those words deep into my heart. Even when I got exactly what I'd wished for, I still wasn't content.

"Will you be in New York for long?" I asked him.

"I'm not sure. It depends on work. How's the modeling going?"

"It's going well. The work is steady. It keeps me busy. It's fun. I'm getting so many offers that I'm turning down jobs. That's a refreshing change."

Was I rambling? I didn't know what to say to him. Nothing seemed right. I didn't want to offend him, and I certainly didn't want to bore him, but he was set so firmly against me that I felt like I was destined to do one or the other.

"Well, that's good," he said, sounding disinterested enough to fall asleep. He knocked back the rest of his bourbon, and the waiter reappeared, taking his old glass and setting down a fresh one.

He downed that one in under thirty seconds. Our waiter had another one ready before Calder could set his glass down.

"I don't have a two drink rule," he remarked sardonically when he was brought a fourth drink some short time later.

I'd gathered as much. I sent him a sideways smile, but he wasn't looking at me. He was looking down at his glass as though contemplating whether he should finish off another round.

It couldn't have been clearer that he'd rather be anywhere else. Unsurprisingly, our first 'date' was not going well.

I hoped that it was too late for him to send me back with a full refund.

CHAPTER
7

"Have you received an invitation from Millie Bancroft?" he asked.

Our first course had arrived, and I was stirring my roasted carrot salad around, pretending to eat it. He'd already cleared his plate.

I wasn't expecting the question, so I had to think about it for a moment before I could answer. "Um, yes. She invited me to a girls' night a few weeks from now. She and some friends are going out dancing at a club." I looked at him as I spoke, assuming he'd tell me not to go. The nightclub scene was hardly a good look for his wife.

He shrugged, still staring at his drink. "You should accept. She's the wife of one of my closest friends. She was your maid-of-honor. It would be nice if you two could at least pretend to play nice with each other."

I hadn't expected that. The more time I spent with his circle of friends, the more apparent it would become to them that our marriage was a sham. I'd assumed he'd want to avoid that.

"How would I even get into the club?" I asked him. "I did look it up when I received the invitation. It's twenty-one and over."

"God, I keep forgetting about that." He said it like he found it somewhat horrifying. "How old *are* you, anyway?"

"You don't know how old I am?" I wasn't offended. I was surprised. Eighteen on the dot cost extra in the Bride Catalogue.

"I know that of course you're legal, but I don't remember the details. To be frank, I don't know anything about you and I don't want to."

I stared. "You don't know *anything* about me?" I repeated back, trying to unwrap his words.

"That's what I said," he enunciated slowly. "I picked you out of that catalogue because your face made my dick hard. Aside from that, I didn't really care enough to learn more."

I hadn't known that he'd been the one to pick me out. I'd more than half suspected that his father had done it.

Why, out of all of the awful things he'd just spouted at me, did my mind only focus on that little detail?

And moreover, why did I feel a keen little unwanted thrill at the knowledge?

I realized after a time that he wasn't going to speak again.

"So all of the rest . . ." I began haltingly. Genuine confusion warred inside me. "The IQ tests. The psych evals. The background checks. The compatibility tests. The medical exams. Your people researched me down to who I sat next to in third grade."

He shrugged, his eyes raking over me in a cursory manner then darting away. "I didn't care about any of that. That was my father. The *whole thing* was my father's doing. I didn't want to be married. I still don't. I was lucky I even had a say in what you looked like. It was nearly a deal breaker."

That added up, I supposed. That didn't mean it wasn't a little jarring to hear it come directly out of his mouth. And with *such* contempt.

"Back to your question," I said slowly after it was clear he was done speaking. "I'm eighteen."

He flinched, looked away, then back. His eyes caught on my drink. He picked it up and set it decisively away from me. "You're too young for that," he muttered.

"So about Millie and the over twenty-one club," I said. "I'll tell her no."

He didn't roll his eyes at me, but I could tell it was close. "If you think you're going to get carded, you haven't been paying attention," he bit out, obviously annoyed. "Let your security handle those kinds of details, and tell Millie yes."

I almost answered with a sarcastic, Yes, sir, but restrained myself. Barely. "Alright," I managed to get out instead.

Our main course arrived, and silence reigned again for a time.

I took a few bites of my branzino while he devoured his grass-fed beef.

"You don't like it?" he asked me when the waiter took our plates away.

"It was great, but I filled up on salad."

"No, you didn't," he contradicted. "You had two bites of that salad then pushed it around your plate for ten minutes."

"I don't want to go over my calorie count," I leveled with him. It was the truth. I had a photo shoot in the morning that involved skin-tight clothing.

He'd been lifting his fifth bourbon to his mouth, but he stopped mid-motion at that, setting his glass back down. "You hardly ate anything."

I turned my head to meet his eyes and tried to keep my expression perfectly blank. "I'm on a strict diet. For the job." He may as well get used to my eating habits.

"What you ordered wasn't enough food to feed a rabbit, and you barely touched it," he sounded angry, and a little drunk. "Define *strict*."

"I'm restricted to eleven hundred calories a day," I admitted.

"*Eleven hundred calories?*" he asked incredulously. He didn't understand what models had to do to stay coat-hanger sized. He knew how to fuck them, but clearly had no clue how to feed them. Eleven hundred actually wasn't even bad. It was generous. That was the maintenance number. When I was actively trying to lose weight, it could vary from nine to as low as five hundred.

Eventually I nodded, studying his face.

He looked more pissed than usual for some reason. His lip curled up in distaste and he tossed his napkin on the table. "Well, that nonsense is coming to an end. I'll speak to your chef."

I stiffened. If you messed with a model's diet, you messed with her career. If he hated our arrangement enough that it might make him want to sabotage me that would be a good way to do it. I almost stood up to him, but I forced myself to back down. Whatever he tried to do about my diet, it wouldn't matter. I'd act amenable, pretend to eat whatever was put in front of me, move the food around my plate, etc., but if it went over my calorie count I just wouldn't consume it. I was used to denying myself. Rigid self-control was an old friend of mine.

He called the waiter over. "My *wife*," he stressed the word in a certain way, like he found it so distasteful and oppressive that he wanted even strangers to know it, "would like dessert. A praline mousse roulade, I think. And I'll have another round. Thank you."

I waited until the man left before I said quietly, "I can't eat that."

He sent me a less than friendly look. "Indulge me. My father forced me to fly all the way here from London just to take you on a *romantic date*, so I think you can go over your calories for one night."

Dessert arrived, and with a sigh I did indulge him, all the while calculating how much more time I'd need on the treadmill to compensate for the extra calories.

We didn't speak for a time, and the quiet between us felt less awkward/hostile and more charged. Charged with something interesting.

Yes, he hated me. But he'd also kind of admitted that he was attracted to me. In spite of myself, I was kind of attracted to him too. It was hard not to be. He was as beautiful as he was mean.

What's he thinking? I wondered, studying him as I took a very tiny bite of my decadent dessert, stirring the rest of it around on the plate to make it look smaller.

God, he's gorgeous, my fuzzy buzzed mind told me.

I wanted to touch him, to lean into him. *Mostly* I wanted to read his mind.

That last one was out of the question, but what would he do if I tried out the first one? If I just reached over and brushed that oh so touchable lock of silky dark hair back from his temple?

That was the problem with him. He seemed *touchable* no matter how untouchable he may actually be. Well that was *one* of the problems, another being the fact that I was married to him and he couldn't stand me.

He turned his head, his eyes meeting mine with an intensity I couldn't place. He grabbed the spoon, scooping up a small bite of mousse. "Do you want a taste?" he asked, the words succinct.

My mind wasn't on the dessert as I exhaled a breathless, "Yes."

He put it to my lips. Our eyes stayed locked as I sucked it clean.

When I was finished, he drew the spoon away. He set it down beside the dish, watching me closely. I couldn't look away. His eyes had a way of holding me captive. I resented it, but it made me feel *alive*.

"Look at that. We barely know each other and here I am feeding you."

I drew in an unsteady breath, then another.

He'd had his elbow on the table between us, keeping up a clear barrier. As I watched, he moved his arm, placing it along the cushioned seat behind me.

"Come closer," he told me softly.

I leaned toward him, bringing my face near to his.

"Closer," he said, voice softer still. His eyes were on my mouth.

The arm along my seat back wrapped around my shoulders, tugging me closer still until our lips were a breath away from touching.

"Do I need to spell it out for you?" he breathed the words right into my lungs and yet somehow the words were remarkably dispassionate. "You're supposed to kiss me now."

I couldn't refuse, but moreover, I didn't want to. Closing my eyes, I pressed my mouth to his. I thought it would be brief and neat. Quick and clean.

It was not. It was pure filth.

His mouth on mine was not fit for public.

At first it was just that brief soft press, our lips rubbing together, back and forth, back and forth. The briefest teasing contact. It didn't matter. It was enough. It was too much. I took in a deep shuddering breath for a beat.

I wasn't even sure how a kiss could be so indecent when he was barely touching me.

His delectable lips locked on mine and it was an R rated attack on my senses. R made slow progress into X as his soft lips slid over mine, his tongue licking deeply into my mouth, drawing my tongue out to play with his.

I was inexperienced at kissing, to say the least, and I'd certainly never expected a kiss like that. I had no defense against it. I went a little limp against him, breathing him in, letting his presence overwhelm me.

He tasted like alcohol, but sweeter, the flavor of *him* mixed with hard liquor. He stroked his tongue against mine in a rhythm that brought to mind another, less pleasant act.

He hooked one of my legs over his knee beneath the table. It was hidden under the long white tablecloth, but I was still aware of the fact that this brought my already short skirt up high on my thighs, exposing my panties.

He pulled away slightly.

I watched his face, trying to read his intent.

His palm was on my thigh, rubbing and moving up at an alarming rate.

CHAPTER
8

"I'm curious," he said, his hand never stopping its distracting movement. "Tell me something. I was told that you were *trained,*" he stressed the word, "for the marriage bed. What does that even mean?"

"How much would you like to know?"

He mulled it over, his eyes enigmatic, his big hand rubbing and kneading at my inner thigh. "Give me all of it."

"I know how to get myself ready for you. Or how to . . . compensate in the event that I want something . . . like that . . . and you don't feel like tending to me." The words were a jumbled mess and I could barely look at him after I said them.

He stared. "Are you saying that they taught you how to masturbate?"

I couldn't look at him, and my whole body

felt flushed with embarrassment and something else. Something warm and shameful. "Among other things, yes. With my own hands, and with toys, though I couldn't put anything but my own fingers inside of myself. Of course I had to keep the proof intact until our wedding night."

"Of course," he agreed with utter sarcasm. "So what did you learn? About your own pleasure. Where do you like to be touched?"

"The usual places."

His brows rose. "Be more specific, please."

I wanted to sink into the floor, but I didn't hesitate. This was a test, and I had studied hard for it. "My breasts, nipples, and clit, of course. My inner thigh—"

"Like where I'm rubbing right now?" he interrupted, squeezing my leg.

I sucked in a sharp breath. "Yes."

"Keep going. Where else?"

I had to clear my throat before I found my voice again. "That spot you're hitting, all the way up to my groin. And my back is particularly sensitive. My nape, shoulders, and the spot where my shoulders meet my neck."

"You touched your own back?" There was a bite to the question.

"A masseuse was brought in to find all of the spots I couldn't easily reach."

"Who was it?" he asked.

"Excuse me?"

"The masseuse. I'd like a name."

Something in his voice caused the strangest bit of dread to creep up my spine, but I answered promptly. "Thomas. I don't know his surname."

"I see," he said hotly.

"What do you see?" I asked.

"They had another man put his hands on you to get you ready for me. I don't see how that would help you pleasure yourself, and *I* certainly never agreed to it." Temper, temper. "But continue. What else do you think is expected of you?"

"When you come to the—our bed, I'll lie on my back, put my heels on the mattress, and spread my legs for you. I'll offer to suck you off. I was also instructed that, whether it hurts or feels good, I'm to endeavor to keep a pleasant expression on my face. If prompted, I'll talk while you're doing it. I was told that you like dirty talk when you're inside a woman."

"My God. I know I've said it before, but I'll repeat, they didn't miss a trick, did they?" His question was incredulous and crisp with a bitter edge.

I got the distinct impression that he found the notion as distasteful as I did.

"They were very thorough," I reassured him. I had no doubts that if they thought I'd somehow disparaged their efforts, they'd make me pay for it.

"I wanted them to make sure you understood what to expect from me, but I didn't realize they'd be quite so . . . zealous about it. Well, at least you won't harbor any illusions about this arrangement."

"I will not," I said succinctly.

He was silent for a time, then, "You said you'd offer to suck me off. Did they teach you how to do that too?"

"Of course."

"Of course," he repeated slowly and sardonically. "Tell me what they taught my obedient little *wife*."

The alcohol was helping. I wasn't sure I could have managed any of the words without it, but a cursed blush still crept back up my cheeks as I spoke, "I don't excel at deep throating . . . I have a gag reflex . . . so I've learned to suck hard and use my hands a lot . . . with a very firm grip . . . to make up for the shortcoming. I'm told this can be just as satisfying for you if I do it right."

"And what exactly did you learn on?" he asked, and there was a cut to each word. "They didn't bring in a real cock to teach you, I hope," he drawled and I could hear something ugly under his quiet voice.

Why is this making him angry? I wondered.

"No, of course not," I answered finally, then listed off the various objects I'd practiced sucking on for his benefit.

I was too self-conscious to steal even one quick glance at him.

He fingered the edge of my panties. "Don't worry, wife. Tonight is our first date, and mandated though it is, I feel like *tending* to you."

I squirmed, looking around. He wouldn't. Not in public. Would he?

"No one can see my hand," he assured me, voice pitched very low. "I'm going to get you off. Right. Here."

A bone deep shudder seeped into me. Not a shudder of revulsion either. It was one of *delight*. What was wrong with me? My eyes shot to his. My cheeks were flushed. I was well and truly scandalized. "But we're in *public*."

"We are," he agreed. "This is a very crowded place, and it's getting more packed by the second. You're going to have to behave yourself. Contain your reactions. Keep very quiet. Do you think you can do all of that?"

I shook my head. "I have no idea."

"Are you telling me they didn't train you for

this?" I thought he might have actually been teasing me, but I was too alarmed to try to figure it out.

"They didn't."

"Well, try your best, okay?"

"Okay."

"Give me your mouth again," he coaxed in his deep, cold voice.

I did and I couldn't stifle my gasp as his finger pushed past my panties and reached the lips of my sex. It was disorienting. And arousing. He rubbed me there, his touch feather light, his lips firm and warm and *delicious* against mine.

One of my hands gripped the table, the other holding onto the lapel of his jacket as I sucked at his mouth, hyperaware of every minuscule movement of his hand beneath the table.

He drew his mouth away just far enough to speak. "You're wet," he pointed out, his tone full of something warm and addictive, and started kissing me again.

Abruptly he jammed a finger into wet me. I gasped into his mouth.

He held it deep inside me, stroking at the most addictive spot. With a whisper soft touch, his thumb started softly toying with my clit.

"You're not as cold and dispassionate as you appear," he remarked with ironic dispassion.

I didn't respond with words. I couldn't. His actions were monopolizing all of my oxygen. I panted against him like a bitch in heat.

He spoke into my mouth, his voice rumbling low and rich, at last showing the weakness of his desire. "You're not cold at all. You're burning up, and tight enough to hug my finger. Do you have any idea what that does to my dick?"

I was still incapable of answering. Liquid heat flooded me. He'd started pumping in and out of me with concise, measured strokes. He kept his thumb against my clit, the pressure against it ebbing and flowing with every measured drive of his hand.

He stroked his tongue into my mouth. Instinctively I sucked at it. He worked it in and out until it was fucking into me just like his finger.

With a sexy little groan, he plunged a second finger into me and started stroking at that spot deep inside of me again.

By then I didn't care that we were in public. I didn't care if anyone noticed what was happening under the table. I wrapped both arms around his neck and drew desperately at his mouth.

He fucked me with his relentless fingers, working in a steady rhythm until I felt my eyes rolling up in my head, the whole world going fuzzy as my climax took me in heavy, melting waves.

He kept his fingers deep inside of me, pulling back from our kiss to watch my face.

My eyes opened, and it was a struggle, but I made myself meet his gaze as I came down from my sensuous high. My sex was still rippling around his fingers.

It was quite gratifying to see his hard face go a little slack with desire.

"Good girl," he murmured in a hoarse voice. "Sometime very soon I'm going to taste you. I'm going to bury my face in your pussy and memorize every last little dip of you with my tongue."

He caught himself, features hardening again almost instantly into their normal cold, stoic mask.

It didn't matter. I'd seen it. He wasn't as immune to me as he'd pretended to be all night. The realization made me bold.

He started tugging his fingers out of me. The delicious drag of them made me squirm as I said, "Is that all?" It felt like I was blushing from head to toe, but I was proud of myself for getting the words out.

He studied my face, his nostrils flaring. "You know what? I don't think so. We're not taking it that far tonight. The last time we fucked it didn't turn out too well, if you'll recall. It was obligatory, thanks to my controlling father. I think I'll train you better before we try that again."

I blushed harder, but for different reasons. Was that the reason I hadn't seen him for a month? Was I flattering myself to assume that he even needed to *have* a reason not to see me?

I made myself meet his eyes and speak clearly. "It was my first time. And I'd never had that much to drink. I wasn't sick because of *that*."

He almost had his fingers out of me, but at that he pumped them back in to the hilt. "Well, that's a relief."

I gasped, ready to go all over again. "Please," I whimpered.

He took my mouth briefly, his fingers dragging free of me. He spoke against my lips, but his words did not match the softness of his touch. "Show's over. It's time to go. Put yourself together. Straighten your dress. Once your legs are steady, go to the bathroom and fix your hair and makeup. And for God's sake," he continued harshly, "try to wipe that fuck me look off your face."

I pulled away from him with deliberate slowness. It was an effort not to flat out recoil.

There was a knot of sick tension in my stomach as I did as he'd instructed, putting my dress to rights, grabbing my bag, and walking with as much dignity as I could muster to the restroom.

My mind was spinning with the way he went hot and cold on me with every step I took away from him, his last words echoing in my mind. Talk about mood swings.

I took my time in the powder room, smoothing out my hair, touching up my makeup.

I wondered what went through his head. I wondered if I really wanted to know. He probably just found me foolish and irritating. It was a chore for him to even *pretend* to go on a date with me. And the one time we'd had sex . . .well, that hadn't endeared me to him much.

I exited the restroom with an optimistic mind toward turning it all around. There wasn't much I could do about his affections or lack thereof, but the attraction between us was so real and visceral that it had its own pulse. We could at least make that one thing between us live up to the potential that was obvious to even no-experience practically still a virgin me.

Or at the very least, we could work toward making it an upgrade from our wedding night.

I was determined that this time when he left me, it would be with better memories than watching me rushing to the toilet and throwing my guts up right after he finished.

When I returned to the table, he was scowling at his phone.

"Something wrong?" I asked, sliding back into the booth beside him.

He instantly put his phone away, features smoothing into neutrality. "No. Are you ready to go?"

I nodded, rising again.

He didn't touch me as we moved through the crowded back dining room to the more crowded lounge. Even when we made the short trip from the front door to the backseat of a limo, there was no contact at all.

I thought that was odd. If this was all for show, why was he being so visibly distant in such a public place?

I studied him as the car started moving and realized that, going by his demeanor and expression, he was deeply upset about something. I wanted to ask him again if something was wrong, but made myself refrain. He'd made it very clear that he didn't care for those kinds of questions from me.

I glanced toward the front of the long cabin. The partition was up. I didn't even know who was driving. Was it his regular driver? Did he have a regular driver? I assumed he did, since I'd been assigned one, but it was only a guess. I knew next to nothing about his day to day life.

"Let's find out what you've learned," he broke

the silence. The words were so unexpected that I didn't respond at first. I only stared at him. He motioned me closer until we were nearly touching.

Abruptly he opened his slacks, pushing them down to expose the thick, heavily veined length of his shaft. Without another word, he cupped the back of my head and pushed it down.

I was shocked but I caught on quick. I took him in my mouth. I rubbed my lips around his thick tip. It felt like velvet. I eased him slowly deeper. He was larger and harder than I was expecting. No wonder it had hurt so much our first time.

I cupped him in both hands, caressing him from root to tip. I liked the feel of him, warm and eager and overwhelming.

He groaned. The sound made me want to purr.

I took him deeper, inching my lips up his silky length, laving him with my tongue as I worked him deeper. It was heady, the taste of him, the feel of him rearing against the roof of my mouth. I liked it. I was already primed from what he'd done to me in the restaurant, but I knew innately that performing this act would have turned me on on its own.

Well wasn't that some ironic icing on my precariously arranged cake?

I didn't realize I'd paused midway down his length until I felt him move under me. His hips churned. He held my head still, his erection thrusting up at me impatiently.

With a hungry moan, I took him as deep down my throat as he would go. I started moving on him, my head bobbing slowly up and down, my hands gripping, sliding, stroking, getting mixed up in my saliva until it was a smooth glide. My hands worked his base while my mouth sucked and stroked at him from mid-shaft to tip. I worked into a well-balanced rhythm, sucking him as deep as I could and jacking at him firmly with my hand. I was so involved that a few times my lips met my own hands and I was caught off guard at the contact.

I paused when he gripped my hair suddenly, rolling my eyes to glance up into his face.

Holy shit. I actually liked the half-crazed look in his eyes, the way the skin around his cheekbones was taut with strain, his telling grip.

"Fuck," he muttered. And that wasn't all. He was making these delicious noises, raw, little keens escaping from the back of his throat. The noises were harsh and male and I loved them. "Damn it. Suck it harder."

I tried my best with genuine interest and enthusiasm. So far his fingers and my mouth were far more enjoyable than the act of sex itself. Who knew?

His climax was a lot more interesting, quick, and messy than I was prepared for. I knew the mechanics but those did not take into account how my own musings and reactions would distract me from the job at hand. It was an easy enough mouthful to swallow, but somehow half of it ended up *on* me, running down my chin, my neck, my collarbone, and deep into my cleavage.

I lifted my head when his hand in my hair went slack.

His eyes were running over me, over the spots where I'd spilled his cum on myself. "Did any of it manage to make it into your mouth?" he asked, breathing hard. I would have answered, but as he spoke he was fingering the shoulders of my top, pushing them aside and down my arms. It was a revealing dress. Just that easy, I was topless. He stared at me some more, his breath slowing eventually but not by much. He fondled me.

I looked down at his hand on me. The sight made me squirm in my seat. My nipples were hard, his cum was all over my skin, and his hand looked and felt so good on me that I couldn't stop staring at it.

"Fuck," he said roughly. *"Fuck."*

Abruptly he took his hand away, pulling my straps back onto my shoulders, folding me back into my dress.

"Was that okay?" It took a few minutes and lot of my courage to work up to asking that question.

He put himself away and didn't look at me once. He didn't speak for an unbearable length of time. He seemed to be gathering himself for something, and I doubted that would bode well for me.

"Do you want me to be honest?" he asked in a dead voice, his eyes trained out the window at the swiftly passing buildings. He didn't wait for me to answer. "I feel I was misled about your skill level. All that training, I thought you'd be better with your mouth."

It felt like I'd been slapped. My eyes stung and I had to blink rapidly and look away to hide it. It was the unexpectedness of the assault that made it hurt so bad, I told myself. I was completely unprepared for such brutal directness.

"Apparently," he continued ruthlessly, "practice means nothing if you don't have the right tools. We'll have to work on that."

I felt my jaw set stubbornly. "If you insist. Would you like to do it now or do you need more time to recover?"

He was staring at me now. It wasn't a good

stare. There wasn't even a hint of friendliness in the curve of his mouth or the glint of his eyes. "Why'd you do it?"

I stared back.

"Why would you sell yourself to someone who doesn't even *like* you?" he added.

"Not all of us get to be born rich," I told him. Simple and bitter like one of his drinks.

"You *sold* your virginity. Your hymen had a *price tag*. This is certainly a first for me."

"Excuse me?"

"You're the only virgin I've ever broken in and had to train, *and* the only woman I've ever had to pay to fuck me."

Shock robbed me of all response. All I could do was stare at him.

"So I guess you could say you're my first whore, and I'm your first John."

"John's don't buy the cow," I was angry enough to point out.

His pretty mouth twisted and it was ugly. He parted his lips to say something horrible in response but his phone rang, distracting him, thank God.

"Hello, Father," he said into the phone with utter contempt. "Yes, I'm here. Yes, I took her out. Oh, we're getting on famously. I got her off with two fingers in the restaurant, and she clumsily serviced me in the limo. I'm not sure anyone told her she's supposed to swallow the cum when it shoots down her throat. Enough details for you?" He paused. "If you don't like hearing that, quit interfering in my life."

He hung up his phone with angry motions just as we were pulling up to our building.

My husband was back to not looking at me. "I'd see you up," he told me coldly, "but it's been a long day, and I can see Chester waiting to do the honors, so I'll let him."

"You're leaving?" I asked him. It was unexpected.

"I have some work to do, and I don't know if anyone told you, but I prefer to stay at my own place when I'm in the city."

He had a separate apartment for me. How had I not known that?

How *would* I know that? Asha loved keeping me in the dark, and *who the hell* kept multiple apartments in the same city?

Old money did. And they also had strange notions about marriage, apparently. He treated me more like his mistress than his wife.

"Well, thank you for dinner," I told him stiffly.

"Good night, Noura." He didn't spare me a glance.

I didn't look at anyone as I made my way on

shaky legs up to my apartment. I was grateful when Chester didn't say a word.

I showered and went straight to bed. It had been an enlightening first date. My husband couldn't stand me, and I needed some better lessons on sucking his dick.

Things could have gone better.

Why then was I still turned on? It was hard to fall asleep with the relentless throbbing in the pit of my belly that would not subside, but eventually I fitfully dozed.

CHAPTER
9

I decided the next day that living alone in my apartment was a huge a relief, although the alone part was short-lived, and my husband had nothing to do with that.

A girl named Jovie did.

I was backstage changing into my street clothes after a runway show. My part was over, and I was all set to leave when I was stopped in my tracks by a loud fight between two other models. I was across the room so I didn't hear everything that was said, but the end result was one of them storming off, a triumphant smile on her face, and the other one bursting into tears.

This wasn't all that unusual, and I might have minded my own business but for one little thing: the crying girl was young. Painfully young.

She didn't look a day over fourteen.

It wasn't unheard of to see a girl that young at this kind of show. It was an immensely high fashion dressmaker, and they loved fresh faces for the really avant-garde stuff.

Hell, I'd been her age when I'd moved to New York to model full-time.

I wasn't in the best mood. I felt the night before in a sharp pain under my eyes and a constant clench in my gut. I wanted nothing more than to go home and be alone, but her broken sobs swayed me.

With a sigh, I walked across the room.

"Are you okay?" I asked her.

She sized me up with a pretty glare, like she thought I might pinch her. "I'm fine. Why?"

"You looked . . . upset. Is there anything I can do to help?"

She scoffed. "Unless you have a spare room for rent starting *tonight*, then *no*."

"You need a place to crash?"

"Men are scum, you know that?"

I thought it over. "Yeah, I know that. Are you okay?"

"Do you really care?"

I thought that over too, studying her. God, she was young and as innocent looking as a little lost lamb. "I do."

"I've been better, to be honest," she eventually

answered. "I just got dumped by my boyfriend, and now I need to find an apartment in Manhattan, which is like impossible, ya know?"

"How old are you?"

"Fifteen." She saw my expression. "Practically fifteen. In less than two months," she added defensively.

"And you were *living* with your boyfriend?"

"Yeah, so? My parents were taking all of my modeling money, so I paid my lawyers a small fortune and emancipated myself. I don't like being alone all the time, so I moved in with my boyfriend. It was working out just fine . . . until today."

"What's your name?" I probably should have known it, I'd seen her around, but I'd been preoccupied with my own issues for a while now.

She didn't seem offended. "I'm Jovie."

"That's a cool name."

"Thanks. I made it up myself."

"What's your real name?"

"Jovie is now. I had it legally changed. I went with just the one name. Like Halsey. Or Beyonce. Or Madonna. Doesn't it sound like the name of someone who's going to be famous?"

I nodded encouragingly. "It for sure does." She looked like someone who was going to be famous too. She was drop dead gorgeous, obviously biracial with stunning coloring: light brown skin, golden blonde hair, and sky blue eyes. "Nice to meet you, Jovie. I'm Noura."

"Oh, I know who you are. You're the snobby, famous, *rich* one who doesn't talk to *anyone*."

The rich part of that I was still getting used to, though it was accurate and didn't bother me a bit. I'd done a lot for that money, and it was still fresh enough that the idea didn't taste bitter. Yet. The snobby part now, that stung a little. I kept to myself, but I *wasn't* a snob. I didn't think I was better than anyone, I was just doing the best I could, though it wasn't the first or even the tenth time I'd heard that said about me. "I'm talking to you, aren't I?" I pointed out.

"But look what a fool I had to make of myself first," she said with a disarming smile.

That startled a laugh out of me. The tears weren't even dry on her face and already she was joking around. What a strange, interesting girl.

"What did she say to you?" I asked her. Jovie had seemed fine until the other girl had spoken to her.

"Ambrosia Hurst? She's the one he left me for. You know how it is with these model chasers. They want a piece of us all. And she called me a baby prostitute."

That made me so mad I felt my face turning red. "What a stone cold bitch."

"I know, right? I absolutely *hate* being called a baby."

There was a hint of a smile around her mouth as she said that last bit, and I couldn't help but be charmed.

"I have an extra room," I said impulsively. "You can crash there if you want."

She eyed me warily. "I don't want charity. I can pay for the room. I mean, until I find something more permanent. 'Kay?"

I shrugged. "Whatever. We'll figure it out later. Are you hungry?"

Her face fell. "I'm staaaarving, but I went over my calorie count at like nine a.m."

"You're only fourteen. You're probably having a growth spurt. You need extra calories to grow. You should eat."

She studied me like she was trying to figure out whether I was putting her on. "You think? I'm only five eight. I'd love it if I could grow three more inches. I hate it when other models tower over me."

I nodded. "I bet it is a growth spurt. I kept growing until I was seventeen, and those extra inches are an advantage. Let's go get dinner."

We went to a tiny pasta place in Little Italy that Chester recommended. He'd been trying to talk me into going there for weeks, but since pasta was my favorite food *and* the bane of my existence, I'd been using all of my self-control to avoid it.

That night I indulged, and it was worth all the extra work I'd have to put in later.

Jovie and I shared a plate of manicotti that literally made my eyes roll up into my head with every bite.

"Oh my God!"

"Can we swing by my boyfriend's place after this and grab some of my stuff? I'm afraid if I leave it there too long, he'll just throw it away."

"Of course," I said, glancing at Chester, who'd been silent while he ate enough food to feed a small village of models.

He shared a look with Vincent, who was also packing in food like he'd been starving along with me.

"I'll go in with her and help her carry everything," Chester told me. "But you'll need to stay in the car."

I stared him down. "Why?"

"This is a break up thing, right? That sort of thing can go badly. The boss wouldn't like it if you got caught in the middle of some domestic dispute."

When he said boss, I never really knew who he meant. My husband or father-in-law? And

I never asked, because it was humiliating that I didn't already know.

"Raoul probably won't even be there," Jovie assured him. "He's a club kid. He likes to go out late like every night 'til five a.m."

"How old is this Raoul guy?" Vincent asked her.

I eyed him warily. Vincent didn't talk much, so when he did, everyone paid attention.

Jovie shrugged, but it was a tense movement. The question made her uncomfortable. "Twenty-five or twenty-six? It doesn't matter. I'm never speaking to him again."

"And how old are you?" Chester asked her, his words coming out very slowly.

Uh-oh. The guys' hackles were up. So were mine, for that matter, but the last thing I wanted to do was scare Jovie off.

"Almost fifteen," she said, looking back and forth between the two men.

Vincent spit over his shoulder.

Chester started cracking his knuckles.

Not good. "Guys, tone it down," I told them firmly. The last thing we needed to do was push her back to the creep.

Jovie was looking back and forth between the two of them. "You know, never mind."

"They won't do anything," I told her. "They'll

help you grab your stuff and that's it."

"I hate violence," she said slowly.

"There won't be any violence," I told her.

"You promise?" she asked, still looking at the guys.

They both mumbled out that yes they promised.

"We won't touch him tonight," Chester added with a bland smile.

Well, that did not bode well for Raoul the Creep, I mused.

It took her less than twenty minutes to grab her stuff from the creep's apartment, and he never made an appearance, thank God. Chester threw two overstuffed suitcases in the trunk as Jovie slid back into her seat beside me.

"That's *all* your stuff?" I asked her in surprise.

"I'm a minimalist. It suits me. You never know when you'll need to bolt."

I used to be like that. Before the wedding, my life could've fit into two suitcases, as well, so I don't know why it threw me off. Perhaps because I couldn't travel overnight without more junk than that nowadays. How quickly I was becoming accustomed to my strange new extravagant existence.

The instant Jovie entered my apartment something changed. Something about the space and something about my life. Both became more full of an intangible something I hadn't known I'd been *craving*. Chester and Vincent were great company, all things considered, but Jovie was something else. Her vivacious energy was food I hadn't known I was missing.

We stayed up way past my bedtime talking for hours and doing all the fun girly shit we could think of.

I got her hooked on DramaFever and she got me hooked on BTS. It was very easy. Both were highly addictive.

"Where's your husband?" she asked at some point. We were drinking unsweetened green tea kale smoothies and she was braiding my hair.

I shrugged. "Working probably." It was only a little lie.

"Did you tell him I was staying here?" she asked, pausing her quick motions against my scalp.

I shrugged again. "It doesn't matter. He rarely stays here. This place is mine." I felt pleasure as I said it even if it wasn't strictly the truth. It was true enough.

She was quiet for a while. "That's cool," she drew the words out. "But if he doesn't stay here, where does he stay?"

I tensed up. I'd literally signed my rights off to

give away candid details about my marriage, but I wanted to spill my guts to this girl I'd only just met. It was stupid, and I made myself exercise caution.

"Hey listen," she finally said when it was obvious I wasn't going to answer the question. "Forget I asked. I'm way too self-absorbed to be all up in your business."

I smiled because that was bullshit.

She proved me right a minute later when she just couldn't help but pry more. "Is marriage how you always hear it is?" she asked.

"How do you always hear it is?" I couldn't help myself either. I wanted to hear her fourteen-year-old take on it.

"You know. Mistresses, resentful blowjobs, and fights about serious shit that really doesn't mean anything. Like grownup stuff."

We laughed for a long time at that, and I never did have to answer the question.

I went to bed after midnight with a smile on my face. I couldn't remember the last time I'd had so much fun.

At about two a.m. there was a light knock on my bedroom door.

It was Jovie. She didn't want to sleep alone, so I let her bunk with me. I didn't mind. The big bed always felt too empty with just me in it.

Soon after she got settled, she started crying very quietly then louder until she'd worked herself into wrenching sobs.

I tapped her on the shoulder and she rolled over, burrowing her wet face into my neck.

I held her as she cried. She didn't stop for hours, saying over and over, "He was supposed to be my family."

"I don't have a family, either," I whispered to the night. "We'll be okay though. We can lean on each other."

"What about your husband?" she whispered back. "That's a family."

"Not for me, it's not."

"Well, then you can leave that asshole. We'll figure it out. We both get plenty of work. We don't need him. You could have any man you want."

"Don't worry about me," I replied. "I have everything that I want."

"Okay, okay," she sniffled. "How long can I stay here? I never want to leave. I'm so lonely, Noura."

"As long as you want."

"Thank you, thank you, thank you," she sobbed.

By the time she cried herself to sleep in my arms, my heart was a puddle of mush at her adorable, baby model feet.

CHAPTER
10

I didn't hear directly from my husband again for weeks.

It bothered me more than I was comfortable with.

I'd walked into our marriage for reasons that had nothing to do with love or affection. I'd gone into it with my eyes wide open. My motives were money and security, and at one point, before I'd set eyes on him, there was nothing I'd have loved more than a wealthy husband who ignored me as much and as often as possible.

It bothered me how much that had changed with just a few brief exchanges. I didn't want to be ignored. Not by him. I wanted the opposite. Mean and nasty as he was, I wanted his attention.

I wanted his fingers in me again. I wanted his cock in my hands, down my throat.

His insults after were *still* ringing in my ears, and *still* I wanted a repeat.

How messed up was that? I knew how much, and it didn't matter. I wanted more destructive contact with him. Enough to think about it too much. Enough to fixate on it. Enough to *do* something about it.

Two weeks and two days after our one month anniversary and our first 'date,' I accidentally stumbled upon a way to get it.

Up to that point, I'd followed all of the trophy wife rules to a T.

They weren't easy rules. And there were a lot of them. They were a consuming set of arbitrary commands designed to keep me in my place and blending in seamlessly with my new fake family.

I was bound to break one or two of the little ones at some point. And when I did, it gave me a powerful weapon against Calder, because I learned something valuable.

If I wanted his attention, all I had to do was misbehave.

It was simple, and honestly it came more naturally to me than what I'd *been* doing.

So far in our marriage I had, for all intents and purposes, been very well behaved. I went where I was told to go, wore what I was told to wear, and tried my best to keep quiet and out of trouble.

Through it all, I'd only seen my detached husband one obligatory time.

I found out, quite by accident, that a little bit of trouble was the quickest way to get a response out of him.

It started with one impulsive, racy Instagram post. It was uncharacteristic of me, and I can't even explain what gave me the urge. Since the wedding, I didn't run my own social media. I was signed in on my phone on every platform, but I'd never posted personally. My timelines were generally filled with professional shots shared directly from modeling jobs. There were no captions, just pictures tagging whatever clothing I was being paid to sell. I'd never given any of it much attention.

If I had a free moment, I spent it joking around with Chester and Vincent, or watching DramaFever on my phone, not stalking my own social media profiles.

It all began with a snag in the paper thin couture dress I was supposed to be modeling for an editorial in Vogue.

I was all set to go, hair piled high up on my head and laced through with an extravagant crown of dusky pink roses. My makeup was heavy glam, with a dramatic cat eye and dark red wine lips.

The gown I was modeling was a risqué

ensemble to begin with. It was so sheer that I couldn't even wear a bra. This was why I was wearing nothing but the tiniest nude thong in the world, itty bitty pasties, and four-inch high transparent stiletto sandals while I waited for the alteration.

Normally I'd have a robe to walk around in, but they'd taken the dress from me mid-change, and what was supposed to be a quick fix, wound up taking longer. Two minutes turned into an unexpected thirty as they carefully hand sewed the tear and hid it enough for the shoot.

I was bored. I'd already sat in the hair and makeup chair for two hours, and I was waiting again, just standing there all made up and bare at the same time. Luckily all of the blaring lighting warmed the room enough that it wasn't chilly.

I noticed the good lighting at right about the same time I spotted a floor length mirror.

I contorted my body into its best angles, hiked my leg up, and banded an arm across my breasts to cover them up. I snapped a few shots like that, then immediately went into my camera roll to check them out.

They were good. They were flattering without being vulgar, and I loved my glam makeup and flower crown.

I put my favorite shot up on Instagram. The

caption was silly. I posted it because I was bored and I thought it was kind of funny.

Loving my latest look from Balmain but I think they forgot something. #extraaf

I was nearly nude, and the picture made it look like I was totally nude, but it wasn't like anything was showing. All of my essentials were covered up.

I didn't imagine anything like that could bother my husband. I modeled for a living. Hell, I'd just landed a lingerie campaign. My modesty had been thrown out the window *years* ago.

I posted it then went back to texting with Jovie and watching my current K-drama obsession on my phone while they finished fixing the dress.

When I was finally dressed, we got back to work. The shoot took another three hours, and by then, I'd completely forgotten about the picture.

"What do you want for dinner, Duchess?" Chester asked me as he walked me out to the waiting car.

I sighed. "Do you mind if we go to that salad place you found for me a few weeks ago?"

He grimaced, handing me into the car.

I nodded to Vincent, who nodded back.

Chester walked around to the other side and sat down in the back with me. "I thought you were off that awful diet Asha had you on."

"I am. Now I'm on an awful diet I put myself on. I have a shoot where I'm practically naked on Monday."

He shot me a look. It was his disapproving father look.

"What?" I asked him, stifling a laugh. I didn't mind it when he lectured me. For some reason I found it cute. Probably because I knew he did it because he cared.

It had been a long time since someone cared about me.

"Speaking of being naked," he said in his best dad lecturing voice, "I saw that picture you posted. What was that all about?"

I was surprised he'd seen it. And a little embarrassed. I shrugged. "I thought it was funny. It wasn't funny?"

He ran a hand through his red mane of hair, still staring me down. It became harder for me not to laugh. His face was a perfect combination of amused and exasperated. "It was *naked*, Duchess."

"It felt more like a nude to me," I said with perfect composure.

That finally broke him out into a smile. I looked up front. Even stone-faced Vincent was smirking.

"You do know that nude and naked are the same thing," Chester pointed out.

"Not really," I tried, out-and-out grinning, "nude is classier. Nude is *art*."

I'd gotten him to laugh, and I loved it. I laughed with him. "You know," I told him honestly. "Having you two around all the time is the probably best perk about my marriage."

It was the truth.

When I'd been told I'd have a full security detail, I hadn't understood the need for it—still didn't—but I hadn't really thought much of it. I hadn't put any thought into whether I'd like or hate the constant company.

I hadn't realized, until I spent so much time with people whose company I enjoyed, just how lonely I was. How alone I'd constantly been for *years*.

I was finding out, for the first time in forever, that I liked having company more than I liked being alone.

It was nice.

Chester gave me a look that was outright fond. "And you're my favorite body I've ever guarded."

I waved him off. "You're just saying that."

"No, I mean it. You're always polite. You treat us well." He looked at Vincent. "Back me up here, man."

"I agree," Vincent said simply, eyes on the road. "And you're not terrible to look at, either,"

Chester added teasingly. "I've been working for the Castelos for almost fifteen years, and I've never enjoyed working for them more than I have in the past month."

I flushed head to toe in pleasure. "Thank you," I told him, feeling shy. "Are you not normally . . . friends . . . with the people you guard?"

He laughed. "No. No one usually bothers to talk to us. And I've *never* had anyone ask me if they minded where we ate."

"Are all of the Castelos assholes?" I couldn't help but ask.

He waved that off. "Not at all. They're better than most. They're just . . . Well, they are what they are. They're old money, and we're the hired help."

I looked out the window. "Well, I don't see it that way. You guys are my friends, and I like having you around."

"It's mutual, Duchess."

We grabbed a quick dinner at a salad place I liked called *Greens*. The guys mimicked my order of kale salad sans dressing and all greens smoothies for the road.

"You aren't going to like it," I warned them when we got our food.

"Oh I know," Chester agreed. "We did it to see what you have to live with. Maybe it's more filling than we imagine."

"You're twice my body weight," I pointed out. "It's not even going to put a dent in your appetite."

"That's not the point," Vincent put a rare word in. "If you can starve, so can we."

I was amused more than anything. "It's my job to maintain my weight. You guys need to stop worrying about my diet. I can either count my calories or do coke. Which do you think is better for me, Dads?"

Chester laughed.

"Not funny," Vincent muttered, going back to his salad.

"Be honest," I said when we were in the car again, headed home this time, "you're both going to order takeout now, aren't you?"

"Damn straight," Chester agreed instantly. Just then his cell rang, and he checked it. His brow furrowed, his eyes shooting over to meet mine as he put it to his ear.

He answered with, "Chester here."

I was stunned when I realized it was my husband calling him.

He hadn't called me directly, but I could hear his voice through Chester's phone.

Because he was shouting on the other end of it. I couldn't make out the words at first, but I could still tell it was him.

"That was just what she was wearing as she was waiting for some repairs on the dress she was modeling, Mr. Castelo," he was explaining in a formal tone. "She wasn't modeling nude."

"—telling me she just hangs around the set like that?" Calder's voice got louder, enough so that I could make out some of his words. "She's just walking around *naked*? How many people were in that room?"

Chester glanced at me.

I held up six fingers.

"Six," Chester said into his phone. "And she wasn't actually nude." He was looking at me sternly. "She had a thong and pasties on."

"Were *you* in that room with her dressed like that?" my husband shouted.

"No," Chester answered. "I was waiting right outside for her. I stay away from the backstage once I know the area is secure. There tends to be a lot of scantily clad women running around at these things, and I prefer to give them some privacy."

Calder said something I couldn't make out, and Chester handed me the phone with a clenched jaw.

"Hello," I said, and it came out more hesitant than I meant for it to.

He didn't yell at me as he had Chester, but his

tone was mean enough that it didn't feel much better, "Why did you do that?" He bit each word of the question out with acute hostility.

"The-the picture earlier?" I asked. I knew that's what he was asking about, but I was stalling for an answer. I didn't know what else to say.

"Yes," he snapped. "The picture you posted online a few hours ago. Why did you do that?"

I couldn't figure out why he was reacting like this. Had it really been such a shocking picture? "I-I thought it was funny. Everything was covered up."

"Funny?" he ground out. "Everything was covered up?" His deep voice was inching toward a shout. "I'm looking at a lot of bare fucking skin right now. My *wife's* bare fucking skin. No one but me needs to see this much of you, Mrs. Castelo."

"Okay," I said woodenly. His mean tone was having an unexpected effect on me. I was shocked at myself, I rarely cried, but it was an effort for me not to burst into tears. "I'll take it down."

"I already took it down," he shot back, voice calmer now, though nowhere near friendly, "but it's out there forever now. I'm sure I'm not the only one with a screenshot of it."

"I didn't realize it would displease you," I told

him stiffly. "What can I do to make up for it?" I had to choke the words out.

My husband's voice was biting and strident. "Here it is: No more naked pictures online."

"I was *not* naked," I couldn't help but point out.

He ignored that. "No more changing in front of everyone. No more hanging out in your panties with six fucking other people in the room. Who were the six people, by the way?"

I had to think about it. "Hair dresser. Makeup artist. Lighting guy. Photographer. A designer and a tailor." Yep, that was six.

"How many were men?" he growled.

My brows rose. "Three."

I listened to him breathing through the phone for a solid minute. He was really going through something on the other end. A rage or a temper tantrum, I couldn't decide which and I wasn't sure what the difference was.

"Only one of them was straight," I finally added.

"It doesn't fucking matter," he snapped. "I want you to start showing some decorum on the job. Some *modesty*. Change behind a curtain, wear a robe when you need to. Are we clear?"

"Crystal."

I hung up and handed Chester's phone back to him.

"So now I have a *changing room* dress code?" I asked sarcastically. I wanted to cry, but I thought I was hiding it well.

Chester sighed. "You do, Duchess." He didn't have to say it but we both thought it. This was the life I'd signed on for.

It was hours before it dawned on me what it all really meant. What I'd done and my husband's reaction. It had been hostile, volatile, and quick.

He couldn't stand me, but he wasn't *immune*. He kept closer track of me than I'd realized, and he'd just shown me how to get a rise out of him, one that made him incapable of ignoring me.

It was an advantage.

CHAPTER
11

When the day came around I was in no mood to go out with Millie Bancroft and a bunch of rich girls I didn't know and had nothing in common with.

I was dreading it, but I knew I had to go. It had been a direct order.

I'd been trying to rally myself to get ready for the evening ahead for the last half hour.

I was sitting in my living room watching E! with Jovie and the guys when the doorbell rang.

Vincent answered it, and I was surprised when three familiar faces filed in.

My husband had sent my regular hair and makeup girls and my personal shopper with an outfit picked out specifically for this outing.

He didn't want me to embarrass him by

looking a mess in front of his friends. I supposed I couldn't blame him since I'd been planning to do the very bare minimum to get ready.

My glam team did the opposite of that. They did me up like I was about to walk a red carpet.

My hair was twisted into an artfully messy topknot. My foundation was light, my eye makeup heavy, and my lips were painted a soft matte nude.

My outfit was a tiny, high-waisted, cream micro mini skirt paired with a boat-necked gold sequin crop top that bared my midriff. Gold hoop earrings and tan stilettos finished the look.

The overall effect was very over twenty-one sex kitten.

"I'm coming with you," Jovie said. Our eyes met in my oversized vanity mirror. She'd been there the whole time, nicely distracting me while my team got me ready.

I loved having her around in general, but I'd noticed an added perk to it recently. Asha seemed to disappear more when Jovie was around. It was wonderful.

"You can't," I told her reasonably. "You're not old enough.

"Neither are you."

"Yes, but Chester will get me in, and he's already specifically told *you* no."

"You shouldn't have to face those barracudas alone."

"I'm not altogether sure that they're barracudas." I was pretty sure though.

"Fine. You shouldn't have to face those prissy society princesses alone."

They were that. "They might be nice. It's not their fault they were all born rich."

She begrudgingly agreed but her parting words were, "My phone is glued to my hand. The second you text me for help, I'm coming, even if I have to wrestle a bouncer to get in."

That had me walking out the door with a laugh, but it died as we took the elevator down to the garage. I was still unaccountably nervous about getting in the door due to my age. It would save me having to go, though, so it wouldn't be all bad. Just embarrassing as hell if I was turned away.

"What if there are paparazzi, and they catch me going into an over twenty-one club?" I asked Chester as he handed me into the car. "Won't that look bad?"

He got in beside me before he answered. "Your husband's friend owns the club," he explained to me. "And there's a back entrance. You don't need to worry about stuff like that, Duchess. That's my job."

"I've never been to a club before," I confessed. "The closest thing I've done were a few modeling parties, but they *really* weren't for me. They were all about networking and they're *intense*. I started avoiding those things early on."

"Just try to relax and have fun," Chester encouraged. "You're off the clock tonight."

I couldn't think how to respond to that. This outing was not about me having fun. I'd basically been ordered to go hang out with strangers. And didn't he know by now that I was *always* on the clock?

We arrived at the venue and Chester escorted me easily through the back door security and straight to Millie's VIP booth. It was a big booth, with enough room for at least twenty people.

And there was no one there.

A dark-haired waitress was waiting there. She greeted me with a big smile, introducing herself. She was wearing black boy shorts, a white crop top that hit her mid-boob, and platform boots that had to be at least six inches high. She was pretty, but her makeup was caked on and her fake tan was a few shades beyond excessive. She asked me what I wanted to drink.

I couldn't think of a thing. "Champagne," I said automatically. It had become my go-to social drink. When in doubt, champagne.

I didn't sit down, instead hovered right outside the booth. I locked imploring eyes on Chester. "Since no one else showed up, I can leave, right?"

He sighed. "I think they're going to show. You're just the first one, but you can do whatever the hell you want, Duchess. Just tell me what that is, and I'll lead you to it."

The waitress brought me a drink and I thanked her. I sighed, then took a long sip.

"I'm going over my two drink limit tonight," I said grimly.

"I don't blame you," Chester remarked from somewhere close behind me, then added, "I believe some of your friends have arrived."

I turned to look. It was an effort not to point out that they weren't *my* friends, but I managed to keep the words in.

Millie was striding toward us with three women I'd met at my wedding and two more I didn't think I'd ever seen before. They all looked like carbon copies of each other with only slight variations.

Like they'd all come from the same intimidating rich girl factory: Same height, same shoe styles, pretty faces, similar black mini dresses. Even their hairstyles were cut into similar bobs, though two had blonde hair, two light brown hair, and two were brunettes, and they all had varying skin tones.

I wondered if they all looked alike on purpose, or if they were just that influenced by each other.

Millie spotted me and gave me a huge smile and wave.

I smiled and waved back shyly. I had no idea if Millie actually wanted to hang out with me, or if she'd just invited me because of my husband, but I strongly suspected the latter.

She gave me a big hug when she drew close, then pulled back and introduced everyone.

I studied each briefly as she went down the line.

"I know you met some of them at your wedding, but you met so many people that day, so I'll give you a refresher course." She pointed to the two brunettes, who were standing side by side like they were choreographed by hair color. "That's Veronica, Camilla." She pointed to the two light brown-haired girls. "Beatrix, Hadley." She pointed to the other half of her own blonde pairing. "And that's Addison. We all went to school together, and we've all been friends since we were kids. Me, Hadley, and Veronica are married and all of our husbands are friends with yours. We're a very tight-knit crew. You'll fit right in."

I smiled as politely as I could, but I knew I

wouldn't fit in with them. I would just be happy if I could remember most of their names.

And of course, I was instantly out of place—I was the wrong height, wrong pedigree, wore white while they all wore black— I was flashy instead of tasteful. They were everything I wasn't, and vice versa, and I felt it keenly, but I was used to hiding that sort of thing. Every ideal is a judge, and insecurity was a monster that my occupation made me battle daily. I'd gotten quite adept at stomping it before it sank its claws too deeply into me.

They all sat down, huddling together in one small corner of the big booth.

I sat down a few feet away. I wanted badly to look at Chester, I don't know exactly why, perhaps to feel less alone and estranged, but I restrained myself.

Instead I downed the rest of my champagne.

It wasn't lost on me that I was the only one that had their personal security with them in the club, and I wondered again why my husband and his family insisted on such strict measures.

I wondered, but I wasn't upset about it. I enjoyed having Chester around. Often he was one of the best parts of my day.

The waitress came strutting up with two bottles of Grey Goose lit with sparklers. She waved them around theatrically while the ladies cheered her on.

I couldn't help it. I glanced at Chester. We shared an amused look.

Millie asked the waitress to pour us all shots.

I took mine without protest. It seemed like a good night to try a shot, and I sure as hell wasn't going to admit to these filthy rich princesses that it was my first one.

Worst case scenario: Chester was big and strong enough to carry me out.

I barely choked it down, though it wasn't as bad as I'd been expecting—it was something surprisingly sweet—but it was still more than I was used to.

I looked around. There were several other VIP booths in the large room, but for the most part the place was deserted. "I thought it would be busier," I remarked.

"It's not actually open yet," Millie admitted with a laugh. All of her friends joined her as though they'd been cued. "It opens in a half hour, and this is a private room. The main club is through there." She pointed across the room.

One of the girls, Addison, I thought I recalled correctly, asked the waitress for another round of shots.

"Oh," I was surprised. "So we're not going to the main club. We just stay in here?"

Millie shrugged, laughing again. "We do whatever we want!"

I digested that as I took another shot with the group. This one went down easier. I pointed at the empty glass. "I like these," I said more loudly than I needed to.

Shit. Was I already drunk?

The group erupted into fresh peals of laughter at my expense. My face stiffened, cheeks reddening.

I was embarrassed, and I tried to quickly recover with a serious (and I thought neutral) question, "So what do you all do? Like for work?"

More laughter, this time louder.

I wasn't in on the joke. I knew they were rich, duh, I got that message loud and clear, but didn't every adult need something productive to do? Going by the fact that they'd all gone to school with my husband, they were all around twenty-six years old and none had kids yet.

What did a twenty-six year old do without a job or children?

It was particularly strange to me since I'd been working and supporting myself full-time from the ripe old age of fourteen.

Oh yeah. That's when my fuzzy mind

remembered. They're a different breed than me. Not *working class*.

"We're full-time socialites," Millie explained with a kind smile. "I'm sure you're getting into the swing of something similar, when you're not busy modeling. We represent our families *socially*."

"It might sound superficial to an outsider," one of the brunettes (I thought it was Camilla) added, "but we all have Ivy League educations. And we all do a lot more for society than a typical *working* woman."

My eyes tried to climb straight up to my hairline for that one. "Do you now?" I tried really, really hard to keep my tone even and neutral.

Millie sent her friend a look. "What Camilla means is that we *try* our best to contribute. We're all involved in charity work, and Hadley," she pointed to one of the light brown-haired ones, "even got a law degree just to help represent her husband's cancer research foundation."

My hackles were still up from Camilla's comment, but I managed to let it go. I wasn't here to judge anyone (why would I be?) and charity work was certainly something I admired.

To each their own, I chanted in my head. Being born rich and privileged was not a crime.

I tried my hardest not to have a chip on my

shoulder about that kind of thing, but sometimes it was harder to hide than others.

If I was honest with myself these types of women were one of the reasons I'd agreed to such an arrangement. I hated the idea that there was an upper class and that they were *better* than.

I didn't want anyone to have something over me like that. If there had to be a social ladder, I wanted to climb to the top and stay there. To dig in roots and make it mine for generations.

I wanted to change my family tree.

I shook off the thought. Now was not the time.

Someone had the waitress make us another round of shots, and I took mine gratefully.

The group just sat there for a while.

I wondered if there was going to be any dancing, or if they actually were lame enough to come to a club and do nothing but sit and *talk*.

It was looking that way.

They shared a *lot* of gossip about people I didn't know. No one so much as glanced my way for a solid hour.

I kept drinking and tried to school my features into an expression that resembled politely interested, but it was hard to keep my mind from wandering.

Why was this so much harder to sit through than my nightly galas? I should have been used to talking to strangers about things I didn't care about by now.

This felt more pointless, I decided. This small group of elitist women were never going to like or accept me. Why had my husband wanted me to try to be included?

Eventually the alcohol did its job and I just didn't care. I kept making silly faces at Chester because it made him smile.

"Do you guys dance at all?" I finally just asked them. Why go to a club and not just a restaurant or bar if they were only going to sit there?

I'd interrupted a tirade one of them had been spouting about some woman who'd had the nerve to wear a dress they thought was out of fashion to one of their parties. Blah blah blah.

Millie nodded, her face shaped into its usual pleasant smile. "We're just getting warmed up."

"I need to powder my nose," Addison said, standing suddenly. "Come with me, Noura?"

It wasn't my favorite idea, but I went along with her just for the sake of being agreeable. Also I needed to pee. I did not have a good liquor bladder.

Addison hooked her arm through mine like we were best friends. I let her, but I glanced back at Chester, who was following us.

Addison finally seemed to notice him. "Will

he go into the bathroom with you?" She laughed hard at her own question.

I smiled weakly. "No. He'll wait outside. He's just doing his job."

She sent him a second look. "He's kind of hot. Have you fucked him?"

I nearly stopped in my tracks. She'd managed to genuinely offend me. And embarrass me. I couldn't even look at Chester. "Of course not. You know I'm married, right?"

Sometimes I didn't feel married, but I sure as hell was acting like it.

She rolled her eyes at me. "Like that ever stopped anyone." She sent Chester an unctuous smile. "I have a question for you, Ginger," she told him. "Does the carpet match the drapes, and what does a girl have to do to find out firsthand?"

I wondered just how drunk she was.

"Not going there today, Miss Du Mont," he answered, sounding amused. At least Chester had a good sense of humor.

"Pity," she purred back.

CHAPTER
12

I was relieved when we reached the bathroom, and I dashed inside.

Addison touched up her makeup while I used the restroom and washed my hands.

She casually offered me coke at the sink, right in front of the bathroom attendant.

I politely turned her down.

She scoffed at me in the mirror. "Oh please. You're a model, right? Don't act all innocent about it with me."

I leveled an annoyed look at her, one of my brows arched high. "I count my calories and work my ass off. Not all models are cokeheads. Certainly not the ones that keep getting work. It ages you. I wouldn't do it *because* I model, and I don't want to age out of it by twenty-five."

Yeah, it was a dig. She was clearly a cokehead

and past twenty-five. She glared at me. "Suit yourself," she said. She bent down to the counter, partaking liberally.

So it was going to be that kind of a night. Not so very different than the industry parties I tried my best to avoid.

I cringed at all of the nasty germs she was inhaling with her cocaine. There was so much wrong with this picture.

It didn't escape my attention that the bathroom attendant didn't bat an eye.

What a pro.

I tipped her a fifty on our way out.

"I bet you didn't tip like that before you married *rich*," Addison remarked, her tone amused.

This bitch. My head whipped around to look at her.

She was smiling with a smug something in her eyes that I really didn't care for.

I realized that she was *trying* to goad me.

Not today, Satan.

"I was always a good tipper," was all I remarked.

If this was some sort of self-control test, I was going to pass it, I decided then and there.

None of these entitled princesses were going to get a rise out of me.

We went back to the booth and I sat as far

away from Addison as possible. She was one of six. How hard could it be to avoid her?

The waitress handed me a fresh glass of champagne and I thanked her.

"So, Noura," Addison started in almost instantly. "Why is it that Banks' friends were the only ones in your bridal party? Where were *your* friends?"

I just stared at her for a long, awkward moment. I hadn't expected the question, and I didn't have a good answer for it.

I'm a loner, was a pathetic answer, if accurate.

I didn't even think to invite anyone I knew to my fake wedding, was even worse.

"Don't mind her," Millie said. I was starting to catch on that she was the peacemaker of the group. "She's still salty that she wasn't asked to be one of your bridesmaids."

I couldn't think of a good, non-humiliating way to tell her that I'd had no say in who my own bridesmaids were. Anything I said would only fuel the fire.

"And she's jealous that he chose you instead of one of us," Beatrix added almost under her breath.

But I'd definitely heard it, and it more than piqued my interest. "Excuse me?"

"We all figured he'd impulsively get married

after Fatima's wedding—" Beatrix piped in.

Millie shushed her.

I waved it off. "I know about Fatima. Keep going."

"Well, we all figured he'd find a bride just to spite her for the betrayal, but we also assumed it would be one of us."

"Beatrix, enough!" Hadley snapped. "You sound ridiculous."

"And not a commoner," Beatrix added.

"A commoner?" I repeated, trying to look more amused than offended. Who the hell did these people think they were?

"Oh, come on," Addison joined in. "You must see that one of us, one of the girls from his social circle, someone that *grew up with him*, would have made a lot more sense as his wife than a random model out of nowhere."

"So if I'm a commoner, do you all consider yourselves American *royalty*?" I asked, a sardonic edge to the question.

I was the youngest there by several years, but I was quickly realizing that *they* were the sheltered ones.

Millie waved that off. "No, of course not. I think they've had a few too many." She made a drinking motion with her hand, smiling to try to cut through the tension of the moment.

I respected her effort, but it didn't work.

"Of course," Addison answered with honest snobbery. She really believed the nonsense she was spouting. "We're the closest thing America has to nobility, something you could really only comprehend if you're one of us."

"Do tell," I said with a brittle smile, my eyes cold on hers.

She did. "We were taught impeccable manners practically from the womb. We all attended the same finishing school together, and it was the best there is. We were born to marry powerful men like our fathers. Men like your husband."

"I guess he had other ideas," I pointed out.

"We are fluent in social etiquette," she plodded on as though I hadn't spoken. "You don't even know what that means, do you? I'm sure you received a crash course in it, but everyone here knows the difference. Except for you. Do you know that you're not even holding your glass correctly? I won't even tell you how many embarrassing faux pas you've committed since we got here."

"Are you showing impeccable manners when you point out someone else's faux pas?" I asked her, tone deadly calm. The more vicious she became, the less it affected me. If debutantes were created to show impeccable manners, models were made to endure harsh criticism. This twit had nothing on any random savage casting agent I'd ever had a run in with. "Just curious," I added pleasantly.

Three of the other girls started to speak at once, and at first I thought for sure that they were backing up their friend.

I was wrong.

"Calm your tits," Camilla scolded Addison.

"What the fuck, Addie?" Veronica exclaimed.

"That was rude," Millie said to Addison in a sharp tone. "Apologize."

Addison rolled her eyes, glared at me, and stood up. "You know what? If you're going to unload on me just because I'm the only one here that's not being fake as hell, I'm going to dance. Peace." She held up both hands in peace signs as she strutted away.

I watched her until she'd disappeared through the door that led to the actual night club with envy. It had to be more fun in there than it was in here.

Three of the five women left apologized for their friend's rude comments, and I shrugged it all off.

Was I offended? A little. Was I surprised? Not at all. Snobbery was the least of what I'd expected from the rich girl club I was being forced to hang out with tonight.

I contemplated taking the Addison route—just ditching them all so I could go dance with some strangers—but decided against it. I was still at the point where I was trying to play nice with them just to prove to myself that I could. If I was honest, though, I was about one easy strike away from ditching the whole crew.

Things had grown quiet and awkward after Addison's dramatic departure. Everyone had taken to playing on their phones.

I did the same, wondering if they'd notice if I dug out my headphones and started watching some K-drama. It sure would pass the time.

I was still entertaining the idea when Millie started bouncing up and down in her seat, making excited noises.

I looked her way politely, since she seemed to want everyone's attention.

"We have company coming!" she squealed.

"Did you hire some strippers?" I asked deadpan.

No one laughed. I glanced at Chester, who was trying to hide a smirk. I smiled back. That was reward enough for me.

"As you know, our husbands," Millie said slowly and dramatically, "are out drinking together tonight."

I nodded, pretending that I'd known that, but of course I hadn't.

"My Preston," she continued, "just told me that *all* they can do is talk about their wives." She beamed at me. "They miss us! How sweet is that?"

It didn't escape my notice that the two single girls remaining at the table were rolling their eyes at each other. Who could blame them?

"It's *so* sweet," I answered woodenly. Millie seemed to expect it.

"That sounds like my Bradley," the one I thought was Hadley said smugly.

Hadley and Bradley? Really? Had their parents planned that shit out?

"Of course they do," Veronica said with unshakable confidence. "My Royce *hates* going out without me."

Millie nodded emphatically. "My Preston is the same."

"What about you, Noura?" Beatrix piped in. "Does your Banks *hate* going out without you?"

There was a certain something in her voice. Something catty and almost knowing. I wondered what she'd heard, and some part of me wanted to be brutally honest. Some part of me wanted to just spill the tea to the whole gossipy lot of them just to see how scandalized they'd be. *No, my husband doesn't hate going out without me, in fact he's only gone out* with *me once.*

But I knew I couldn't do it. I'd signed away all my rights to being a truthful person when I'd signed that prenup. Hello, money. Goodbye, honesty.

I just smiled blandly and said that he did.

"You guys are basically still on your honeymoon," Millie added without an ounce of irony. "*God*, I remember those days. I miss being a newlywed."

That prompted the women into telling various romantic early marriage stories.

I listened attentively. Hearing about happily married people sure as hell beat out the gossip about random women I didn't know.

This went on for a while and when they eventually tried to draw me into telling them a story about my marriage, I quickly redirected the conversation. "Did you say they were coming *here*?" I asked.

"Yes! The husbands are on their way. Isn't it nice that they're such good friends?"

I agreed that it was nice.

"We need to find Beatrix, Addison, and Camilla husbands that fit in with our men," Hadley added. "It's a small pool to draw from, though. Not many eligible, single men left from our circle."

"They can only marry men from your circle?" I asked. I was past being offended and into honest curiosity. How these people thought was a complete mystery to me.

"I mean, they can marry anyone they want. It would just be nice if it was an insider instead of an outsider. No offense."

I shrugged it off, but of course her saying no offense only made it more offensive.

There was a commotion at the back entrance, and I saw that several tall men had just entered the room.

Our booth fell silent. Everyone's attention was grabbed.

I barely noticed the other men. My husband was the stand-out of the group.

He spotted me and grinned.

My heart took a sharp little jump in my chest.

My reactions to him were unexpected and unwanted.

I couldn't explain how he made me feel. I'd never experienced anything like it. Excited. Agitated. Electrified. Conflicted. Stimulated. Distressed.

I hadn't been having a great time, but I'd had enough to drink that I was buzzed and feeling relaxed in spite of the awkward company.

Suddenly I was a tight ball of confused tension.

I hadn't expected to see him. I wasn't sure how to react.

I had so many questions every time I saw him. Questions I knew I couldn't ask.

Had he been planning this all along? Why did he look like he was happy to see me? How did he make it so convincing? Was he maybe a little bit *happy to see me?*

The men approached the booth, and I rose for some awkward re-introductions.

I knew I'd met his friends before, but they hadn't made an impression. I'd been too nervous on my wedding day to notice much beyond my own acute misgivings.

There was an unmistakable camaraderie between the men and the gathering as a whole.

There were lots of inside jokes being passed right over my head.

There was a sense of fond affection when the group of them were all together.

Seeing him with his friends stung a little.

He wasn't cold with them. He wasn't distant. He wasn't mean. He wasn't untouchable.

It was a dangerous thing for me to witness.

CHAPTER
13

We all sat down, wives next to their husbands, the single girls on the end.

There was plenty of room, so I sat gingerly about six inches away from Calder.

"Closer," he prompted in voice that managed to be both soft and hard.

It only took one word from him, one look, for my body to change. Go from solid to liquid. Chilled to heated.

I met his eyes as I obeyed.

He put his arm around me, pulling me close.

"How much have you had to drink?" he asked quietly.

I bit my lip and his eyes followed the motion. "I don't know," I said honestly, "I've lost count. More than my two drink limit."

"How do you feel? Not going to be sick, I hope?"

"No, I'm fine."

"Good." He smiled. It was a handsome hot smile, and I couldn't tell who it was really for but it made my blood pound through my body a little faster. He leaned closer. "I was in the middle of a meeting when I saw that picture you posted," he murmured into my ear. "I turned hard as a rock. Do you know how awkward that was for me?"

I shook my head.

"And then later," he continued silkily, "when I was alone, I jacked off to that image. Is that what you wanted?"

He leaned back to meet my gaze.

I shook my head. I couldn't tear my eyes off him.

Why did that make me wild? The idea of him pleasuring himself to a picture of me got to me in all kinds of ways.

He thought about me when he wasn't with me. Before that picture I'd been so sure I was completely forgettable to him. Less than an afterthought. Easier to wipe from his mind than the damp circle left by his morning coffee.

"Do you know how many other men must have seen that picture before it was taken down, and *did the exact same fucking thing?*" His tone was different suddenly. Switched from seductive to mean. Holy mood swing.

It dawned on me then that this was another dressing down. He'd just taken his time getting there.

"I didn't think it showed that much," I spoke as quietly as I could. I didn't want anyone we were with to realize that my husband was chewing me out. My pride had taken enough of a beating with this crowd. "I covered everything."

"Don't do it again," he warned.

"Okay," I said. A plaintive note slipped into my voice as I added, "We already went over this, you know."

He leaned forward, suddenly animated. "My *wife* posted a nude selfie online for the world to see. For every creep in the world to jerk off to. Excuse me if I feel the need to go over it *twice*."

"It's been erased," I pointed out.

He gave me a pointed look. "I saved it the *second* I saw it, and so did countless other people."

We stared at each other for a long, strange moment. Why did the fact that he'd saved a picture of me hit me straight in the gut? It didn't mean anything. He was probably just saying it to prove a point. "Did you really?" I asked, my voice little more than a whisper.

He cleared his throat. "Forget it. Just use a little sense next time."

"Got it," I replied.

He leaned close.

My eyes were on his lips. They were so plump. I reached a fingertip up to touch them. And so soft.

He moved closer. "Let's go dance." It wasn't a request.

I nodded and he stood, holding out his hand. I took it.

He told the group that he was taking me dancing. We received several toasts into the air in response.

He led me out of the booth, across the private room, and through a doorway that led to a much more crowded club.

An attractive hostess met us at the door and led us to another, smaller VIP booth in a corner of the main club.

Calder kept hold of my hand, pulling me close behind him.

I glanced back once to find Chester trailing us. I don't know why, but it made me blush. I'd forgotten he was there.

We sat and the hostess fixed us drinks. I tried to order more champagne (which he switched to OJ), and he ordered bourbon.

We were sitting close, hips touching. I turned my head to meet his gaze. My eyes devoured his handsome face. Why did he have to be so good-looking?

"I thought we were dancing," I remarked.

It was much louder in here, and he had to lean his ear close to my mouth to catch my words.

He leaned back just enough to look at me, then put his lips to my ear to answer, "We are. In a minute."

"Will we dance right here or over there?"

He pulled back enough to see my face.

I pointed at the grinding, gyrating mass of people in the center of the club. We were several floors above, overlooking them.

He gave me a look that told me he thought I must be joking. "*Here*," he stressed the word, his breath hot against my neck. "I'm not letting you near that mess. You'll be groped six ways to Sunday." He seemed to think about that, then leaned in again. "And not just by me. By strangers."

"So no groping," I said, unable to hold in a smirk.

"No one said that," his voice was a low, delicious rumble in my ear.

I shivered, a shot of lust wracking through me. My nipples went hard, my sex clenching. I had no idea what he was planning, I never did, but I was still somehow looking forward to it. Craving it.

We received our drinks, but barely took one

sip before he was standing. He moved to Chester, waving the older man over so he could be heard over the overwhelming din.

I didn't catch what he said, but I knew it was a dismissal when Chester shot me one worried glance and departed.

Calder took his suit jacket off, tossing it carelessly onto a seat. He rolled up his sleeves, his eyes on me.

He said something, and it was directed at me, but I couldn't hear it. I stood, moving closer, pointing to my ear to indicate that I needed him to repeat himself.

He wore no tie, and the top button of his dress shirt opened enough to show off his appealing, tanned throat. My face was pressed there as he spoke into my ear.

God, he was tall. And big. And he smelled divine. Like bergamot, vetiver, and heaven all wrapped into one big, edible man. I wanted to lick him.

"He really likes you," his voice vibrated against me, his mouth was so close to my skin.

I had no notion what he was talking about. He'd completely distracted me by standing so close.

"Who?" I asked him.

"Chester. He's very attached to you. I could tell he didn't want to leave."

I shrugged, not meeting his eyes. "He's nice to me, which is a good thing, since we're always together. And he's very good at his job."

I was looking at his delicious throat, but I felt him staring at my face. He stood still like that for a long, awkward moment before he let it go. I knew the subject was dropped when his hands went to my waist, pulling me closer.

My eyes were on his body, on his too close, too tempting chest, on the big, cut biceps rolling under his shirt.

His hands slid down my hips and over the curves of my butt. He pushed my body flush against his.

A hot, slow trickle of arousal gathered in my core.

"I've barely touched you, and I'm already hard," he murmured into my ear. "I've been thinking about fucking you again. About teaching you what a proper fuck *is*."

My breath was panting out of me. Every word he said, no matter how crude, was like a drug to me. I couldn't get enough. I wanted him to want me. Needed it.

I wanted to say something, wanted to ask him why, if he wanted me that much, he'd basically ignored me since we said *I do*, but I couldn't bring myself to say the words.

I was a coward, so I chickened out and just nodded.

He tilted my chin up to him with one finger, and the heated look he gave me then was dazzling.

I was in so much trouble.

He started moving to the beat of the song that was pumping through the club, and without any conscious permission from my brain, my body started moving with him.

It was good. We both knew how to move. We danced like we'd made love beautifully a thousand times instead of fucking regrettably once. Regardless of our history, or lack thereof, our chemistry was undeniable.

Our torsos flush, he pushed his thigh high between mine, and buried his face in my neck, rubbing his nose back and forth along my tender skin while his ever moving hands played havoc on my hormones with every heady pump of the bass.

His hips moved against me in a slick, greedy rhythm. As we moved, his chest brushed against my face. I licked it. His flavor was like a sweet, heady liquor.

God, I wanted more. I wanted to touch him, to run my lips all over him, to climb up his body right then and there.

I wanted him to fuck me again when my body

and mind were like this, relaxed and languid, hazy and ready. I wanted a real consummation, his body invading mine for reasons other than bloody sheets and doctor probes. I wanted to do absolutely everything with him. Not for business but for pleasure. I wanted him to teach me what that meant.

God I was a little drunk. Whether it was on him or the various shots I'd done, I wasn't sure. But it didn't matter. My mind was awhirl and lucid all at the same time, making it ripe for picking unwanted truths out of my own brain.

I was becoming obsessed with my own hostile husband.

My only excuse was that he was an easy man to become obsessed with. Effortless. The perfect line of his stubbled jaw, the spark in his gorgeous eyes, the lush curve of his mouth, the playful fall of his dark hair, every inch of his hard body— all of these things haunted my dreams whether I willed them or not.

I'd reassured myself repeatedly that my obsession was superficial, and that at least it was not affection. But that night those reassurances were shattered straight into dust.

It was so easy to like the him he was with his friends; warm and easy. Laughing and joking. Charming and fun.

The way he touched me was the first cut. That night was the second. The barrier inside of me was being bombarded. And he didn't even have to try.

I needed to snap out of it. I needed to rally. I needed to stop the feelings I was feeling before this all got out of hand.

The agony of feeling something for my own husband needed to be avoided at all costs.

And forget about the L word. That was straight up out of the question. I blamed the liquor that it even came into my brain. Love was always a heavy burden, but loving a man like him would drag me down into the dirt, of that I was certain, and my head wanted no part of it.

Unfortunately my body didn't agree, and my heart kept trying to pound its way out of my chest, kept trying to bring real emotions into this fake marriage.

CHAPTER
14

Our small booth was in a corner, and he moved behind me suddenly, tugging out curtains that I hadn't realized were there.

A light dawned. I glanced around. "Is this some sort of a sex club?" I hadn't asked the question loudly, but I was close to his ear.

He heard me, glanced back, and smirked. He leaned over to my ear to answer. "No. I know of a few in the city if you want to check one out, but this is just a regular club with some perks for the owner and his friends."

He pulled the curtains out until they encircled the entire booth, leaving us in near darkness.

A heavy breath shuddered out of my enervated, trembling body.

An instant later I felt his hands on me, his breath panting against my lips.

He shoved my crop top up to my collarbone and snapped open the front of my bra.

He cupped my breasts and fondled them. Flattening out his palms, he rubbed my nipples in circles.

A moan escaped me.

He tugged at my nipples, rubbing them harder.

I moaned louder, but the sound was drowned out by the noise of club.

He bent down to my breast, drawing the tip into his mouth. He sucked it while his fingers rubbed my other nipple. He did this thoroughly, moving from one side to the other.

The sensations overwhelmed me. I clutched at his hair, holding him to me, and didn't bother to hold back my moans as he sucked my nipples until my eyes rolled up in bliss.

I squirmed, my hips moving, seeking something, anything, just *more*.

Could he make me come with just his mouth on my breasts? I didn't think so, but I had a genuine moment where I thought he just might.

The question left my brain as he moved down my body, dropping to his knees on the hard, dirty club floor.

I was shuddering like a leaf. In anticipation. I had already learned that when this bitter man put his mind to pleasuring me it was oh so sweet.

He shoved my skirt up to my waist and tugged my panties down to my ankles. I stepped out of them, and he casually thrust them into his pocket.

He pulled one of my legs over his shoulder, burying his face against my sex. He inhaled me.

I nearly came right then, but he was only getting warmed up.

His fingers softly parted my folds, and he burrowed his face deeper against me. His tongue fluttered whisper soft over me as he teasingly licked my cleft.

I clutched his hair and held on for the ride. It was all I could do to stay upright.

He rimmed my trembling slit with the tip of his tongue, taking his time at it, moving slow as dripping honey.

My heart was stuttering wildly, my wet tongue kept licking at my lips as though that would make my throat less parched as I cried out in quick, breathy pants.

He kissed my pussy for a very long while, going at it like it was romantic, like he was in love with it, like he was making out with my mouth instead of my sex. His head moved back and forth with his movements, kissing, licking, sucking, nibbling.

I'd thought he was good with his hands. He was an artist with his mouth.

Finally, after all the drugging tastes and teases, his tongue speared into me, shoving as deep as it could.

I screamed in pleasure. The club noise drowned it out the second it hit the air.

I knew he heard it because the second he did, he went wild. He started fucking me with his tongue, fucking with the concentrated purpose I'd only ever seen him use when he was trying to get the bottom of a glass of straight bourbon.

He was making these exquisite little noises as he ate at me, noises I felt more than heard, hungry noises like he was licking the bowl for the last spare trace of cream.

I loved it, loved the way he made me feel, the way he made me come alive under his hands, his mouth.

I gripped his silky hair in both hands and rocked my hips, swiveling my aching cunt into his face.

I cried out a protest as his tongue withdrew, but it turned to encouragement as it stroked its way to my clit. He lapped there gently for one lick, two, three.

It was so excessive and yet lacking, it was too much and somehow I needed more, everything, now.

"Please," I begged him, not caring if he heard,

not caring who heard. I needed more. I needed to ignite again.

He shoved his fingers into me and started punching them in and out hard. I felt my own juices dripping down my leg. It almost hurt, but even that felt good.

He pinched his lips oh so softly around my clit and drew on it until I felt my flesh teasing between his flat straight teeth. It was a tender draw at first, but suddenly and without warning, he sucked *hard*.

The nerve endings in my loins shredded. I screamed into the chaos.

Yes. There it was. That ignition inside of me. He'd done it before, but this time was more, deeper, hotter, hungrier. I came with my whole self, with shivers that ran the length of my body in a rush of heady ecstasy that spread down to my toes.

It took me a long time to recover. I was pretty much useless while he righted my clothes.

I couldn't look at him.

He refastened my bra, caressing my sensitive breasts as he did so, kneading at my flesh and pinching my erect, sensitive nipples like he couldn't help himself. He sucked on them while he tugged my skirt down and straightened it, smoothing the material down my thighs. He pulled back and positioned me so I was sitting up on the seat. I wanted to lie down. I wanted to spread my legs and beg him to do it all again.

He righted my bra and put my top back in place.

"My panties," I reminded him, my voice drowned out by all the noise.

He heard. "Just keep your legs together and try to be modest, if you even know what that means."

I flushed. How could his mouth be both the nicest and meanest thing I'd ever encountered?

He opened the curtains and I shut my eyes against the bright strobing lights. Darkness was better, especially after *that*.

I still couldn't look at him. I was sitting somewhere between mortified, disgusted, and completely smitten.

There was really no hope for me.

He sat back down beside me and threw an arm around my shoulders, pulling me into him. My face was hot. I felt his breath against my skin a beat before his soft lips kissed my temple. It was almost sweet.

What was that? What were we doing here?

"Well, you're better at taking oral than you are at giving it," he murmured. "At least you're good for something."

Ah, there it was. The venom hadn't gone away, not for one second.

I didn't even realize we'd been joined by a few of his friends until he leaned away from me and started casually chatting with one of them.

I stared in a daze at absolutely nothing. I was drunk on more things than the champagne.

After a short while, we went back into the smaller, private room. Our groups' booth was empty. Everyone else was out dancing now. Calder didn't seem to care.

We sat in silence for a time. I sipped sparingly at the virgin OJ he'd autocratically ordered for me while he tried to drown himself in bourbon.

Something was bothering me, and I knew it was a bad idea even as I felt the question leaving my mouth. "So why didn't you marry one of the debutantes?"

He paused mid-drink, then resumed, finishing the glass, and giving me a thorough, less than friendly once over.

Personal questions were not welcomed in our marriage, and I'd had the gall to ask one anyway.

I'd displayed very bad fake wife manners.

I cared less and less about that.

Finally, surprisingly, he answered, "First and foremost, I didn't want to. Second, I had no desire to marry someone that I and at least half of my close friends have plowed."

I winced at his vulgarity, his misogyny, and his snobbery. "Isn't that a double standard? Have you been a saint?"

"No, I haven't and yes, it is, but that doesn't change anything. I don't know what to tell you. I was never going to marry one of them. That was never on the table. If one of them implied otherwise, they didn't get the idea from me."

"Because you wanted a virgin."

"I told you. That wasn't my stipulation. But now that it's all said and done, I'm not sorry about it. It all worked out for the best."

Well, I'll be damned. Almost a compliment.

"Not the marriage," he corrected hastily. "I still fucking hate being married to you. But I don't entirely hate that your body's my *exclusive* territory."

And there it was.

His hand slid shamelessly between my closed thighs. They parted for him in spite of my shame, and he fingered me. "No one else has been here," he whispered and promptly withdrew.

He proceeded to ignore me in favor of his phone.

I withstood it for a solid thirty minutes before I broke. My mind snagged on something, fixating on it to the point that I found myself stewing until I finally just addressed it out loud. "So am I getting this wrong, or did you imply that you've slept with most or all of my bridal party?" I asked him.

His face stiffened. He turned his head and eyed me with spectacular detachment. "My, my, aren't you full of questions you don't have any right to ask?"

I thought that was his answer, and we lapsed back into silence for a time.

"I never slept with Millie or Veronica," he said suddenly. "As for the rest, we were all dumb, horny teenagers together. What can I say?" He saw the look on my face. "Don't ask questions you don't want answers to. And need I remind you? This is not a love match. Where I've put my dick is not your business. So I think it's fair to say this whole discussion is less than productive."

It was only the brutal truth. I'd walked into this knowing I'd have no ownership of him.

The thing was, I hadn't been fascinated with him then. There was no obsession in my bloodstream when I'd put ink to that paper. I wasn't sure how or why, but a lot had changed since then.

I tried not to show how much I was appalled by what he'd just revealed. A part of me had been expecting and hoping he'd deny it, but this was not going to go my way. "I don't suppose it is. Making me hang out with them is also less than productive."

He had the grace to at least look somewhat uncomfortable. "I didn't know Millie was bringing the entire messy crew," he said stiffly. "But it is what it is. This is your social circle now. It's what you signed on for."

"Understood," I said smoothly.

We lapsed back into silence, and I could feel him staring at me. I kept my gaze trained down at my hands.

"You're very composed," he remarked after a time. I couldn't tell if it was a compliment, insult, or simple observation. "Are you always so quiet?"

I chewed on my lip, stealing a look at him. I couldn't seem to get a word out. I could feel the blush staining my cheeks. My mind was stuck firmly on what he'd done to me earlier. I hadn't been quiet earlier when he was making out with my cunt and making me scream.

He smirked. It wasn't friendly. It was some mean mix between self-loathing, irony, and utter disdain. "Well, I guess not always, huh?"

CHAPTER 15

CALDER

I could still taste her, still feel her on the bed of my tongue. I hated her guts but, she tasted like paradise.

It was a mistake to come here, to go anywhere near her. I'd known it was a bad idea from the start. I didn't want to do it, but I was still fully culpable. I had let my friends talk me into it with barely a struggle.

The second I saw her, I regretted coming. Two hours later, I was regretting it even more. I wanted nothing to do with her, had in fact vowed to neglect her as much as it was possible for a husband to neglect an unwanted wife, but that didn't seem to matter exactly the *second* she got close enough for me to touch her.

Eating her out and getting addicted to the

taste of her in the process had not been in the plans. Training her to melt at my touch, to ignite when my lips made contact with her were counterproductive to my intentions. All of my actions were at odds with my goals for the evening and in general: to drive her away through humiliation, estrangement, or flat out cruelty. In other words, by any means necessary. I despised this sham marriage, and I wanted her to know it, feel it, resent it as much as I did.

I wanted her to hate me more than she loved the millions she'd sold herself for. Hate me enough to call the whole thing off. I couldn't do it, but if *she* did, I knew that would prove a very important point to my father: this scheme of his was doomed from the start.

I'd left her sitting alone some time ago. I couldn't be that close to her. Across the room was too close.

I'd set up camp at the private club room's small bar, downing one drink after another to erase the honey sweet flavor of her. So far it wasn't working.

She was looking down at her phone, and I couldn't stop watching her for more than short stretches of time. As I stared, a few of my friends joined her. She looked up and responded to a question, her lush lips shaping the words attractively, her flawless face somber and serious. I could see the little dimple in her lush bottom lip from across the room. That fucking dimple.

My balls hurt. My dick was still hard as a rock. I'd had to drape my jacket in front of my raging erection after the incident behind the curtains in the main club. If she so much as brushed up against me again tonight, I was going to come in my pants. Another solid reason to resent her. She made me lose the control I'd come to take for granted at this stage of my life.

I wasn't used to denying myself like this, but I'd made a resolute decision not to let her get me off tonight. I didn't need more memories of her enthusiastic, artless mouth locked around my cock, her elegant fingers wrapped around it. She'd sucked me off like she *loved* it. After watching her fall apart tonight, I was starting to suspect that she might.

Hell, maybe I'd bought myself a slutty little virgin.

Or perhaps she was just a very good liar. I liked to think so. She didn't deserve the benefit of the doubt. Not by a long shot.

She'd sold herself into marriage. That was fucking calculated. But just *how* calculated was she?

Calculated enough to fake an orgasm that

made her lose her fucking mind? Yes, of course. But was she talented enough to pull it off *so well*? Who the fuck knew? Not me.

She laughed at something my friend Bradley said. She threw back her head when she did it, her gorgeous tawny blonde locks flowing back like she was a fucking Disney princess. Her laugh tinkled like a bell. It grated on my ears. Her teeth were white and perfectly straight, her big aquamarine eyes tilted up like a cat's. And her soft, lush pink lips were every wet dream I'd ever had as a teenager. Hell. As an adult.

What on earth was I thinking when I picked her out? What a short-sighted thing to do, marrying someone that I wanted to fuck this badly. I hated myself for it, but I hated her more.

I glared at Bradley but he wasn't looking at me, he was looking at my too gorgeous for her own usefulness wife.

My jaw clenched as I saw her face relax into happy lines. Not a fake smile for the cameras. Not a photo shoot. A genuine, candid smiling moment. It wasn't something I'd been privy to personally. I didn't like it. She was even more beautiful when she smiled like that, and it was already fucking enough.

Flashes from our wedding night came to me,

as they tended to do at odd moments even when I wasn't this close to her. Her lean, luscious body lying sprawled on the bed, long legs spread, blood and cum on her thighs. The perverse pleasure of feeling her virgin cunt squeezed around my bare dick. Skin on skin, *Jesus*. I'd never fucked without a condom before that night, and I'd certainly never had a *virgin*. The idea was *still* appalling, but the sentiment was shallow. I hadn't lasted thirty seconds once I was inside of her. The feel of her gripping me like I was her last lifeline was too much. It had flat-out done me in. I hadn't gotten off so fast since my first time inside a woman. That'd been twelve years ago. I flinched as my mind made that connection, while I'd been fourteen at the time, the woman had been older than my wife was now.

That night at least I'd had an excuse to touch her. Consummation was a nonnegotiable part of the deal.

What I had no excuse for was the rest. I never should have felt how wet her sleek cunt could get with just the barest brush of my fingers. I never should have let her wrap her lush lips around my cock. Never should have fucking *tasted* her. Never discovered how wet and hungry her smooth little pussy was.

She was setting a worse trap for me than my

father had, and I couldn't even tell if she was doing it on purpose.

The more I watched her, the more a dense fog of desire enveloped me. My balls were so fucking heavy I didn't think I'd last ten more minutes let alone the rest of the night.

Resolutely, I turned to the bar. I wouldn't so much as glance at her again, I decided. Out of sight, out of mind, out of fucking myself to death distance.

"Hopefully the women weren't too rough on her before we came by," my friend Preston spoke as he moved in beside me at the bar. He was the sweet, caring one of the group. He and Millie were perfect together. "Millie says it was a bit tense. I don't know what that even means, but I hope they didn't scare her off. Sorry, man."

I shot him a glance. He was turned the opposite way of me, facing the room.

I shrugged both of my shoulders. It was a restless motion, more for me than him. "She's a grownup. She can fend for herself."

"I hope she didn't have to is all I'm saying," he remarked.

I didn't respond to that. I didn't know what I hoped for. Nothing I felt lately made any damn sense.

"What do you see when you look at her?" I

asked him. I had my back to her, but I knew he was staring at the incomparably gorgeous creature I was married to.

My best friend appeared distinctly uncomfortable. "Your wife."

I laughed, and it was actually amused instead of bitter. "Look deeper. And get rid of that stick up your ass. The question wasn't a trap."

"A beautiful woman."

"Look deeper."

"Unbelievably beautiful. A bombshell. A modern day Brigitte Bardot."

"Deeper."

"When I look at that woman, I see the best sex of your life, you lucky bastard. How's that?"

It was my turn to look uncomfortable. We'd always been honest with each other. It was one of the reasons we'd stayed friends since childhood. "Yes, of course she's beautiful. An irresistibly attractive shell on her part was a condition of our union. But do you know what I see what when I look at her?"

"What?"

"My ruin. My own self-destruction strutting around on killer legs. Chaos. The ruination of my peace of mind. The way I react to her looks is the death of my principles. The way I respond when I feel her pussy is the vindication of a tyrant."

"The tyrant being your father, I presume?"

"Of course."

"Who the hell cares?" he said harshly.

"Excuse me?"

"Who the hell cares what your father thinks? You've always been at war with that man, and it's got nothing to do with that poor girl. Yes, your father can be a tyrant, but *she's* not."

No, she was a whore, I thought, but I didn't say it aloud. It was one thing for me to think it, but no one else got the privilege.

The thought made me freeze. Hell no. I would hold *nothing* sacred about her. About us. "She's not a tyrant," I agreed. It surprised me how much effort it took me to muscle the next words out. "Tyrants have brains, and voices, and choices. She sold off all three. You know what she is?"

He was staring at me with wide eyes, giving me a look that said, *what are you even thinking, man?*

I answered my own question. "She's a piece of art that my father bought for me to fuck on the regular. An expensive blow up doll. A gorgeous fucking cum dumpster. She's my own private whore."

"Banks, stop," my best friend said in a very careful voice.

I turned. She was standing right there. I wondered exactly what she'd heard. I felt color climb up my cheeks in a guilty flush, but I told myself that I didn't care. She deserved everything I'd said. It was nothing but the brutal truth.

"May I go?" she asked with quiet composure. It made me want to shake her.

"No," I said, feeling cruel. "Go earn your keep and mingle with my friends."

Without a word, she turned away.

"And Noura," I called out, voice hard, dick harder.

She turned to look at me. Her eyes were insolent.

It made me wild.

"Yes, husband?" There was a bite to her words.

She had some spirit. I found that almost unbearably provocative.

It made me lash out all the harder. "I know this is asking a lot, but try your best not to embarrass me."

Something fascinating happened to her face. It barely moved, but her eyes snapped at me, and her lips trembled.

I couldn't tell if I'd broken her spirit or lit a fire in her. Why did I perversely want to do both?

"Is that all?" she shot back.

I raked my eyes over her, top to bottom. Her nipples were erect, and it was visible through her top.

Well, hadn't that backfired in a hurry?

"No," I drawled. "You may be a whore, but you're *my* whore. Stop flirting with Bradley."

Without another word, she turned and walked away.

"Jesus, Banks," Preston sounded shocked. "What the *hell* is wrong with you?"

"Her. She's what's wrong.

"You're going to have to get over this."

"You're not the one who had to marry some dumb model."

"Do you even know that she's dumb? One thing I know for a fact about your father, he would not allow you to breed with someone with a low IQ."

I knew he was right about that one small point. I even knew that I had access to all of her information, from her shoe size to her SAT scores, but stubbornly I refused to look at it.

"Did you see that picture she posted a few weeks ago?" I changed the subject.

Preston nearly choked on his drink. I glared at him. That was answer enough. "Stop following her on social media, you fucking pervert," I ground out.

His eyes tried to bug out of his head. "I only follow her because I thought it was the polite thing to do. I was the best man at your wedding!"

"How sweet. Well, stop. And you better not have that fucking picture saved on your phone."

"You've lost your mind."

He probably had a point.

CHAPTER 16

NOURA

For some reason I could not fathom why my husband drove back with me to my apartment. I even got past my helpless rage enough to speak to him once. "Will you be staying at my apartment tonight?" Because why the hell else was he in my car?

He didn't bother to look at me. "No. I'm going home. I need sleep. I haven't had a solid night of rest for days, and I know I'll sleep better in my own bed."

Fair enough. Good riddance. I wanted free of his company ASAP. It was nothing but a relief.

It was also a relief to catch him letting loose that hateful tirade at my expense, I told myself. I'd been going a little soft for him. *Can't have that.* I knew deep in my gut that I couldn't show him an ounce of weakness. Showing your belly to your enemy was always a stupid move.

I bid him a cursory goodnight. He didn't bother to respond or so much as look my way. Asshole.

Chester escorted me up to my apartment in silence. I knew he had opinions about my husband and my marriage, but he always had the grace to keep them to himself. I knew there had to be some conflict of interest there.

Jovie was still awake. I let her coax me out of my foul mood. It didn't take long. She braided my hair while we watched an episode of our latest K-drama and told me a story about a runway show she'd done where they'd made all of the models dress like terrifying clowns.

Eventually the tension in my shoulders and the clenching of my fists eased enough that I warmed up enough to share. I gave her an edited version of the night. I left out my jerk of a husband's words and all the things not fit for fourteen-year-old ears. She agreed that my husband's privileged rich girl friends were all skanky bitches and hoes. Her company was just what the doctor ordered. I reflected, not for the first time, how lucky it was that we'd found each other.

We called it quits after about an hour. I felt

worlds better, courtesy of my newly adopted baby model. Jovie had acclimated to sleeping by herself, mostly, and she gave me a big hug before skipping to my spare room which was now firmly *her* room. I wondered to myself how long she'd stay with me and secretly hoped it was indefinitely. Sometimes you don't realize how lonely you are until you find just the right company.

I went to bed alone and with a smile on my face.

I woke up in the dead of night, hot and bothered.

And I wasn't alone.

Calder's large form was stretched out on top of me, his arms bracing tightly outside of mine, bracketing me in. The thin T-shirt I'd gone to bed in was gone. My panties were gone, too. I was completely bare.

One of his muscular thighs was shoved high between my legs. I was rubbing wantonly against it.

"I thought you were staying at your own place." The words came out of me in soft, unwanted pants.

"I tried," he murmured into my ear.

"I thought you needed sleep," I said.

"Forget what I need." His mouth slid along my jaw and down my throat. "Give me what I *want.*" As he spoke he pressed his palm low on my belly, touching my clit oh so softly with his thumb. I pushed myself against it.

He fingered my sex with the softest whisper of a touch and *purred* his approval into my ear. "Good girl. Already wet for me. I could slip my cock inside you right now, but I won't. Not just yet." His words were low, soft puffs against my flesh. "First, I'm going to make you come. I need to taste you again. I'm going to eat you out before I fuck you. And not like the first time. This time I'm going to fuck you right. You're going to be ready this time. More than ready. You're going to beg me for it. I'm going to show you that you love having my cock buried balls deep inside you."

"Oh, God," I breathed, embarrassed and aroused.

I opened my mouth to say I don't know what, but words were not what escaped me as he started to push one of his big fingers into me. It entered me slowly, carefully.

My eyes shut at the aching sensations pulsing through me. It was sobering, how vulnerable I felt as he invaded me with just that one thick, curious finger.

He took his time feeling me, testing my cunt.

"You're squeezing me like a vise. This is just

my *finger*, Noura." His breath was ragged in my ear. "Imagine how tight you're going to hug my cock."

I didn't whimper, but it was a close thing. I didn't know if it was his dirty talk, his touch, or my name on his lips, but he was getting to me good. How could I let someone who held such disdain for me affect me so? I hated it and loved it all at once. Everything I felt only added to my arousal.

He tugged his finger out of me abruptly, moving to stand.

"Lie down on the edge of the bed. On your back." He paced restlessly as he spoke.

I sprawled where he'd instructed. A small part of me wanted to shut my eyes in shame, mortified at what I was submitting to, embarrassed at how he affected me.

A larger part of me, the part of me that won out, couldn't take my eyes off him.

He stopped in his tracks. He was staring at my body. He caught his lip between his teeth as his gaze traced over me, avidly and thoroughly.

He moved back to the bed. He hooked my leg over his arm, hitching it up, spreading my legs wide.

I was trembling, my nipples drawn tight, everything bared to him. Sensations overwhelmed me, everything inside of me warring with itself. Shame, chagrin, desire, hunger, shock, confusion.

Desire won. I squirmed. Not in discomfort. In anticipation for the return of his touch.

He reached between my legs with both hands, and parted me oh so softly with his fingers. "You're lovely everywhere," he told me quietly. "So tender and pink. Just for me. Say it. Say this is just for me."

"This is just for you," I said, voice thready with need.

Painstakingly and with utmost care, he slid two thick fingers into me.

I watched him, eyes dissecting his face with avid interest as he breached me. I loved how absolutely he was focused on me, his lower lip bitten as though in deep concentration.

"I'm going to make you come so hard, Noura," he crooned as he pulled his fingers out and thrust them gently back in.

I clenched eagerly around him, my breath panting in and out.

He pulled out, dragging the pad of his fingers along every sensitive nerve inside of me, then pumped back in. "You're even a snug fit for my fingers. I can't stop remembering how good this hot little cunt felt when it was hugging my cock." He drew out and shoved back in, this time going deeper, harder until I had to shift, trying to ease the pressure.

"I'm going to ride you *bare*," he bent lower, nuzzling between my breasts as he spoke into my skin. "I'm going to fill you with my cum."

His mouth surrounded the peak of my breast and oh so softly *bit* right as his fingers pulled out. He started pumping them in and out, quick, smooth and shallow.

I didn't know what to do with myself. I was keyed up and turned on. I started jerking my hips, trying clumsily to match his movements. My arms were flung out, my fingertips digging restlessly into the sheets.

I whimpered out a protest when he tugged his fingers out.

"Shh," he breathed into my skin, his mouth working soft as a whisper along my flesh. He moved lower, his lips running along my ribs, down my belly, not stopping until his gorgeous face was wedged between my legs.

He stretched me open with his big hands and touched the very tip of his tongue to my clit.

My hips jerked and I cried out.

He nuzzled against me, then started licking, lapping luxuriously from taint to clit.

"Please." He wrung the word out of someplace deep inside of me.

He raised his head, looking up my sweat slick torso, through his thick black lashes at me. "Please what? What are you asking me for?"

I didn't even know. Only he did, and he was well aware of that fact. I said it again.

He smiled, and lowered his mouth back down to my sex.

He locked his mouth over my cunt, thrusting his tongue into me, over and over.

My hands were in his hair before I could stop myself, clutching him against me, my hips bucking, shoving myself into his mouth.

He said something into my flesh, but I couldn't make it out over the roaring in my ears.

He latched his lush lips over my clit and started sucking.

I barely held in a scream.

One of his hands was at my breast, kneading, plucking, rubbing. The other hand stayed between my legs, two of his fingers shoved into me. He pounded them in and out.

He did all of these things to me, all at once, and I lost all sense of time and reason.

I didn't just come. I was moved. I felt. I yearned. Wanted. Coveted.

In that moment it was apparent to me that there was some sort visceral, primal connection between us. It was powerful and undeniable.

The way he touched me.

Kissed me.

Held me. Savored me.

Breathed me.

Like I was necessary for his next breath.

It was *such* a lie, but I needed it.

I'd been prepared to submit for *his* pleasure, to do whatever was necessary for it, but I had not been in any way prepared for my own.

I had assumed that since I'd been instructed that I was not ignorant.

Oh how wrong I'd been.

Finding my own stingy, small release in private was not the same animal as having it *wrung* out of me by his hands, his lips, his tongue.

I was mortified to find that the feelings he pulled from me were somehow more than physical. They messed with my chest. My head, too.

And they were powerful. I couldn't reason myself out of them.

Somehow it was much more of a violation than the act of his body invading mine, this turning of my body and emotions against me. I'd never imagined this part of the arrangement, let alone agreed to it.

And just as soon as I came down from the high, out of body experience of coming so hard

I forgot my own name, I promised myself I'd be resenting the hell out of him for it.

CHAPTER
17

I was a boneless, thoughtless puddle on the bed. The only thing working were my eyes, and they followed his movements as he pulled away.

I hadn't even noticed that he'd been fully clothed between my naked thighs until he started to strip.

He was moving with swift impatience, but it was still a good show.

He looked down as he worked impatiently at the buttons of his shirt. His hair fell forward, his lashes falling into thick shadows against his taut cheeks.

He was as handsome as a fallen angel with silky, inky black hair, and deep olive skin.

He shrugged out of his shirt. It was a sight, the powerful muscles of his shoulders working under his crisp white material as he worked. I drank in the sight of his ripped, tanned torso as he started working on his trousers.

I'd known that he was large and muscular, but his shoulders were stronger and wider than I'd imagined, hard muscles moving under his skin, jumping and flexing with his every movement. His chest was large and built, his pectorals swollen, his small brown nipples hardened into tight points. The hard ridges of his abdomen were starkly defined, his body arrowing down to hips that were a slim contrast to his wide shoulders. God, he was beautiful.

He wasn't just a playboy or a businessman. He'd earned a body like that. He'd worked for it.

In reality I didn't own any part of him, but in that moment I felt a keen, perverse thrill that this magnificent creature was my husband and that no one else had that honor.

My breath punched out of me as he pushed his slacks down over his hips, boxers and all.

His sex was thick and long, curving up to his navel. He was fully aroused, and it was as intimidating as it was enthralling.

I felt a primordial thrill move through me. Strange as it was, our bodies were made for each other. One owning the other. His cock was an instrument of power, and he was moments away from claiming me with it. And I wanted him to. Needed it.

When he was fully nude he paused for a moment, and we took each other in.

I was sprawled, legs open, still limp from my orgasm, but alive, so alive, and so wet and ready for more.

His tall form was tensed, looking a second away from pouncing, eyes hungry. His long, athletic legs flexing with the effort to stay in place.

We watched each other for one pounding heartbeat, two, three, four. He was teasing us both.

His hand started stroking his rigid length, and my eyes were drawn to the sight. My body went from boneless to rigid with anticipation. I wanted more. I wanted him fully. I wanted a true consummation. I craved having him inside of me.

Finally he moved, striding to the bed. He lowered himself over me, pressing kisses to my belly, working slowly up to my breasts. He sucked at each of my nipples before making his way up to my neck.

He lined his cock up to fuck me. I tensed. The first time had been painful, but that had been another world, another dimension, a different copy of me. He hadn't bothered to tune my body to the music of his touch then. I hadn't been ready. I was beyond ready now.

He pulled his mouth away from my skin, looking down between our slick, naked bodies. My eyes followed his.

He held himself up with one arm. The other reached down. He gripped his thick length and teased me with the tip, rimming my sex. His breath was panting out of him.

My heart was pounding so hard in my ears that I wondered if he could hear it. If he could see it moving in my chest.

"Touch me," he hissed out between clenched teeth.

I reached for him, and his arousal fell heavily into my hands. I squeezed him. The fingers of one hand barely fit around the thick girth of him. He was so hard, but his skin was like velvet. The contrast of something so hard wrapped in silk was delightful. Thrilling. Intoxicating. I stroked him, feeling all of him with my palms. With hungry enthusiasm I fisted him with both hands, root to tip.

I was just getting started when he tugged my hands away with a curse. "Too much," he warned me. "I'm too primed right now, and I want to come inside of you."

"Yes," I said, voice agonized, thready with

need. My arms fell back onto the mattress. I could count the seconds since he'd gotten me off, but it wasn't enough. I was empty again. *Aching* and I wanted him inside of me, filling me utterly. I wanted it all, and only *that* part of him was enough.

He kept himself propped up on one elbow, the tension in his muscles making them stand out starkly in his shoulders.

His other arm was busy guiding the wide crest of his thick length against my entrance.

Both of our eyes were trained on his rigid member as it breached me. He let out a tortured moan as he fed his cock into me with utmost care.

I tried to suppress my own moan as he slid in oh so slowly. His long, hot, velvety shaft stretched me with every bit of progress. My tender muscles clutched at him, my breaths coming short and fast.

He was still looking down between our bodies, his features slack with desire. I knew instinctively that he was too far gone to slow down, let alone stop. Good. Stopping wasn't an option. I *needed* more.

I took his thick length all the way to the root. There was no pain this time, just a delightful, overwhelming, racking stretch.

It was almost too much and *exactly* enough.

"God," he said, his deep voice hoarse with delicious agony. "I'd convinced myself that I'd *imagined* you felt like this."

His heady words, the way he spoke them, were undeniably flattering. And a shock. It was news to me that he'd enjoyed any aspect of our wedding night. I tucked the knowledge away for later consumption.

He started to move, not pulling out but shifting around, *feeling* me, massaging a sweetly tender spot inside of me that I hadn't even known was there. But *he* knew. He navigated his way inside me like it was second nature, like he'd been there a thousand times instead of once.

My nails dragged into the sheets, my legs curling naturally around his hips.

"You ready?" he panted into my skin.

"Yes, keep going," I huffed back.

"Keep going? I haven't even gotten started."

And with that, he started fucking me. It was only my second time, but he didn't go soft or easy on me.

Exactly and precisely the opposite.

His rigid cock nailed me straight into the mattress.

It was devastation.

It was heaven. It was hell. I was overcome.

Turns out, I loved fucking. Took to it like a

natural whore. Oh the wonderful, bitter irony.

Once he started, he didn't let up at all.

He had me in a tireless tempo. In a perfect, strident battering of body and wills. A giving and a taking of flesh pounding flesh.

There was a brutal, concentrated focus to the way he fucked that got to me. It was art. It was poetry. It was creation. Perverse chaos done in explicit order. It was the wonder of nature and the debasement of humanity.

Oh my body. I said goodbye to it then. It was his. He really did own me now. In law and in fact.

Was it always like this, or was this all him and I? Something that we owned alone. A private piece of paradise just for us.

He grabbed my hips, tilting me into an angle that had the plush head of his shaft rubbing me just right with every drive home.

His hips churned as he rutted in and out, in and out, his thick length pulling out until his blunt crest rimmed me before slamming back in, balls deep every time. And *fast*. Urgent. Frenzied.

Every single plundering lunge was satisfying and complete.

He called me a whore, but he was the one who fucked like it was his job. His very purpose in life.

I kept my eyes closed the whole time.

I never pictured his face when he was inside of me. I never said his name. I did those small things right.

Still somehow I lived and breathed for his touch. His possession.

He drummed in and wrenched out of me with a desperate, masterful rhythm, his hips oscillating in and out, drawing back and driving in, again and again with increasing tempo.

The pressurized tide inside of me built and built, finally letting loose on an upsurge right as he hit the end of me with a soft, desperate grunt.

I came in a torrent. In a deluge. My anxiety, my fear, my anger, my *soul* poured out of me. I tried to keep my eyes shut tight like that would keep some of it in.

My sex gripped his thickness in beating, milking pulses, sucking him deep and holding him there.

My eyes opened somewhere in the middle of it in spite of my efforts. Our gaze clashed. It was a raw, aching moment, vulnerable and naked. I wasn't alone here. He was going through some earth shattering of his own.

I was too shaken by the moment to feel even an ounce of self-satisfaction at the reveal.

He swore harshly, yanking out of me with one sudden, savage wrench.

I looked down between our bodies and for one fleeting moment I saw that he had pulled out mid-climax. Cum was still spurting out of his tip.

In a flash he rolled me over and up onto my hands and knees then started pumping into me again, hips slamming against my ass with each forceful plunge as he rubbed out every last twitch of his orgasm, rooting his cum out deep inside of my sensitive flesh.

"What the *fuck*?" he panted in a rough, agitated voice.

He held me up with a strong hand fanned out against my belly, and he kept me prone like that, buried deep while he emptied himself with drawn out spasms.

It went on for quite a while. He savored his climax to the very last drop. "Worth every penny," he muttered into my ear at the end, like he hated it, but not nearly as much as he loved it.

My body was confused about what was happening to it. I was coming down from the high of my climax, a little mortified at my wanton response to him, a part of me had definitely gone a little numb, and in spite of all that I was still turned on.

When he was finally finished, he dragged himself out of me.

I sucked in a breath at the sensation of that slow, slick pull.

He finally tugged himself free. There was a wet little pop as my cunt reluctantly let go of his broad tip.

A second later his palm left my belly, and I felt his heavy form shift away and leave the bed.

I held my own weight for maybe three seconds before I collapsed. I was boneless. Used up. Spent. I didn't think I had an ounce of energy left in my body.

I don't know what he did after that. I fell asleep straight away.

CHAPTER
18

CALDER

I woke up with a raging hangover and a relentless hard-on. What the *hell?*

I didn't even know where I was.

Oh, wait. Yes, I did.

In my *wife's* bed. I'd caved in and gone to her the night before.

So many excuses had led me here. I'd lasted exactly two hours from the time I dropped her off to when I broke. Refusal turned to denial which led quickly into empty justifications.

The fact was that I'd wanted her more than I cared about my reasons for hating her. I'd needed to fuck her. *Needed* it.

So I'd changed my mind. Twisted all of my rationalizations. This might be a travesty of a marriage, but there was no reason I couldn't make the best of it. I'd use her body however I pleased and keep hating her, I told myself. Maybe I'd get lucky and she'd fall in love with me so I could break her money-loving heart.

Even I knew it was an empty excuse. I used it anyway. Anything to bury myself inside her for a few hours. And if that wasn't bad enough I'd actually allowed myself to *stay the night.* My father would be unbearably smug when he heard.

It was untenable but I should've been used to the feeling. Lately my whole life was untenable.

Two years ago I was on top of the world. I was independently wealthy. I was happy. I was a romantic. I thought love conquered all. I thought love existed.

And then everything had changed. A few unfortunate happenings caused it, but all that mattered were the results—I lost everything of value in my life.

My business went belly up. My father disinherited me. The love of my life married another man. In that order.

The result? I'd become hardhearted. A cynic. And there was *nothing* I hated more than a fortune-hunting female.

Except perhaps my father for leveraging me into marrying one.

And now I was sleeping with her without

any coercion whatsoever. And this wouldn't be the last time. I knew it in my gut. I hadn't had enough of her. Not even close.

Still, I tried to rally. I swore to myself I'd leave right away.

Right away after some aspirin, coffee, and one more *quick* orgasm.

Reluctantly I turned my head, taking in my first sight of my wife in the morning light.

It wasn't a smart thing to do. I should have just walked away without looking back.

It was very early, but she'd left the blinds open completely and the morning sun was just peeking in with streaks of sunrise.

She was lying on her stomach, nude from when I'd undressed her the night before. Her hair was a silky tangle of tawny blonde waves that covered most of her shoulders and half of her face. That face was turned to me, innocent in slumber and flawless in the dawn light. I'd never seen her without makeup on before. Her skin was smooth and perfect and pore-less as a babe. She looked like the crossover child of a Victoria's Secret model and a Disney princess. It was an intriguing, unsettling, stirring combination, to say the least.

So clean and so dirty. So innocent and so tremendously, immeasurably fuckable.

Moreover, I'd never seen her face relaxed, without artifice or guile. It was shocking. It was fascinating. I wanted to brush all the hair away and study her at my leisure. Every inch of her, inside and out. I wanted to ferret out all of her secrets. I wanted to know what made her tick.

It made no sense. I knew all I needed to already. She was a gold digger. The most predictable creature on earth. She shouldn't have interested me in the least.

But I'd be damned if I wasn't absolutely fascinated. Fascinated and disgusted. Disgusted enough that even when she looked this innocent I wanted to lash out at her.

I wanted to hurt her. I wanted to fuck her silly. I knew I'd do both, but for the life of me I couldn't manage to do it in that order.

I slowly slid the sheet off her, running my hand along her back as I did so. She stirred but didn't wake. Her silky skin curved into my palm as it skimmed her, like a cat seeking firmer contact. My little pet bride.

When she was uncovered, I ran my hand over her back again. She sighed contentedly in her sleep.

I throbbed. When my palm cupped her ass, it perked right up into the air. I fingered her cunt. Her legs shifted, letting me in. She was soft and ready. Warm and wet.

I could count with my fingers the times I'd gotten her off, but it was already too much. Excessive. I'd gone too far.

I had trained her *too well*. She caught fire when I touched her now. She was my creature. I made that.

I loved it and resented the hell out of her for it.

I used two fingers to get her off. I watched her face while I did it. Watched it go from slumber, to waking, to the wonder of orgasm.

It was an addictive thing to witness. Distracting. The sort of thing that diverted you from your day's plans.

Your life's plans.

Our eyes were locked together. I was sucking my fingers clean, wondering if I could hold back long enough to get her off again before I shoved myself balls deep into her cunt. It was an unforgettable moment.

And our door opened.

No knock. No warning at all.

A small, middle-aged woman with a tight, hard expression on her face walked right in as though it were the most natural thing in the world.

I stared. She was vaguely familiar looking. I was so shocked at the intrusion that I didn't react at first. I just stared.

The baffling woman glared at my wife.

Glared. At my wife.

"There's no time for you to be a sloth this morning, Noura," she said with strident disdain. "You're an hour late. Out of bed, lazy girl. It's weigh-in day."

My stunned gaze swung to my wife. How would she react to this strange, awful woman?

To my chagrin she didn't. Or rather, she did. She rose without a word and obeyed the older woman.

I was distracted watching her bare ass move from the bed to the bathroom. The terrible woman followed her.

When they were out of my sight, I shook my head. Hard. Twice. *What the fuck?*

I got up, wrapped the sheet around my waist, and followed them.

My wife was standing naked on a scale. The woman was glaring down at it.

"Up two pounds?" she was saying coldly. "Must have been quite a night. Hope it was worth it for you. Looks like you'll be skipping breakfast. No milk in your coffee either."

My gaze flew to my wife. Her face was utterly stoic. And for some unfathomable reason, she didn't speak one word of protest.

Why wasn't she putting this shrew in her

place? Well, if she wouldn't . . .

"What the fuck are you doing?" I burst out at the stranger. "Who do you think you are, talking to her like that?"

"Excuse me, Mr. Castelo," she spoke to me in a completely different tone. Her very demeanor changed. "I'm Asha. The handler. Just doing my job."

"Well, you better rethink how you're doing it."

"How so, sir?"

I didn't even know where to begin.

Wait. Yes, I did.

"Get. Out. Of. Our. Room. And do not enter it again. Without. Knocking!"

For her part she reacted quickly enough to suit even me in that moment.

I threw on my clothes from the night before and went on a bit of a tear, going through the apartment, gathering my wife's entire staff.

Strangely, a teenaged girl was in the mix. She was studying me coldly, like *I* was the one who didn't belong in my wife's apartment.

I ignored her, focusing on Noura's team: Asha, the loud handler. Chester, the too-friendly, eyes too warm on my wife security. Vincent, the quiet driver.

I went on a tangent, laying out some ground

rules that I thought should have been pretty fucking obvious.

"Don't walk into our bedroom without knocking. Ever. In fact, stay out of our bedroom alto-fucking-gether."

That was for all of them.

"Don't raise your voice to my wife. In fact, don't even think of speaking to her with an *ounce* of disrespect in your tone. Don't so much as look at her fucking funny. Noura's the one in charge here. No one else." I glared at Asha all throughout this part of my rant. It was for her. "And if I hear that you've been telling her what to eat—that you've been telling her *not* to eat." I had to collect my temper before continuing. *"So help me God, there will be hell to pay!"*

Mouthy Asha didn't have a thing to say to that.

"Is all of that crystal fucking clear?" I asked, making solid eye contact with each of them.

Why was the teenager grinning like a loon now? I ignored her again.

Asha's eyes snapped at me, but she didn't hesitate. "Yes, sir," she replied firmly.

"Crystal," Chester drawled. He was clearly holding in a smirk.

"Certainly," Vincent agreed cheerfully.

I left them without another word, returning to my wife's quarters.

CHAPTER 19

Noura was just stepping out of the shower, toweling herself off. So clean. Not for long. I watched her for a time, wondering why she had nothing to say.

Finally I broke out with, "Why'd you let her treat you like that?"

She shrugged. It drew my eyes down to her barely covered, edible tits. "That's just how she is. I was too tired to fight her today. Besides, I'm supposed to listen to her. It's part of the arrangement."

"Fuck the arrangement," I said succinctly. "No one gets to tell you what to do. Certainly not her."

She raised her perfect brows at that. Insolent, succulent little piece.

"I mean it," I stressed. "You're a Castelo.

Don't take any shit from her. Don't take that kind of shit from *anyone*."

"Except you."

I glared. She may have had some sort of a point, but as far as I was concerned it was irrelevant to the conversation. "You don't have to take orders from her. Consider whatever that was stricken from the arrangement, okay?"

She didn't smile at me. God forbid. But her face did soften into something so warm I could barely stand to look at her. "We don't have to be enemies, you know," she said with quiet solemnity. "There's no reason we can't be civil to each other. Pleasant, even. I'm game if you are. Truce?"

A peace offering. It would have been sweet if I didn't despise the very idea of her. And worse and even more despicable, the need I felt building in my blood for her.

No. No. No. *No.* I wasn't parting ways with this grudge. I'd hold onto it for the rest of our lives if I couldn't find a way to be rid of her sooner.

Instead of answering, I moved closer. I grabbed her chin and studied her face. "I'm not used to seeing you without makeup," I told her. "I don't like it." (A lie.) How was she even more beautiful like this? She dazzled me.

"You look too young," I added. (The truth.)

She raised her face to me, tempting me to take her mouth in a kiss. I resisted. "I'll take that as a no." She sounded almost sad.

"No truce," I agreed, taking off her towel. I lifted her onto the closest counter, parting her thighs.

I'd infuriated her and I liked it that way. I wanted her hot and furious.

I didn't undress. I just took out my dick and started fucking her like my life depended on it. Because it did. If I couldn't rut my need out inside of her Right—*Oh*. This. *God*. Second. *Yes*—I was convinced I'd die on the spot.

She raised her lips to mine for a kiss but I managed to resist, turning my face away.

Instead I bent down to suck on a pebbled, perky nipple.

"You're so cold," she told me in a ragged breath.

I ran my mouth up her collar, along her throat. "Are you kidding me?" I rasped into her ear. The words weren't voluntary. They were torn from me. "I'm on fire."

I pulled back to watch her face as she started to come, but I couldn't take it. I didn't want that between us, that unspoken intimacy. I rallied myself to pull out and turn her around, but I didn't even manage that. The best I accomplished was to bury my face in her neck so I didn't have to see her gorgeous eyes while I shot my load deep inside her fortune-hunting cunt.

I stayed there until I was sure she'd milked out every last drop. Betraying every stubborn principle I had never felt so good.

When I finally pulled out, I didn't look at her face.

She didn't join me in the shower, and I was relieved. She stepped in after I stepped out, and I was still maintaining my self-control well enough not to look at her.

"Do I have a change of clothes somewhere in this place?" I asked her blandly.

"There's a rack of men's clothes in the closet. I suppose we can assume they're meant for you." Her tone was even blander than mine, the brat. I almost joined her in the shower just to slap her lightly on the ass for that bit of sass, but resisted. If I so much as touched her again, we wouldn't be leaving for some time.

I caught her just toweling off again when I exited the closet. I managed not to look again, point for me. "Who's the teenager?" I asked her.

"Another model. She needed a room . . . temporarily. I have extra room, so I offered."

I looked her way at that. She was still toweling

off. Why was it taking her so long to get dry? Maybe she needed my help? I shook off the thought.

"This isn't some child model halfway house," I said sternly. I was determined to regain the control I lost every time I got my dick wet inside her.

"I'm aware of that," she said with unfathomable calmness. It heated my blood. I had an almost uncontrollable urge to shake up that calm. I stared at her lips, remembering how they felt wrapped around my shaft.

"Send her back to her parents," I ordered.

"Not everyone has parents, Calder."

I blinked, trying to focus on the subject at hand. "She's an orphan?"

"She's emancipated. It's complicated. I have an extra room. She doesn't cause any problems. She's a kid, she needs me, and I like having her around."

I stared at her. "You've adopted a teenager?"

Did she just roll her eyes at me? And. *How far would they roll back with my cock rammed down her throat?*

"Please," she uttered.

I liked that word on her lips. "Say that again," I rasped.

She glared at me. I liked that too. "Please," she gritted out.

I grinned. "Aren't you a bit young to be someone's mommy?"

That lit a challenging, almost smug look in her eyes. I knew it meant she was about to goad me in some kind of way. "We're friends. She's only a few years younger than me. Actually, she's a lot closer to my age than *you* are."

Gorgeous little brat. It worked. Point to her.

Abruptly, I dropped the subject and left the room.

There was no food being prepared in the kitchen. I took up the job myself. No breakfast my ass.

I'd make sure she ate something decent (*only* because I knew she wouldn't eat if I didn't) and then I swore to myself that I was outta here.

The rest of my wife's team had gone back into their holes.

All that was left was a teenaged model drinking coffee and watching me like I was her favorite TV program.

I studied the contents of the refrigerator. At least it was adequately stocked.

"Does she like omelets?" I asked the girl.

"I have no idea," she answered. "We don't really have breakfast around here."

"So I've heard. We're having it today."

"I'm Jovie," she told me cheerfully.

"Banks," I responded automatically. *Everyone* had always called me by my middle name. Everyone except my wife. Why did that realization make me flinch all of a sudden?

"So are you like living here or something now?" she asked bluntly.

I sent our bold little houseguest a flat stare. "Are *you*?" I returned.

"Yep," she answered without hesitation. "I'm your wife's roommate," she added with incorrigible sass. "And her bestie. We've been inseparable since we met."

I felt a pang of something unpleasant move through me. Jealousy, thick and bitter, shifted around inside of me, making itself right at home. It settled deep, lodging itself down into my gut. I knew the emotion, but I wasn't certain of the why of it here. I couldn't possibly be resentful that my wife had a *friend*. Even I wasn't that much of a bastard, right?

I was dishing up the first omelet when my wife walked up to the bar that looked into the kitchen. I placed it in front of her, trying not to take in the sight of her in more than the smallest bites.

She was wearing gym clothes, if you could even call them clothes. A white sports bra and teeny tiny shorts. I tore my gaze determinedly away from her body.

She opened her mouth, to turn down food, I was sure, but I stopped that in its tracks. "You're eating. I know that you drank more than you're accustomed to last night, and you need food. I don't want to hear a word of protest."

She met my eyes squarely. "Thank you," she said simply.

She took the food to her large, round dining table.

Damn, she was hard to read.

I made two more omelets. One for Jovie and one for myself. Right before I took my plate to the table, Chester and Vincent returned to the apartment and made themselves right at home.

I felt a tick start up in my temple as I watched Chester casually take the seat next to my wife.

The *only* empty seat left next to her, as Jovie had her other side.

The bastard had some nerve.

He seemed to notice me for the first time. He grinned. He leaned back, kicking the chair opposite him out from underneath the table. "Here ya go, boss."

The tick intensified. I tried my best not to react. I calmly sat and started eating.

"What are our plans for today, Duchess?" Chester asked my wife. He was smiling fondly at her, looking directly into her eyes.

And *her*. She was smiling back at him with unabashed warmth! Vaguely I heard my fork clatter onto my plate. I glanced down. My hands were both in fists.

I looked around the table. Chester and Vincent were looking at her with unmistakable affection.

Like they were one big happy family.

What the hell was happening here? These men were paid to guard and drive my money hungry wife. Yet here they were acting like she was a Disney fucking princess and they were a couple of mice about to burst into song.

My wife was speaking, answering his question, but I couldn't hear her over the roaring in my ears. Chester said something and she laughed. It was a real laugh, beautiful and genuine, and I hated that she was laughing like that for *him*.

Eventually I got the word out that had lodged itself in my throat. It came out in a loud growl that burst through the room and interrupted the happy little fucking exchange. "Duchess?" I asked.

Her face froze. Her smile fell. She flushed. "It's a nickname," she explained. "I'm not even sure how it started. Chester's just always called me that."

I looked at him. He met my eyes, not backing

down whatsoever. "Doesn't it suit her?" he asked casually. Insolently. "She always struck me as a proper lady."

"It's perfect," Jovie piped in. My gaze swung to her. She was smiling with some sort of keyed up, wicked glee. "She's a total, extra as fuck Duchess. You nailed it, Chester."

Abruptly I stood. "I'm late for a meeting," I said. A cursory excuse, though it might have been true. I couldn't remember any of my plans. It had been a strange, completely out of my control morning. I took that control back by leaving without another word.

"Have a great day, Banks!" Jovie shouted cheerfully at my swiftly retreating back.

CHAPTER 20

NOURA

After my husband left like my apartment had caught fire, I didn't expect to hear from him again anytime soon.

I tried not to think of him again that day, but when I did my lips and fingers trembled. If I didn't turn my mind in another direction, the shaking moved to my hands, my arms, my shoulders. Usually I had enough self-control to stop it there, but in weak moments, when I let my mind stick on messy thoughts of him, it kept going, that trembling. It throbbed through me, always unpleasant at first, but if I let it keep going, let it move to my chest, the tips of my breasts, to my churning stomach, my aching loins, that's when it became truly disturbing and not so very unpleasant at all.

And worse, my mind kept going back to the way he'd stood up for me with Asha. Why had he done that?

And why did it weaken me so? It didn't change anything. One kind act didn't change the hard facts: My husband held my whole life in his careless hands, and he did not feel one soft thing toward me.

Luckily I had a busy day. I didn't have two spare seconds to rub together. It helped.

I was one of the lucky models selected for the VS fashion show. It was the runway event of the year. The most televised, viewed, obsessed over walk in the world. And, thanks to my fake marriage and newfound fame, I'd been selected to model two looks.

The show was coming up in mere days, and prep was well underway. The fittings lasted more than ten hours, and I was utterly exhausted by the end.

Presumable, it may have been a shorter day if not for a drawn out argument between the VS people and mine. I heard (indirectly—through Asha, of course) that my husband (or my handlers, it was never clear which) wanted me to only model all white/cream looks that covered X amount of my skin, and they were insisting on full approval rights.

The VS designers wanted me in one black, one white outfit, and they weren't backing down on how much of my skin they wanted to show.

Eventually, late into the afternoon, Asha finally took a bathroom break.

"Just agree to what they're saying and then put me in whatever you want," I said quietly to Marian, the designer.

There were three other women in the room with me—Marian, who was working furiously on modifications on her laptop, a tailor fitting giant white feathered wings to my back, and another down at my feet measuring my legs for the thirtieth time.

They all froze.

"You're okay with that?" Marian asked tentatively.

I rolled my eyes, shrugged and smiled. "My husband is being unreasonable, newlywed stuff I'm sure, but he'll get over it, I promise. Just do what you planned, and whenever Asha makes some ridiculous request, act like you're going along, and continue exactly as you please. It's what I do."

"You're an absolute doll," she told me with a conspiratorial grin.

After that, we were done within half an hour. I only wished I'd thought of it sooner.

I got home at eight p.m. I'd skipped lunch and dinner. Being measured in your underwear for ten hours was an unbelievably effective appetite suppressant. I was starving by then, but I was planning to ignore my hunger in favor of a good night's sleep. It was the perfect day for it. More often than not, Jovie talked me into staying up late to watch something with her, but she had a shoot across town that she'd texted me was going to run late into the night. I was planning to responsibly take advantage of her absence and make an early night of it.

I forgot all those plans the second I walked in the door. My apartment wasn't empty.

My husband was back. He was standing about ten feet from the front door.

I was wearing sweat pants, a hoodie, and a ball cap. He was wearing black jeans and a distressed charcoal gray pullover that hugged his shoulders and skimmed his collarbone. His wavy black hair was pushed carelessly back from his face. There was extra scruff on his jaw.

He was fallen angel beautiful. I wanted to lick him, head to toe.

His hands were in his pockets, eyes predatory. It seemed the feeling was mutual.

"Hello, Calder," I said. I wanted to pat myself on the back for how steady the words came out.

Nothing else about me felt steady. My pulse was rioting loud enough to fill the room.

"Call me Banks," he corrected.

My brows rose. I knew why he'd ordered me to call him Calder at our wedding. I even agreed with it. His friends and family called him Banks and as far as he was concerned I was neither of those things.

What I didn't understand was why he was changing it now. It seemed like a trap. I wasn't falling for it.

I opened my mouth to reply, but his eyes had moved past me. "Leave us. She won't need you again tonight," he said curtly.

I didn't need to turn to see it; I *felt* Chester's reluctance as he left. Everyone else had already retired for the evening.

We were alone.

"Have you eaten dinner?" Calder asked me after the door shut behind me with a decisive click.

I almost lied. I tried to, but I was too hungry and intrigued not to see where this was going. "No."

He smiled at me. Why was he doing that? It was only us in the room. "I brought takeout from Omar's."

My stomach rumbled. "Omar's?"

"Have you tried it?"

I nodded. I had. Their chicken shawarma, falafel, and hummus were to die for. I loved their food, but could rarely afford the calorie hit.

"I got a little bit of everything. Care to join me?"

What could I do? I agreed to share an intimate, at home dinner with my husband.

He plated my food and served me, just as he'd done for breakfast.

We ate together. He sat so close our knees touched throughout the meal. Every so often his hand would rest familiarly on my thigh. Every so often he fed me a bite from his own plate.

It was delicious and dangerous.

Every time he showed even an ounce of humanity, I wanted to fall onto my back and open my legs.

And worse, I felt myself soften toward him a little.

What the hell was wrong with me?

By the time I was done, I'd eaten too much and I was squirming in my seat. Every time his hand returned to my thigh it moved a little higher. Was he teasing me or testing me?

I experimented by placing my own hand on his thigh.

"Don't touch me," he said softly. "I can't last a *second* with your hands on me."

I leaned toward him, tilting my face up to him.

He stared hard at my lips, but he didn't kiss me.

I'd almost forgotten. He never kissed me on the lips unless we had an audience. It was always for show. In private, he pointedly avoided it.

I was glad I'd thought of it. It made my soft heart harden a little. Enough to keep me sane. Enough to ground me back into reality.

"So I hear the VS people were giving you a hard time about my conditions," he stated blandly.

So they *were* his conditions. "Not me," I responded. "But they certainly got into it with Asha."

"I understand that they agreed to everything I requested. You'll be adequately covered for the show?"

I kept my expression perfectly blank. "It seems so. Asha was happy."

"Good," he nodded. "Good. You show enough skin as it is. The world does not need to see you in lingerie."

It was literally a lingerie show. What the hell else did he think I'd be wearing? But I didn't say any of that aloud. I wanted the job and the exposure that went with it. I'd deal with his reaction after the fact. If and when it came.

"I was surprised to find you here," I admitted to him. A change of subject wasn't a bad idea at all.

His mouth curved into something between a smile and a frown. Whatever it was, it wasn't happy. "You make me feel deprived. Do you know that?"

I felt a minor quake move through me.

"What do you mean?" I asked carefully.

He touched my trembling lips, rubbed them softly with the tips of his fingers.

A major quake now.

"You're *mine*," he whispered.

A sharp liquid throb started up in my loins.

"Legally and literally. I'm with you *right now*, but I feel like I'm doing without. I have you, but it *feels* like you're eluding me. How do you do that?"

Of course I didn't answer him. I didn't *have* an answer. But it was a fact that I felt it too. *Exactly* as he was describing it.

He didn't seem to need an answer. Abruptly he pushed his chair back from the table. In one impressive motion he grabbed me by the hips and perched me on the heavy table in front of him. I didn't have to ask what he intended when he started tugging my sweat pants and panties off, slowly peeling them off my hips and inching them down my legs. They were loose and soft, so it was an easy job. When he had my bottom half bare, he pushed my legs wide apart with his hands and just stared at me for a time.

He shoved his chair closer until he was settled comfortably between my legs. I could feel his breath against my sex as he looked up at me through his lashes. It was an intoxicating thing to behold.

His mouth twisted up into some self-deprecating version of a smile. "I didn't come here for dinner, Noura," his voice rumbled deeply from his chest into my core. "I came for dessert."

His words barely registered as sound. But they were felt. Oh. God. Were they felt.

"Open your shirt," he ordered, nuzzling into me.

With trembling hands I unzipped my hoodie. All I wore beneath it was a bra.

"Take your breasts out," he told me.

I obeyed.

"Cup them," he rasped into my skin. "Pinch your nipples. Rub them. I want you to fondle yourself while I," he licked, "tend to you. Got it?"

I rubbed my aching, sensitive breasts, rolling my nipples against my palms.

His eyes followed the movements for a long beat, two, three. He looked enraptured. It was very much mutual.

"Good," he murmured and started to feast.

He ate me out like he was indeed deprived. I responded likewise.

He got me off like it was his job instead of vice versa.

Afterward he rose, setting me on my feet directly in front of him.

I had to hold onto the back of his neck to keep from falling down. Or lying down.

He tilted my face up to him with a light touch. The barely there contact somehow sent a shockwave of awareness through me. "Look at me, Noura."

The sound of my name on his lips made my knees try to go full liquid.

I looked at him.

"Undress and wait for me in our bed," he ordered brusquely. "Don't touch yourself."

I couldn't even hide the shiver that visibly moved my body at those words.

I obeyed.

I'd forgotten I was bare from the hips down until I started to undress. I forgot everything when he put his hands on me. His mouth. Oh God, that mouth.

I lay naked on the bed, pulling the sheet up to my chin. I was shivering, head to toe, but not from cold.

He made me wait a solid half hour before he joined me, a bourbon in hand. He set it on the nightstand.

He pulled the covers to my ribs, smoothing it flat along my skin.

His eyes were dispassionate on his hands as he played with my breasts. He was arousing me like it was his weapon.

It was like a different man had entered from the one I'd just shared dinner with. And dessert.

Abruptly he rose, shrugging impatiently out of his pullover and the shirt underneath. He dragged his jeans and boxers briefs off like they'd personally offended him.

He was fully aroused, his hard dick bobbing with his every move as he dragged my sheet off.

"Get up," he said, the words cutting out of him angrily.

I stood.

He sprawled out on my bed, his back propped up against the headboard. He grabbed his drink, took a long swig, and set it back down.

He patted his lap, his eyes insolent. "Hop in the saddle, *wife*. Tonight's the night you learn how to ride a cock."

I hesitated, both at his nasty mood shift and his order. I wasn't sure how to go about it.

He stroked his cock, and in spite of myself I moved closer to watch. Close enough that I was almost touching him. Watching him touch himself got to me. A hot, drenching rush of sensation clamped down on my loins. Even when he was a bastard, I wanted him.

He lost his patience. He grabbed my hips and swung me over to straddle him.

I arched my hips, notching his blunt, thick tip against my cleft. I rubbed on him, coating him in my arousal.

He only watched through heavy-lidded eyes, his hands lightly gripping my hips. Resentment and detachment warred for his expression.

I took him in with a long, smooth glide. Smooth but not easy. He stretched me even more in this position. I felt impaled.

He was virtually silent. All that came out of him was a capital H, an aspiration. I rode him in a slow dance, with full, big movements, dragging him out to the tip before seating myself again. Again. Again. Again. My brain went fuzzy with the mind-bending pleasure of it.

I wanted to go faster, needed it, but it just felt too good to tease him.

He brought his hands to my aching breasts,

palming them roughly. I gripped his wrists, fingertips rubbing against his racing pulse.

I rocked my hips, undulating. A timeless rhythm overtook me. There was no reason I should have picked it up so quickly except that it was dance that was as natural as breathing and as old as sin.

His fingers were on my nipples, plucking and tugging at them gently, then harder, rougher.

My hips jerked faster, breaking the rhythm to seat myself on him harder, deeper.

His teeth were grinding together.

I saw how much he liked that and I paused before each lush downswing. Just to rile him.

Finally, at last, he snapped.

He clutched my hips above him and pumped upward into me, jacking in and out just how we both needed. I was on top, but he was setting the pace now. It. Was. Just. Right.

I didn't know I was going to come until I felt the first tremors of him go off inside me. Actually I wasn't sure who started first. It was a neat trick. He blew right as my cunt started sucking at him. I couldn't honestly say which one set the other off.

I was just moving down, seating myself deep on him, watching his face as his body started to erupt and mine started lapping it up, that first powerful instant of climax, when his eyes snapped open and caught mine.

His jaw clenched. His teeth gritted.

In a flash he had me on my stomach, his chest covering my back, his weight subduing me, his twitching cock digging into the flesh of my inner thigh. He was making a hell of a mess. All for the sake of not having to look me in the eye for another unguarded moment.

I understood, but it stung all the same.

"Look what you've done to my sheets," I remarked. It was said lightly. With breathless nonchalance. A defense mechanism.

He didn't take it lightly. With sudden ferocity, he lunged into me again, rooting balls deep, jarring with blunt force against my cervix. He held himself there, his cock still jerking, still shooting out the last bit of cum.

His lips pressed to my ear. His voice was a deep, furious rumble. "Did you think this room belonged to you? This bed? These sheets? It's all *mine*. But most importantly, *you* are."

CHAPTER
21

My apartment was humming with activity the next morning. I could feel it before I even opened my eyes. It took my sleep befuddled mind several minutes to work out why that was, but I had a very good excuse for that.

I hadn't gotten much sleep. Hardly any, in fact. I'd drifted off several times, but each time I'd woken up with my husband inside of me, mindlessly fucking again. Like he couldn't get enough.

But that had been his sole purpose. To get enough of me.

I knew this because at some point in the sin-filled night, he'd whispered it in my ear.

He'd been on my back again, finger soft on my clit, hard cock buried deep. "I'm going to have you as many times as it takes until I have my fill…" he groaned into my ear, "so I can leave you *for good* without another thought."

It was an outright cruel thing to say, but somehow it hadn't kept me from getting off harder than ever. I wished I knew what the hell was wrong with me. Why did my body operate so oppositely from my brain?

I assumed he'd accomplished his goal. I was *raw* with his efforts. On the other hand, perhaps not considering that that very thought made my loins pool with fresh need.

At the moment he was deeply asleep and plastered against my back. We were lying on our sides and I was using one of his impressive biceps as a pillow. His chin was nuzzled into the top of my head. It wasn't all that comfortable, but it was hot. Hotter was his other arm thrown over my side, his big hand gripping one of my breasts like it was a handful of his favorite teddy bear.

He was an affectionate sleeper and an amorous, insatiable lover.

TMI.

Every encounter with my husband taught me things about him that I didn't need to know. In fact, I needed *not* to know them. If I could, I'd erase them from my brain.

It would do me no good to become attached. He didn't have it in him to return the sentiment.

Not for me. He couldn't have made that more clear.

I was contemplating how best to extricate myself from him when Asha took the dilemma out of my hands.

She opened my door and poked her head in, only knocking twice loudly on the door when she was already inside the room. It was her usual routine, but I'd hoped that would change after Calder's harsh words to her the day before.

I just glared at her.

Calder's reaction was much, much worse. He came out of a dead sleep and went straight into a rage.

"What the *fuck* are you doing?" he roared at her.

She retreated. He was up, had pulled his pants on, and was out of the room, following her in an angry whirlwind.

I'm not sure what he did or said to her after that. I dragged myself into the shower. I'd never needed one more. I still felt his touch everywhere. All over every inch of me. I wondered if it would scrub off.

I ran my hands over my body with a strange feeling of disconnect. My husband was right. My body didn't belong to me anymore. It was his. He'd staked his claim.

Even my own touch only reminded me now of *his* touch.

As if that wasn't enough, he'd *marked* me. Little love bites on my breasts, hickeys on my neck.

On the insides of my thighs were small, fresh bruises shaped like his thumbs.

And inside my chest, were small, fresh bruises from his careless ways.

I'd just dried off and had flung my towel over a hook on the wall when Calder walked in. He'd gotten up in such a rush that he still wasn't wearing a shirt and hadn't bothered to button up his jeans.

I froze mid-motion.

He froze too when he saw me, his eyes raking me up and down.

After the night we'd shared, how could he possibly want more?

But that was the funny thing I was learning about sex. The more you had, the more you wanted. The more you *craved*.

"I left some marks," he noted. "Sorry," he added, his mouth quirking up at one corner.

Sorry. Yeah, right. "Inside *and* out," I agreed.

The smug look disappeared. His eyes flew to my face. "Sore?" he asked.

I shrugged.

He pointed his chin at the nearest counter.

ARRANGED

"Have a seat. Lemme see."

I stiffened. "No, that's okay."

He shot me a flat stare. "It wasn't a question."

A jolt shot through me. Desire, sharp and powerful. With a sigh I propped my completely nude self on the vanity. He pushed my thighs apart, kneeling low between them. He studied me.

Even years of modeling hadn't properly prepared me for this level of immodesty. And nothing could have prepared me for the intimacy of his gaze.

There were mirrors on nearly every wall of my bathroom. I glanced over at the nearest one. My face was flushed. From embarrassment, but not just that. The sight of his big naked shoulders kneeling down in front of my naked body did all sorts of things to me. So much skin. Without conscious thought my hand reached out to touch his messy hair. Without any direction from my brain, it gripped a firm handhold of the silky black waves.

He glanced up, grinning. "Was that a request?" There was a laugh in his voice.

I blushed harder, shaking my head so hard my long hair fell forward to cover half my face.

He went back to studying me, and his smile disappeared. He bit his bottom lip.

Unconsciously my hand gripped his hair harder. He looked up through his thick, too pretty lashes. It was a handsome hot look, and it worked me up in all kinds of counterproductive ways. "Hey now," he said softly. "Enough of that. I can only take so much."

"Sorry," the word came out in a pant.

He went back to his task, bringing his hands up to part me oh so softly with his fingers. His breath came out in a ragged exhale that turned into a curse. "You're very tender," he told me. He sent me another smoldering look. "But you're also very wet. You're sending me mixed signals, Noura. What am I to do with you?"

His face moved closer to my sex until I could feel his every breath. "I think even my fingers are too rough for you this morning," he murmured into my flesh.

"Probably," I breathed back.

"Luckily I have just the trick." He nuzzled gently into me, prodding me lightly with his tongue.

He pulled back. "How does that feel? Too much?"

I answered by gripping his hair with both hands and pushing his face back into me. He didn't ask again. He ate me out tenderly, leisurely. His hands stayed busy elsewhere, one plucking and kneading at my breasts, the other finding its way to my mouth. His thumb rubbed back and forth across my lips, teasing.

I watched us in the mirror, the sight of what he was doing to me bringing me close to the edge every bit as much as the sensations themselves.

His fingers prodded at my mouth, and I opened for him. I sucked his fingers in and out as his lips sucked at my slit.

The act was so tender and leisurely that my orgasm caught me completely by surprise. It hit me in a gentle unfurling. My head fell back. My toes curled. I managed not to cry out his name, but it was a close thing.

After he rose up from between my legs, wiping his mouth. I was still trying to catch my breath.

He moved away.

I closed my eyes. They snapped open again when I heard something soft plop onto the marble floor. I glanced down. He'd set a pillow at his feet. Our eyes clashed. He grinned. I blushed. He pulled out his cock, fisting it.

"You want me to . . ." I began.

"If you don't mind too terribly much." The way he said it was excruciatingly polite and utterly irresistible. Especially with his dick in his hand.

"You didn't seem to like it the last time," I

pointed out. "I assumed I was a hopeless cause."

It was his turn to flush, his gaze flitting away like he couldn't face mine all of a sudden. "The truth is, I—" he began, then paused as though choosing his next words carefully. "I didn't mean what I said after. I was just being a shit." He paused again. "I think about it all the time . . . your mouth on me."

Well, well, well. The words and the way he said them were something akin to an apology. Without a doubt they were conciliatory, and they hadn't been easy for him, I could tell, but he'd still managed to get them out. It was something. Some sort of a turning point for us, though I couldn't have said what all it really meant just yet.

I hopped off the counter and lowered myself to the pillow he'd laid out for me. His eyes ran over my body, and he kept stroking himself.

I gazed up at him, licking my lips. I wanted him to move closer, but I loved the sight of him touching himself too much, so I waited.

"I'll try not to make a mess this time," I said, trying at playful.

His voice was a groan. "Don't bother. I want to leave a mess on you."

I don't know why that turned me on so. I felt heat rush through me, flushing my skin and pooling in my loins. He moved closer and I grabbed him with both hands.

He made a rough, delicious noise when my mouth surrounded his tip. His gripped his hands in my hair and eased his thick length into my mouth.

"Touch yourself," he instructed, "Rub your clit."

I kept one hand on him, jerking off his base as I sucked his tip and fingered myself.

I got us both off at the same time. There was something so heady about that, having the power to pleasure both of us at once while all he could do was moan and pull my hair. I felt it when his body tensed to come, everything going stiff, his balls drawing up tight. The very air changed in that moment. It was utterly intoxicating, and it brought on my own release.

I couldn't help it, I cried out as I came, and my mouth released him with a wet little pop.

One of his hands stayed in my hair, the other reaching down to cover my hand on him. He jerked his cum out into the air. It hit my lips, my chin, my collarbone, and lower. He spent extra time spurting onto my tits.

"I meant to swallow it, I really did," I said when I caught my breath.

He laughed, a breathless, surprised rumble out

of his throat, and pushed himself back between my lips. I licked his tip and was surprised when I felt his cock jerk another little stream of cum into my throat. It just kept going.

"There's always next time," he said, voice low and hoarse.

Next time, indeed.

He pulled out and away, tucking himself back into his pants. Why not? He was good to go, I'd licked him clean, meanwhile I was a complete mess. From the way his eyes lingered on me, I could tell he loved the sight.

"Rub it into you tits," he groaned. I looked down at myself, rubbing his sticky cum into my flesh, massaging the firm, perky globes of my breasts. I kneaded at myself, getting it everywhere.

He moaned, rubbing at his crotch like we might just go another round.

I twisted my nipples between my fingers. I wanted him to suck on them, cum and all. I was disappointed when he told me, "Enough," in a hoarse, heavy voice.

He helped me up, then gave me his back, going to wash his hands.

That was when I noticed his tattoo. I'd never seen his naked back in the light before. I moved toward him, studying it. It was a small rose rendered in lovely intricate detail on his shoulder blade. I wanted to trace it with my fingers. "What does it mean?" I asked him.

His head turned until I was looking at his profile. His mouth twisted. "It means that you can never really know another person. Not their mind and not their heart. It means that you should never trust a gold digger."

Such a bitter explanation for such a beautiful piece of art, I mused. That was when I spotted the letters worked into the flowing lines. Spelled out in small, subtle precision was the name *FATIMA*.

I knew that name. I felt myself go cold.

I stepped back from him instinctively.

He turned to study me, but I was already heading back into the shower. I should've learned by now not to bother getting clean until I was sure he was done with me.

He didn't follow. Good. I told myself I wanted it that way. Certainly I needed a few private moments to compose myself.

When I emerged from my room, I saw that my hair and makeup people were waiting. Probably had been for a while.

Oh yeah, that's right. I had an important charity brunch to host with my mother-in-law at eleven.

I said good morning to everyone.

My husband was still present and watching me. I tried to pretend he wasn't.

He and Asha seemed to have worked out their beef, as they were talking with relative civility.

I sat down for my beautifying.

"What's on her schedule for the day?" he was asking Asha.

"First there's brunch with your mother. She needs to leave in one hour for that."

He nodded like he was somehow involved. Why hadn't he left yet? "And after that?" he asked her.

"She's meeting with her financial team—your father's sitting in—to discuss some potential investments and business ventures. She had a very promising offer to team up with a prominent brand to start her own clothing and shoe line. And there's a fragrance campaign on the table. Your father wants her to strike while her brand has so much free publicity. He says that every time you two are seen together, it's money in the bank."

I watched his lips as they twisted bitterly. "Isn't that the truth?" he mused. "When will that meeting end?"

"At five."

"And…?"

"And then she's going to your parents' home

for a family dinner. That's her last engagement of the day. Ideally she'll be in bed by nine. She has a very early morning tomorrow." She sent me one of her looks. "Think you can manage not to oversleep for the third day in a row, or is that asking too much?" she said it in a snotty tone, but nothing too over the top, at least for her.

I wanted to stick my tongue out at her like a child. Instead I gave her nothing. I'd learned that was the best way to win with her.

"Watch yourself," my husband said to her, voice low and mean. "You're on your last warning with my wife. I won't tell you again."

Her pinched face pinched harder, but she only nodded. "Excuse me. I'll be back when they're," she waved at my hair and makeup girls, "done with you."

When she left the room most of the tension went with her. Jovie popped out of her room like she'd been waiting for the moment. She was humming a tune I thought I recognized. Something from the *Wicked* soundtrack.

Yep, she'd been waiting.

She beamed at me. "Did he make her disappear again?"

I nodded and laughed.

My husband caught my eye. Something

happened to him when he saw me laugh. Something volatile and contradictory. He looked bitter and charmed all at once.

It was fascinating to watch.

I only stopped looking when I had to close my eyes for eyeliner. "What about you?" I asked him, just for the hell of it. "What are your plans for today?"

I could hear the grin in his voice. "What are you offering?"

I blushed. I couldn't think of a single comeback for him.

"So are you like sticking around for a while?" Jovie asked him after an extremely awkward silence.

He didn't have a single comeback for her.

I finally opened my eyes when my liner was done. I studied him.

He had the look of a man who badly wanted to leave but just couldn't quite tear himself away.

Apparently he hadn't gotten his fill of me just yet.

CHAPTER 22

I was still fed almost everything to do with Calder through the filter of Asha, and it was all on a need to know basis. Which was why I was annoyed but not surprised when I learned only a half hour before the dinner with my in-laws that my husband and I wouldn't be driving there together. I assumed that meant he'd meet me there.

I'd spent more time around his parents than I had around him. They'd always been quite pleasant, and they warmed to me more with every meeting.

In fact, a dinner with them where he wasn't present would be considerably less nerve-wracking than the alternative.

Or so I thought before that night. I arrived on time. He did not.

My in-laws greeted me cordially at the door, led me to an impressive dining room, and we waited.

And waited. One hour passed, then another.

We ate without him and made polite conversation.

His parents, Pasco and Diana, didn't even bring up his absence for quite some time.

We had a surprising amount to talk about, considering I'd had a meeting with my father-in-law mere hours before. You'd think he'd be sick of it, but he was very forthcoming with business advice for me, which I valued.

He was surprisingly kind. He was a bulldog of a negotiator. In the business world they called him The Punisher, but with me he'd shown nothing but patience and generosity.

He was a man who clearly knew what he was doing when it came to finances. I saw all access to him as an opportunity. An informal apprenticeship. I wanted to learn as much as I could from him. I couldn't model forever, and I intended to keep building my wealth long after my looks were gone.

I wanted to be so rich that nothing could ever touch me.

Diana and I had just as much to talk about. Our schedules intersected constantly over the next two months as we would attend several family charity functions together.

"I apologize for this, Noura," Pasco told me solemnly after three hours had passed. "My son and I have not been able to see eye to eye for quite some time, and I'd just like you to know that his boorish behavior tonight is a reflection of his contempt for me, and not you."

"I don't think he likes me, either," I noted. I was shocked at my own candor. I hadn't meant to speak those words aloud.

Pasco winced. "Well, then I apologize for that, as well. You deserve better."

I shrugged. "It's not your fault. Thank you for a lovely meal. I should probably go. I have an early shoot."

Diana opened her mouth to say something, but paused mid-motion, mouth agape as the sound of a loud crash boomed through the house. It came from the direction of the entryway.

A moment later, Calder staggered into the room.

It was obvious right away that he was stinking drunk.

I stiffened in my seat. I watched his parents share a look. Diana look worried. Pasco looked furious.

Calder had eyes only for me. "Did you miss me, honey?" he sneered.

So he was a mean drunk. Good to know. Still, I felt like I'd been slapped. Every time I was starting to think he might be nice to me, he went cold, or worse, hostile.

I rose to leave.

"Are you feeling proud tonight, Dad?" he turned to his father. "Look how getting married when you told me *I had to* made me grow up and settle down. What a wise decision, *Father*. Good thing you didn't break your perfect streak of *never being wrong.*"

"I never told you that you had to get married," Pasco said with calm, dignified fury. "I only told you that you had to get married to someone I approved of if you wanted the startup capital to get your business back up and running. I think it was a fair trade considering your history of losing fortunes and choosing the wrong bride."

I thought for a moment that Calder was going to lunge for his father.

"Banks. Please, stop," Diana said softly. That alone seemed to take some of the steam out of Calder.

"I never should have come," Calder said bitterly. "Goodnight, Mother." He turned to leave.

I moved to leave, as well. I hugged Diana. She embraced me back, kissing both of my cheeks.

As I passed him, Pasco's hand gripped my arm as though to hold me in place. "Don't go with him, Noura. You should avoid him when he's like this. He has no manners."

My husband stormed back into the room. "Oh please," he scoffed. "Did you think I was inviting *her* to come with me? Did you think I was going to willingly spend time with *my wife*? Get a clue. I have other plans."

Well, wasn't that sweet?

He left without another word.

After an awkward silence, Pasco spoke, "I know that what I did seems extreme. I've suffered the wrath of my whole family because of it. But you have to understand, or at least hear, where I'm coming from.

I didn't miss the irony that he felt the need to explain this to me of all people, but I just listened.

"Banks was always my most responsible son," he continued. "And the most stubborn. Did you know that he amassed his own fortune before he was twenty-one? He's an absolute wiz at sniffing out solid real estate investments. Everyone could see he was going to go very far." He paused. "And then he met *her*."

I knew the her he was talking about. She was tattooed in beauty on my husband's back. His ex-fiancée. Fatima.

"Do you know who she is?" he asked.

My face was so stiff it felt like it might crack. It'd been a mask of utter stoicism since my husband's arrival and short departure. A defense mechanism I'd learned for my trade. Unlike my roiling gut, my voice was smooth and turmoil-free as I replied, "I do."

"She was a sickness in his brain from the start," Pasco continued. "To this day, he has a *total* blind spot when it comes to her. And the sad fact is that nothing but ruin was ever going to come of it. She was using him. I told him so. He wouldn't listen, even with all the red flags. She comes from a very bad family, something he wasn't concerned about at all. And he knew I disapproved. That's why they got engaged behind my back. When I found out, I was concerned. Frustrated. Livid. I did something I'm not proud of." He took a deep breath and shared a look with his wife. She appeared sad, him remorseful.

I just listened, completely silent.

"I went to Fatima," he continued his rant. "*Her* not him. I told her that if they married, he'd be disinherited. He could keep what money he'd earned himself, which was not insubstantial, but *nothing* else. Ever. Not a dime from his family for as long as they were together. For her part, she didn't leave him right away. Instead she convinced him to go into business with her father. He invested everything, thinking he was betting on their future." His elegant hands were on the table clenched into fists. "We still haven't ironed out all the details, but here's what we know: The money vanished. All of it. He lost everything. That's the kind of family she comes from. The kind that makes money disappear.

"And people," Diana added with unexpected vehemence. There was a bitter twist to her mouth I'd never witnessed before. "They make people disappear as well. They're nothing but common thugs."

Pasco just nodded like that was secondary to the rest, continuing, "Within a month, she'd left him and married someone else. A French Count, as it happens. A billionaire, of course. Banks took it badly, as you can imagine. After that it was clear my son was heading in the wrong direction. He had been for a while. He wouldn't listen to anyone, bullheaded boy. Even after she married someone else, it was clear they were carrying on for God only knows how long. And he was not getting better. When an opportunity arose, I grasped it. He'd sniffed out a golden real estate venture and came to me for the money. But I wouldn't give it to him without a condition: Get married to someone who was not Fatima.

He could have chosen anyone, an old girlfriend, a new one. The Bride Catalogue was *his* idea. He wanted someone who knew the score.

I know my actions seem drastic, but I was desperate. I felt that I had to interfere in his life. To shake it up a bit. Anything was better than leaving it to him." He shrugged eloquently. "He won't forgive me. Truth be told, I figured there was a good chance your marriage wouldn't last, but anything to shift his attention away from that poisonous woman was enough for me. I apologize that you were dragged into it."

"Please don't apologize," I said, voice level but sincere nonetheless. "I wasn't dragged. I'm here of my own volition. I knew there was little chance any of this would be smooth."

My words seemed to calm my agitated father-in-law. He nodded once, twice. "You're more than we could have hoped for. You two could suit very well. I wish my stubborn son could see it."

"I wish that too," I said, with absolute, uncomfortable candor. "And thank you for sharing all of this. I think I can understand his behavior a little better now. It helps."

We said our goodbyes, and I left.

I was surprised to run into my husband at the elevator. I'd thought he'd be long gone. He was using the wall to prop himself up. I couldn't tell if he was really that drunk or if he was just that pissed off.

"Do you need help?" I asked him calmly, pushing the button to go down.

He straightened and glared at me. "Gold digger," he spat out. So it was both.

The car arrived and I stepped inside, looking straight ahead. I was so sick of his judgements. His double standards. Finally, I snapped. "I may be a gold digger," I said succinctly. "But you're a spoiled rich boy. I heard what your father said about your startup capital. You do know that means that you married me for *exactly* the same reason that I married you. You're a hypocrite judging me like that for doing the same thing you are."

I geared myself for his reaction before stealing a glance.

He looked like I'd slapped him. And I had. Not literally but with the truth.

And shock of all shocks, I'd left him speechless.

CHAPTER
23

The VS fashion show happened the next evening. I felt more nerves than I had in a long while on the job.

It was more than a world-wide televised runway show. It was a circus of epic proportions. A camera crew followed every model working the event from their homes to the red carpet, through the extensive press gauntlet, and (once you got through all of that) the backstage, which was as much of a show as the event itself.

All in identical baby girl pink bra and panty sets, with an occasional tiny blush silk robe to cover up outside.

Asha had quite a bit to say about that, but I was getting increasingly good at ignoring her. "Take it up with your boss," I told her every time she tried to tell me to cover up more.

It all went by in a sort of teeth-clenching blur. I got through it with a smooth poise fueled by my own sheer determination to make a mark.

I had to kill it for this. This was my shot at the big time. The difference between being an 'it girl' for fifteen minutes and launching into a full-on lifetime supermodel hall-of-famer. Like my mother-in-law minus the romance.

I'd never had any other talents, so I wanted to be the best at modeling, and this show was my make it or break it moment. If I did well, I'd achieve a long wished-for goal.

Backstage was an absolute madhouse, more of a party than anything else. It wasn't even just the model chasing usual suspects (though they were there of course) it was a who's who of tabloid fodder celebrities, men and women both. I spotted famous singers, actors, reality TV personalities, and YouTube influencers and that was only within the first minute.

Someone handed me a glass of champagne, and I toasted and pretended to drink with some random, gorgeous VS models in matching pink. Everyone was very friendly. More so than at any show I'd ever done.

I didn't have to wonder at the reason for it, since there were cameras everywhere.

One of the show's staff waved me down and

started to lead me to my prep station. It was so crowded that I had to squeeze between strangers to follow.

Some random guy (I thought I recognized him, from television maybe?), tried to wrap his arm around my waist as I attempted to press past him.

"Hello, gorgeous," he murmured, lips *on* my ear, hand gripping my ass, voice delighted. "Where have *you* been all my life?"

He got exactly one second into it before he was dragged away by a beefy, ruddy hand.

I glanced behind me at Chester, who was gripping the man by both shoulders and shaking him. Clearly setting him straight. Good old Chester.

I watched and pretended to take another sip of champagne. No way in hell was I partaking anything with carbonation when I didn't get to wear more than tiny scraps of silk and lace for the next five hours.

Not today, bloating.

After that Chester made the journey across the room simply by throwing an arm around my shoulders and elbowing his way through the crowd. Unsurprisingly, no one else touched me after that.

I knew my assigned camera crew had caught

the whole thing, and I wondered briefly how it might play out, but quickly shook the thought off. No use dwelling. Nothing I could do about it but keep my game face on.

I sat down at my station and let hair and makeup do their job.

"Is your security guard always so protective?" The question was from someone on a mic, pitched loud enough to carry over the noise of the crowd. It came from a friendly woman standing behind my assigned camera crew. I recognized her as one of the people producing the show behind the show.

I shrugged and smiled pleasantly. "When he sees the need. I don't tend to like being grabbed by strangers."

Several people laughed.

"You don't know who that was?" the woman asked. She was smiling engagingly, like she found that fact charming.

I shrugged again, hoping I wasn't being made a total fool of but fully aware that playing dumb had its advantages. "I don't, but I have to say he did look sort of familiar."

The woman addressed Chester, "Do *you* know who it was?"

Chester was scowling, an expression that didn't look to be leaving his face anytime soon.

He was the only one in earshot that didn't seem amused by the whole thing. "Some guy who doesn't know how to keep his hands to himself."

That got a loud laugh. I got the feeling the guy must have been more famous than I realized. "He's Brooks Ainsley," someone called out. I shook my head. Didn't ring a bell. "A recording artist," the producer explained to me. "He has the number one song in the country right now." That explained it. I'd been too busy keeping up with Jovie's K-pop obsession lately to check on the US charts.

"Oh," I responded. "Tell him we said congrats." That got a big laugh.

I knew we'd smoothed it over and twisted it to our advantage as best as we could when the producer moved on to cajole some questions out of the next model, looking very pleased with herself. People would be talking about the incident for days, particularly since it'd all been caught on camera. It was as good for me as it was for their brand, and even the handsy pop star would no doubt be pleased at the extra internet hits on his name, even if he was getting dragged.

Wins all around. Free publicity at its easiest.

The next hour showed me a part of the event I hadn't really understood until it was happening. I was there early for prep, but the array of celebs were there for a different reason entirely. While the models sat wearing barely anything and had our hair teased and makeup caked and baked on, the guests flitted from station to station, studying and judging us like we were pieces of art at an exhibit. It was very odd, more like doing a car or boat show than a runway, where we were on display in a different way.

It wasn't pleasant, but I plastered a fake bemused smile on my face and bore it well. On the upside it kept me too busy to linger on nerves over the catwalk.

Several of the famous attendees even deigned to speak to me, and the ones that did were even nice. Not surprisingly, Chester's scuffle with the recording artist had the whole gathering astir. A famous entertainment reporter had caught the entire thing on her phone and insisted on showing it to me.

I watched initially with reluctance, but as I took it in, even I thought it was funny. The man had grabbed at me and been plucked clean away in one second flat. Meanwhile as Chester was clearly berating him, looking like he might pulverize him where he'd stood, I'd watched the whole thing with calm eyes and sipped casually at my champagne.

"It's already gone viral. They even made it

into a meme. You want to see?" the woman asked me.

I said sure and she showed me a GIF of myself. It was the moment I'd sipped the champagne, watching the scuffle with utter composure. Someone had put thug life glasses over my eyes and captioned it with the word **BADASS** in bold caps.

I found myself smiling. The whole thing had turned into an unexpected confidence booster and it was no doubt good press for me, less so for the pop star, but I supposed that's what you got for grabbing random women.

The whole event flew by in a frenetic rush that seemed to come to a standstill and rush by in a blur at will, feeling both too quick and too slow. The backstage pre-game passed by too quickly for me to process but also felt like it dragged on with agonizing leisure.

After forever of waiting and before I was ready, I was squeezed into various pieces of exquisitely sheer white lace, strapped into a set of angel wings that almost tipped me over on the spot, and sent down the runway.

This was the first of the two looks I was walking for the show, and even though I had to wear pieces of stick-on nude tape to keep it TV friendly, it was the more conservative of the two.

That being said, I was practically naked and felt it keenly with every strutting in five-inch stilettos step.

The usually narrow stage was built wide for the show to accommodate live music acts. I walked to the heavy beat of the drums, letting my hips sway. We hadn't had a real dress rehearsal. We'd had the music but not the band, so it was only about halfway down the catwalk that I realized who was crooning into the mic.

Brooks Ainsley. Awwwkward.

Luckily, I had too much momentum to let it so much as pause my steps. I was wary as I passed by him, but he didn't come near me, in fact tensed up and took a few notable steps away as I moved by. He'd learned his lesson.

I smiled at him and winked. He winced, looked away, and kept singing.

There was a discernible reaction from the crowd: gasps, laughs, cheers. Might as well have fun with it. I added a little jaunty bounce to my steps and an extra sashay air kiss at the end of the catwalk.

I didn't dare look into the crowd. While an awkward rock star might not make me falter in a walk I'd mastered years ago, I didn't think I could react so blithely if I spotted my husband in the throng.

As far as I was aware he'd never attended one of my runway shows, and it was easier to just pretend he wasn't at this one. Finding out otherwise would be hell on my already grated nerves. The man got to me like nothing else could.

At least five pairs of hands started peeling my clothes off my body the second I hit backstage. The show was too frantic to honestly entertain something as frivolous as modesty, so all the dressing room rules were quickly thrown out. I opted for penance over permission on that one. At one point, I clashed eyes with a fuming Asha and it left me no doubt that I'd be getting hell for it later.

Oh well. No time to worry as I was unwrapped from white lingerie and twisted back into a complicated series of thin black velvet straps that materialized into a teddy and somehow managed to show even more skin than the first look. Goodbye, runway virginal color theme. Good riddance.

A small team shrugged enormous black feather wings onto my shoulders, and another helped me step into thigh-high black velvet boots before pushing me gently back into line.

It must have been a quick wardrobe changeover because there were over a dozen models waiting in front of me, eyes plastered to a screen showing live coverage of the show. Everyone was dancing and cheering each girl's walk as they watched. I had a naive moment where I thought everyone was just being nice before I realized we were all still on camera.

I had the whimsical thought that they should do this at every show. Even fake kindness was worlds better than the usual bitterly competitive backstage vibe.

I took my second walk slower, in time to the now sultry music number. There was no exchange between me and Brooks this time, in fact everything was going smooth as could be right up until I hit the end of the runway. I lingered at it, forcing myself to hold my spot and pose when all instincts pointed to moving through that catwalk with all due haste.

I was doing great, giving all my best angles, face calm, mouth relaxed, eyes smiling when I made the colossal mistake of letting myself look at the crowd.

Shit. *He* was in the front row. Banks. Staring right into my eyes like he wanted to fuck and throttle me simultaneously.

I didn't blow it completely, in fact it probably looked like I was just milking my moment to the nth diva degree, but inside I was a wreck as I made my slow way back up the walk.

Why was he here? And . . . What was with that look he'd given me? Why was he so hostile? Why was he *always* mad at me? And . . . How could he manage to turn me on with one brief, contemptuous glance?

I exited the stage thinking that was the end of the show, but I was sorely mistaken. Backstage had turned into an after party between one blink and the next. I was led back to my prep station.

Someone handed me champagne, and I actually took a real sip before another someone took it from me so that a new team of helpers could shrug me out of my wings.

"You okay, Duchess?" Chester asked. I hadn't even seen him, distracted as I was in my own thoughts.

I looked up and smiled winsomely at him. "Great," I replied cheerfully, stepping out of my wicked boots and into some furry pink slides. A new wave of energy had rushed through me at both the thought of being done and possibly seeing Banks again.

I was stripped down to almost nothing and shrugged into a fresh pink striped robe.

I was scanning the crowd for my husband when someone else caught my eye.

A gorgeous woman with a glorious mane of black hair was making her way toward me. She was a standout in a room full of standouts, and I recognized her instantly.

Speak of the devil. She just kept coming up, things about her inserting themselves into my life against my will. Or perhaps they'd been there all along and I was too naive and sheltered to see it.

It was Fatima. My husband's ex. The woman who had ruined him. And she was headed straight for me.

CHAPTER
24

Fatima came directly toward me, not trying to hide the fact that I was her destination. She stopped about two feet away and just studied me with an air of amused disdain. What else could I do but study her back?

The backstage situation post-show was crowded beyond belief, but somehow her confidence and my fear were the only things in the room.

She was the quintessential enigmatic woman. Wicked and mysterious. Her eyes were black and sultry her lashes heavy and thick enough to hide all kinds of secrets. Her skin was a fine bronze with golden undertones that gave her a glow that outshone any makeup. A natural beauty that was all the more stunning with a bit of polish, which she had in spades. Her lips were painted blood red and they were lush, with an exaggerated cupid's bow that contrasted interestingly with the mean twist to her mouth. She was sharply stunning.

And then there was the rest of her.

I was slender, toned and fit, but shapely, my hips and bust exaggerated against my smaller waist.

She was a few inches shorter than me, but still statuesque, and on another level of curvy. There'd been hit songs written about her ass. She was a wet dream come to life. I felt like a skinny child next to her.

Comparison was a man's device, meant to pit women against each other. I knew that, so I tried not to let my mind go down that road, but it was a struggle.

I didn't know what to say to her, but she had plenty to say to me.

When she spoke her voice was low, sultry, and dripping with poison-laced honey. "Ah. You. The bride. I suppose it's time we finally met. I'm Fatima. I assume you've heard of me?"

"I have," I said evenly. There wasn't so much as a hitch in my breath. I was proud of that.

We'd never spoken before, but I knew more about her than I wanted to. Some I'd been told, the rest I'd looked up myself with morbid curiosity.

Theirs was an old-school, tragic love story. Star-crossed, Romeo and Juliet shit. His family was old, wealthy beyond measure, and above all *respectable*. Hers gained and lost fortunes like it was a game of Monopoly and were rumored to be closely connected to the Turkish mafia. Or possibly the Russian mafia. Or both, depending on the website.

In spite of his family's disapproval, they'd been together for *years*. And she'd gone directly from being engaged to him to married to her husband with no downtime at all.

I'd also found plenty of random, useless tidbits about her. She was four years older than my husband, had an unholy obsession with all things Gucci, and her DD breasts were real, fabulous, and had been plastered all over the internet thanks to her penchant for frequent topless sunbathing on her yacht.

"Did you need something?" I asked her, polite as I could manage. She'd been staring at me for moments that had dragged into forever.

"From you? No. I was looking for your husband. We got separated in the crowd."

This was a scenario I'd gone over in my fake wife training. It was in the handbook under: Never admit it's a fake marriage, even to his lover. Of course I'd never realized that when it came up just how it would feel, and how my instincts would kick in much more powerfully than my training.

"I saw him in the front row," I retorted with all the fake haughty pride I could muster. "You weren't with him." After a moment I thought to add, "Because he's here with *me*."

Her reaction didn't show up in the way her face shifted but rather the way it smoothed over into even more perfect neutrality. I'd hit some sort of a nerve there. Score one for the wife.

Of course, it didn't take the mistress long to recover.

"You're not staying at his Park Avenue residence, are you?" she asked archly. "I've never seen any sign of you there."

I couldn't have said what moved across my face at her words, but what moved through my chest felt like jagged claws in the shape of her long, red, *sharp* nails.

Did it hurt? Oh hell yes. But hurt wasn't the whole of it. An unexpected red bloom of rage blossomed in my chest. Righteous indignation fell swiftly in its wake.

Was I just supposed to take this?

I think the fuck not.

"I don't know what you're talking about," I

brazened out, the instinct to mark my territory *now* far overshadowing any misgivings I may have had about incurring my husband's wrath *later*. "In fact, I'm staying there tonight, so I'm not sure why you're even here." I paused. "At *my* show."

"I don't believe you," she returned, though her tone was unsure.

That bit of doubt was something, at least. More than I'd hoped for. It told me that he at least hadn't made plans with her tonight.

I shrugged. "So? It's not my concern whether you believe me or not. Our marriage has nothing to do with *you*."

"You should be concerned," she returned with a cold, ruthless stare. "About me. He will *never* be through with me. I was his first love, and I'll be his last. No one knows him like I do. I'm sure you've seen his tattoo. I wear its match. I know what makes him happy, what makes him tick. He will never be able to smell lemon verbena or so much as look at a rose without thinking about making love to me.

My heart hurt like every word out of her mouth was reaching inside of me and tearing it to ribbons.

"Oh and by the way," she was still going. "He's *always* been indifferent to women that want or need his money. I'll let you figure out where that leaves *you*.

Her message was concise and unmistakable.

I was his wife, but she owned more of him than I ever would.

"You're delusional," I replied, but I barely got it out and my voice sounded robotic. Dead.

"That night that you were at Beautique," she continued mercilessly. "One of the *few* times he's even taken you out, right? I don't think you noticed me, but I saw *you* there. He finger fucked you under the table, didn't he? I know all his moves. But do you know why?"

I didn't answer. I couldn't. My mind was too busy torturing me.

Fractured pieces snapping into place.

Everything, all of it, just to make this woman jealous. My stomach dipped with nausea.

Her laugh rang out, polluting the air.

She answered for me. "He saw me. He saw me walk in and wanted to make me jealous. Do you know why he didn't go home with you that night?"

I thought I might throw up.

She smiled and it was bloodthirsty. "I won't be so crass as to tell you. I'm sure you can guess."

She left with smug condescension painted beautifully across every feature on her lovely face.

Humiliating needles dug deep into my gut. I watched her go, feeling things I didn't want to name.

My eyes were still on her when I caught another figure in my periphery, a tall one that moved intently toward her and caught her arm, stopping her.

She spun into him without hesitation, laughing like the whole thing had been planned. Their dark heads bent together. My husband and his apparent mistress.

They looked right together.

I hated that.

They *were* right together.

I hated that more.

Calder dipped his head low to speak into her ear. He must have had a lot to say, as they didn't move for quite some time.

If he'd had a choice, he'd be married to her.

I saw it all then with bitter clarity.

I'd brought my whole heart into this when he only had half of his own.

She'd claimed the rest.

I never even had a shot.

One thing that I noticed about them brought me some small ounce of relief. He didn't smile for her. He didn't laugh. He showed no outward signs of happiness at being close to her. She was as unwelcome of a surprise to him as she'd been to me.

And more encouraging still, my brooding husband appeared as stoic to her as he was to me. It didn't mean anything, but the opposite would have meant more.

It took some time for my husband to make his way to my side, and I had enough small talk with strangers and glasses of champagne to feel at least a little bit of numbness by the time he got there.

He opened his mouth to say something to me when he drew close, but my own words beat him to the punch.

"If you wanted Fatima to think this is a real marriage," I said in a quiet, terse voice, "you're failing. She knows we don't live together."

Not a muscle moved on his face. Not a tic in his eye, not a twist of his lips, not a wrinkle in his brow. No expression marred his glacial eyes as they bore into me.

I wanted to take a step back from those eyes, but I held my ground. I was beyond cowering to him. And catering to him.

"Don't." His low voice was a warning: *Danger. You're trespassing here. Stay out of this.* "Don't talk *to her.* Don't talk *about* her. The subject of Fatima is off-limits."

I thought I might vomit. Hearing him say her name made me feel ill.

I'd never felt this way before. Jealousy was a terrible thing. I felt wretched. Heartsick with it. Utterly useless and inadequate. Like a silly, unwanted, pretty little doll.

He was grinding my heart under his boot. I didn't think he was aware of that fact.

I also didn't think that if he knew it would bother him one bit.

I was married to a man who was in love with another woman. I'd walked down the aisle with my eyes wide open. What I hadn't understood, though, was that this fact would not stop me from falling in love with *him*.

He seemed to have put the subject behind him (that made one of us) and his eyes raked up and down my body, nostrils flaring, lip curling. He was pissed, and I didn't think it was entirely to do with Fatima.

With casual finality, he took the glass out of my hand and set it aside with a caustically muttered, "You're too young for that." He paused. "At least you put on a robe backstage now," he noted.

I shrugged. He wasn't the only one pissed. "Usually. When I think of it."

He had that look on his face again, the one he'd worn as I walked down the runway, the one that made me ponder whether he wanted to fuck me or throttle me on the spot.

"Okay, you won this round," he said finally. He waved one hand negligently to indicate my body. "You do not possess even *one ounce* of modesty. And you have shown me that in spite of my wishes you can and will find a way to go around my rules."

I couldn't exactly argue with him. And worse, why did his words make me feel about an inch tall?

I thought this was just going to be a thorough dressing down, so I was taken aback by his next words. "Fine. You've made your point. Let's negotiate." I shouldn't have been so taken by surprise. He was a business man through and through. "What would you like in exchange for giving me final approval over your dress code?" He paused, then added with sharp irony, "Final approval that you will actually adhere to."

I didn't even have to think of it. My brief, devastating clash with Fatima had done its damage, but it had also had the unintended effect of lighting a new fire in me. The fire of competition. "I want to see your apartment."

He just stared at me, nonplussed. "You can't be serious."

"I can and I am."

His surprise warred with chagrin on his face.

"Reconsider. You can do better. Think jewelry. Money. I'm willing to be very generous for this concession."

I didn't hesitate. "Take it or leave it," I said stubbornly.

He looked like a man who was trying to swallow a very bitter pill. "Fine," he said through his teeth. "When would you like to see my apartment?"

"Now is good."

"Fine," he gritted out.

And like that we were off. There was a brief moment of conflict when he realized I'd actually come to the show in my robe and underwear. Pissed off anew. In my current mood, I ate it up with a spoon and toppings.

He kept glancing at my robe in the car as though it added a new offense every time he saw it. For all that, it was a silent ride.

We took the garage entrance up to his penthouse, to hide my attire I was sure.

"Would you like the tour?" he asked sarcastically as we emerged from the elevator into his apartment.

"That would be perfect," I said with the cheer of someone who was spitefully getting their way.

He showed me around. It was big, gorgeous, and sterile.

"Well, is it everything you dreamed?" he asked bitingly.

"I like mine better," I shot back instantly.

He blinked. "Why?"

"It's warmer. You can tell a human lives in mine."

"Well, your opinion is as unwelcome as it is inconsequential." For all his disdain, his eyes as he said it had gone sensual and drowsy. His bedroom eyes.

He took me to bed like he was devouring me. Like he needed to swallow me whole.

He was marking his territory, nailing my body to his bed, tattooing our sex into his sheets.

He wasn't gentle, but I didn't want gentle. I didn't need it. I needed something else.

It didn't even start out as desire. It was a more complicated need. It was conquest, domination, rough and hot. And with every touch it became simpler and simpler until it'd resolved itself into the oh so satisfying itch and scratch I was coming to recognize and crave with every pulse of blood pumping through my body.

Afterwards I felt rung out. I felt so relaxed I could've curled up into a ball and fallen asleep on the spot, regardless of my location. In fact I started to.

He wasn't having it. The sex had done nothing

to relax him. He was up and pacing two seconds after he dragged his dick out of me, hand pushing his hair back, looking harried and mean.

I just watched him, eyes beginning to drift closed.

"No one said you could sleep here," he said sharply.

I sat straight up and started looking for my clothes. I was dressed (or barely dressed, as it were) and heading for the door in record time. I should've been numb from his rejection, completely immune at this point, but apparently not. I wanted to escape that realization as much as him in that moment.

He stopped pacing to watch me move. He studied me, cursing. "I didn't mean that," he said quietly. "Listen——"

I waved that off. "It doesn't matter. I didn't want to stay, anyway. Good night."

He followed me through each room and to the door. "You don't have to——"

I was texting with Chester and I didn't even glance at my husband. "Chester's waiting for me downstairs, right outside the elevator. I can see myself out."

And I did. Though I will say that the way he watched me as I did it was as remorseful of an expression as I'd ever seen him wear.

CHAPTER
25

I didn't see my husband again for six days.

It would have been longer, I was certain, but I went out of my way to get his attention. I couldn't seem to help myself. It was an utter failing on my part at self-control.

Because I was starting to crave the taste of him, bitter as the aftertaste may have been.

One of my jobs gave me the perfect opportunity, and it was just too tempting to resist. I was ashamed of my weakness, but even pride didn't stop me.

I had a shoot that day with a male model for the first time since my wedding. Nothing too scandalous, of course, but I had a feeling it would still do the trick.

The model was Tommy Grace, and I was relieved the instant I saw him on the set. We'd worked dozens of runway shows together over the years. We'd never hung out on our off time or anything, but we were definitely friendly. It would make the shoot considerably less awkward.

The photos were for a sexy Guess Jeans campaign, and they dressed us in matching distressed jeans. My sweater just happened to be missing its midriff, and Tommy wasn't wearing a shirt. It was a studio shoot so it was warm enough, which was good, because they also kept us both barefoot. My makeup was heavy on the eye glam, with a thick and precise cat eye, and bare on the rest, with natural skin and lips. They teased my hair up high then pulled it back into a chignon. Pin-up meets vintage high fashion was kind of their thing, and it suited me well. This job was going bring my career to the next level. I knew it the moment I saw how they styled me. This was the look that would cement my recognizability.

We were directed to embrace and gaze soulfully at each other. Tommy was a goofball so it was hard to stay serious, but the photographer liked a variety of expressions too so we went with it.

"Your manager lady looks like she wants to charge in and pepper spray me every time I get too close," remarked Tommy.

He was referring to Asha, of course. And she did. "Ignore her," I said. "She's harmless. She just has a powerful resting bitch face."

Asha was getting easier to ignore by the day. It was glorious.

On a break I fished my phone out. "Want to take a selfie?" I asked Tommy. It was the perfect moment. Asha had left the room to take a phone call.

He grinned. "Of course." I wasn't surprised by his enthusiasm. All models loved selfies. He moved in behind me, peeking his head around my shoulder while I held the phone. We took a few smiling, a few with silly faces.

I glanced sideways at his very close face. "Do you mind doing one where you kiss my cheek? I think it'd be cute."

He didn't hesitate to accommodate me. I made a kissy face at the camera while he laid pecks on my cheek.

"Will you send those to me?" he asked me when we pulled away. "I want to post, too."

The photographer was calling us back into position, but I told him that I would as soon as I could.

I studied the images critically on our next break. The funny thing about Tommy being the model they hired was that at first glance, he resembled my husband. He was olive-skinned, with black hair, broad shoulders, and a stubbled jaw. I didn't think that was a coincidence. The client clearly wanted to cash in on my headline-grabbing marriage.

But in the selfies, there was no way to mistake that he was very much *not* Calder.

I found the best shot for my purposes and toyed with the lighting. Perfect. He was hugging me from behind while he nuzzled into me, and I blew a kiss to the camera. I'd angled the camera high so you could see his naked shoulders, and it looked like his hand was spread over my bare tummy.

I posted it. On its own the picture could have easily been seen as innocent. Just a snapshot of some very chummy co-workers. It needed the right caption.

Spent the day with an old friend of mine. #reunitedanditfeelssogood #imissedhim #ilovemyjob

I put my phone away and went back to work with an added lightness to my step. For some reason, the very idea that something I did might rile my husband put me in a downright chipper mood.

We were getting close to finishing up. The photographer just wanted a few more varying oddball shots, and we'd been working so long that we were all getting a bit silly.

"We should kiss just to see if her head will actually explode," Tommy joked. He was referring to Asha the Dour, of course.

I felt my nose wrinkle up. I studied his smiling face, skeptical.

"Not a real kiss, just a little almost lip on lip contact. More about to kiss than actual kissing, ya know? Gerard would be thrilled," he said, referring to our long-suffering photographer who'd been through several levels of hell dealing with Asha throughout the shoot. "Let's throw him a bone."

"He has earned it, poor guy." Even as we spoke, Asha was laying into him, telling him that he'd had more than enough time to get the shot.

"C'mon," Tommy cajoled. "Let's see how almost kissing close we can get before she hits me over the head with something."

I laughed and made as though to kiss him. Our lips were a breath away. He dipped me a little and my head fell back. He laid one on me. It was a cursory thing. Our lips barely even made contact before we pulled away, still laughing.

I lightly slapped his shoulder. "That was a dirty trick," I muttered.

He grinned, shrugging. "I misjudged the

distance, sorry." He was clearly, unabashedly lying and it made me laugh. I knew it was all harmless and fun.

And of course that's the first thing Calder saw when he walked in the door. Me in another man's arms, enjoying myself.

I glanced up, saw him, and froze. He'd come. It had actually worked. One post and he hadn't just called. He'd shown up. And I knew with one look that I might have bitten off more than I could chew.

Shit. Had he seen Tommy's prank of a kiss?

Calder was frozen too. And as I watched, rage lit his eyes, traveling through his face like fire down a detonation cord.

I straightened, glancing at Tommy. He'd noticed my husband's entrance, as well.

"Uh oh," he said simply.

Yeah. Uh oh. My eyes swung to Asha. Her arms were folded across her chest, a smug expression painted on her face. It was the happiest I'd ever seen her. Figured.

Gerard cleared his throat. "We're good here, guys.

"Should I stay or run?" Tommy asked me gamely. "Which would piss him off less?"

"Run," I said quietly and succinctly.

Tommy didn't hesitate. "Always a pleasure.

Catch you at the next show." He hugged me briefly, kissed the top of my head, and took off.

I watched Calder watch him leave. His nostrils flared like a dog's catching a strange scent.

He was clearly struggling not to either A. Confront the other man. Or B. Outright attack him. It looked like it was a close thing. I was very relieved when it became apparent that he was going to restrain himself from doing either.

I approached him with no small amount of trepidation. I stopped about three tense feet away.

He watched me with cold eyes, not making a move to close the gap between us.

"Calder! What a pleasant surprise!" I said with a big, bright, fake smile. "What brings you to this neck of the woods?"

His eyes ran up and down me with a strange combination of hostility, detachment, and pure sex. "Can't you guess?" he drawled.

I blinked. Well, that was direct. "Excuse me for a minute," I told him in lieu of an answer. I indicated my outfit. "I need to change. These aren't my clothes." I went to change in the dressing room that Asha had insisted upon.

Calder didn't excuse me. Instead he followed me. It was a very small space. He moved into a corner and folded his arms over his chest, dominating it.

"You enjoy wrapping everyone around your finger, don't you?" he asked as I was pulling a shirt on.

I studied him. He had that certain look about him, like he wanted to fuck me and strangle me all at once. He wore it well.

"I don't know what you mean," I finally responded as I bent down to slip on my shoes.

"Oh yes you do. You had your ex drooling over you at the same time you had me dropping everything and rushing hell-bent across town. All exactly what you intended. Tell me, has a man ever not done *exactly* what you wanted him to?"

I straightened. I didn't know where to even start in responding to everything incorrect he'd said. I singled out the strangest one. "My ex?" I asked.

His nostrils flared. I wanted to climb him right there and then. "Are you going to try to tell me you and that guy don't have some sort of history? An 'old friend?' What the fuck does that mean?"

"It means we've known each other for a long time," I said slowly, like I was speaking to a crazy person. "I never dated Tommy."

He looked like the he was struggling to swallow something for a good thirty seconds before he spoke again. "Did you date a lot of male models? That's a thing, right? You're all pretty and you date each other."

I had to swallow a smile before I spoke. "No. I've never dated a male model."

"So what kind of guy did you date?"

"I didn't date."

"You never had a boyfriend before?" Disbelief underscored each word.

I shrugged. "I had other priorities."

"Wait." He shook his head. He looked fascinated in spite of himself. He took a step toward me. "Are you saying that you never went on even *one date* before our wedding?"

I shrugged again. I was blushing. It was an embarrassing topic. "I had other things on my mind."

"Wait. Wait." He stepped closer, crowding me. "Are you saying that you'd never even been *kissed* before me?" he asked, voice pitched low.

I shook my head slightly, tearing my eyes up to his. "Is it so hard to believe?"

He didn't answer that. He was breathing hard, almost a pant. "Are you done for the day?"

I nodded.

"Let's go home." It came out as a husky purr. My knees went weak.

He didn't touch me even once until we were

alone in my apartment. The second the door closed he grabbed my arm, tugging me through to my bedroom and into my bathroom. He grabbed my toothbrush, dabbing paste onto it.

"I told you to call me Banks," he said out of nowhere. It burst out, like it had been eating at him. "You keep calling me Calder. Stop doing that."

"You told me to call you Calder at our wedding," I responded, scrutinizing his expression. "Why did you change your mind?"

He didn't answer. Instead he gripped my jaw and started to gently brush my teeth, the weirdo.

"I can't believe you *kissed* him," he said, a ragged edge to his voice I hadn't heard before.

"*He* kissed *me*, and barely," I said after he finally let me spit. My eyes met his in the mirror. He was standing very close behind me. "And it didn't count. It was just for the shoot."

His answer was to fist a hand into my hair and pull my head back. "It fucking counted. Don't do that again."

He turned me around and kissed me. On the lips. And kissed and kissed.

He'd never kissed me on the mouth in private. He'd only ever done it in public. For show.

Whatever this was, it wasn't for show. It was

for us alone. It was blood-pumping, heart-shattering.

Tangible. It was real.

He kissed me deeply, with barely suppressed ferocity. I felt myself melt against him. I held onto his shirt and accepted his plush, decadent tongue as it plunged between my lips. His mouth fucked my mouth, and it was all I could do to hold myself upright.

He felt my knees buckle and took my weight, lifting me and carrying me into the bedroom and onto my bed. His mouth never left mine. The man didn't do half-assed. Now that he'd decided to kiss me, he kissed me silly.

He undressed us both slowly, breaking our lip lock only when he had to. He kissed me while he pumped in and out. When I gasped into his mouth, starting to come, he pulled back. His eyes captured mine while he followed me. An intimate connection passed between us, something undeniable and palpable and impossible to ever take back.

"Is it always like this, or is this something out of the ordinary?" The words just came out after, and I instantly wanted to snatch them back.

His gaze was shuddered in a flash, his eyes cold.

I felt my whole face flushing with mortification.

I tried to backtrack. "I'm just inexperienced, I suppose. I don't know why I said that. Sex is probably like this with everyone . . ."

It came out of him with obvious reluctance. "No, this isn't normal," he said begrudgingly, not looking at me. "Nothing about this is normal. This is some sort of strange . . . chemistry. . . I've never dealt with before either, okay?"

"Okay," I said softly.

"I'm not sure I like it," he said gruffly.

"Me neither," I lied. I did like it. I loved it. I couldn't remember ever feeling quite so much, and it was hands down the most addictive thing I'd ever encountered.

After that he couldn't even look at me. Like even the sight of me weakened him. Overwhelmed him.

It was almost like he was . . . No. It was too silly to think.

This too much for me, larger than life, gorgeous man could not be scared of me.

So what could he be afraid of?

That if he spent too much time with me, he'd catch feelings?

I knew I was projecting, that the thought only crossed my mind because that was the exact thing scaring me.

The exact thing happening to me.

I wanted my husband to do more than want me. I wanted him to care. The idea shocked me. Was there actually some spark of a romantic left in my cynical young heart? The thought was terrifying. I'd gone too far for any of that.

He was getting dressed, his back to me.

"Okay fine," he finally spoke, his tone begrudging. "Let's negotiate. What do I need to do to keep you from pulling any more shit like that?"

I knew just the thing. "Your phone number."

He didn't hesitate. "Deal. Give me your phone." He reached back without glancing at me. I found it and handed it to him. He fiddled with it for a minute. Without looking up he said, "This is my last warning: If I see your lips touch anyone else's ever again, I won't hold back on the guy, and *you* get to explain to my father why I got arrested."

He handed my phone back to me and left without another word.

It was only later that I checked his contact info on my phone.

He'd saved himself as Banks/My Master. Cheeky bastard.

CHAPTER
26

BANKS

I was taking my wife out on a date per direct orders from my father.

I was reluctant, to say the least. I hadn't seen her in eight days. In fact, I'd been actively avoiding her. I hadn't even been allowing myself to look at/stalk her social media.

I'd failed in that multiple times, but I was going four days strong. Out of sight, out of mind. I repeated the mantra.

And still thoughts of her persisted. The feel of her lips. The way her eyes rolled up in her head as she came. Her looking like an irresistibly wrapped confection as she strutted in barely anything down the runway. The sight of her kissing that annoying fucking model.

Why had she asked for my number but never

·301·

used it? I spent way too much time puzzling over that. Whatever game she was playing, I couldn't figure it out. She was as good at mind-fucks as she'd turned out to be at literal fucks.

Thoughts of her bombarded me in a torrent if I didn't keep them carefully locked away. It was an effort.

Even with all those little defeats, though, the fact remained that I had stayed away from her for eight long days. It was a victory, and I resented my dad for ruining it. Hadn't he already done enough?

I was pissed off and bitter right up until the moment I saw her. Then every thought went out of my head. Or maybe they switched heads. Whatever it was, I stopped thinking about my dad completely and let something else entirely take its place. Enchantment of her.

Let was the wrong word. It happened against my will. To be precise, I had no will once I saw her.

I'd refused to pick her up, insisting that she meet me at the restaurant. We'd been ordered on a date, but no one had specified how long the date had to be.

With that in mind, I'd walked in the door planning to bolt after taking exactly two bites of the main course, but my first sight of her undid all of those plans, because I quite simply forgot about them.

The fact was that I wanted to spurn her, but I wanted to fuck her more. And the imbalance of those two urges only grew more pronounced with every contact.

I took her in as she made her way through the crowded restaurant. The tables were awkwardly close together, and she had to navigate between them by twisting and turning her perfect, decadent body to maneuver through. Ah, New York. Everywhere worth being was packed to the gills.

There wasn't one eye in the room that stayed off her. Men stared, of course, but even the women couldn't stop looking at her. I didn't blame any of them. If her stunning looks weren't enough, her flawless face had recently been plastered all over Times Square for some makeup ad.

She was wearing white with miles of her tanned legs showing and her bodice dipped down into a low V that exposed the delectable skin between her perky tits. When she drew closer my eyes ran down her legs, and I noticed the nude stilettos with red heels that peeked out as she walked.

She could keep those on when I fucked her up against the nearest wall.

I tried to shake off the visual but was only

partially successful. My eyes traveled back up her body. I studied her ensemble, trying to figure out how it came off.

"What are you wearing?" were the first words out of my mouth.

I'd caught her off guard. She paused and glanced down at herself. "Are you asking about the designer? I think it's . . . Hmm . . . Halston maybe? I'm not entirely sure."

"I don't care about the designer. What I'm asking is, is it all one piece? What the hell? What is this torture device?"

"It's a romper, and it's not a torture device. It's actually really comfortable."

"I meant a torture device for *me*. It was obviously designed by someone who never thinks about having sex, let alone having sex in a hurry. It looks great, but how am I ever going to get you out of it?" My voice was grumpy, almost childish, with an intentionally whiny lilt at the end.

She threw back her head and laughed.

I was entranced. Bedazzled. My blood throbbed in my veins. She'd never laughed *for me* before.

She was still smiling as she took the seat across from me. I was still staring.

Our table was small enough that as she pushed

her seat in I had to part my knees to let hers slip between. I locked her knees there, reaching one hand beneath to grip her thigh.

Her smile died and something else went to life on her face.

Every time I looked at her sideways she seemed to melt under my gaze. Like she wanted to lie on her back and open her legs for any scrap of attention I gave her.

She couldn't be as caught up in this ridiculous attraction as I was, I told myself.

She just has a role to play, I told myself.

But it was getting harder and harder to lie to myself.

Harder to vilify her. To deny her charms, her sweet, innocent nature. Her magnetic, constantly trembling lips.

She'd called me a hypocrite, and the barb had stuck. She wasn't wrong. Her motivations were no different than my own. They were *more* innocent, really. She was an eighteen-year-old who came from nothing and wanted a better life. Who the hell was I to look down on that? Spoiled rich boy, indeed.

When I used to picture my wife, I'd had a very clear impression of who she must have been. I'd known, thought, *assumed* she was cold and calculating. Unfortunately I was wrong, at least in part. There was nothing cold about her. She'd become a warm, liquid throb in my veins.

Moreover, she seduces everyone around her. Even me. Especially me.

In spite of my best intentions, a different picture was being painted for me of my wife. She was not who I had assumed. There was something very straightforward, almost undeniably honest about her. And there was no way I could deny that she was hardworking. Earnest. Just trying her best to get ahead.

Despite my highest hopes, she wasn't the bad girl gold digger I'd given her credit for.

In fact, she wasn't bad at all.

She was good. I knew it in my bones. It wasn't sight or smell or anything tangible, but it was there in the air around her, another sense. A *feeling*. I was starting to get a lot of those where my wife was concerned. The realization made my skin feel over-warm, like I was getting a fever just under the surface. I tugged restlessly at my collar.

"You're in an interesting mood," she was saying to me.

I shook myself free of my thoughts. I shrugged. "I suppose." We'd been around each other enough for her to notice a different mood of mine. It was a sobering thought. I was utterly failing to keep her at a distance, and the more contact we had together, the less I cared about that. Therein lay the problem.

We ordered drinks. She tried to order wine, and I changed it to water. "You're too young," I said at her look.

A silent spell fell upon us. I stared at her while she stared down at her lap. My hand was heavy on her leg.

"How have you been?" I found myself asking her. Making small talk like a civilized husband.

She sent me a brief glance, then looked down again. Something about my question put her on guard. I felt my gut dip. Had I been such a bastard that even such an innocuous inquiry made her wary?

The short answer? Yes. I hated myself for it even as I braced myself against falling further under her spell.

"Fine," she said. That was all.

"Have you been working a lot?" I followed up with.

She shrugged, looking around at anything but me. "The usual. I keep busy. I'm supposed to fly to Paris for a YSL fragrance campaign and some other jobs in a few days."

I felt myself tense. "How long will that last?" I remembered when the terms for it were being negotiated, but I hadn't realized it was coming up so soon.

"I should be there for around two weeks."

I processed that and no matter how I unpacked it, it left a bad taste in my mouth. "Is that really necessary? Two weeks seems an excessive amount of time."

She finally looked at me directly. "I'm booked solid. You approved all of it."

I was sure she wasn't wrong. That didn't mean I wasn't bothered. Two weeks in Paris. Traveling with Chester and working with God knew who. No, I didn't like it. "It's not the best timing. I have a lot going on in New York for the next few weeks. Things I can't step away from without a lot of rescheduling."

She bent her head down, brow furrowing in confusion. "Okay," she said carefully. "I don't see how that could be a problem. It's not like my travel plans could affect *you*."

I felt my nostrils flare, a tick starting up in my temple. I knew what I was feeling was unreasonable. Knowing didn't make the feelings lesson.

I didn't want her to leave. I didn't want her traveling without me. When it came right down to it, I didn't want her going anywhere without me. *When had this happened?* Our lives were completely separate. I had insisted upon it. It was preposterous for me to feel possessive about the very wife I'd spurned. The wife I tried my hardest to stay away from.

But I felt what I felt regardless of reason. A jealous itch under my skin. An empty ache in my gut. Denying it hadn't lessened it, in fact it seemed to worsen by the minute.

"Where are you staying in Paris?" I asked tersely.

"The family apartments," she answered, watching me. "Your father insisted," she added defensively.

Well, that was something, at least. The family apartments were a very secure, controlled environment. She wouldn't be able to sneeze without someone in my family hearing about it. Without it getting back to me. Good.

We ordered our food and a silence captured us again. I was determined for her to speak first, but she seemed much more content to keep her thoughts to herself than I was to let her. For my part, I was trying very hard to hold in a question.

I drank and watched her downcast face. Her lashes were so thick and long that I was trying to decide if they were fake or not. Usually you could tell, but with hers it was impossible to say.

"If you wanted my number, why haven't you contacted me since you got it?" The words I'd wanted to say since exactly one hour after the last time I saw her burst out of me.

She took a drink of water, seemed to brace herself, and looked at me square on. "Did you *want me* to contact you?"

That shut me up. I didn't even want to analyze that question, but I was afraid I already very much knew the answer. "Why did you want my number?" I countered.

Her perfectly straight teeth caught her lush lower lip, biting into it thoughtfully.

I was sitting up straight, elbows on the table, but at that I leaned forward, and the hand that wasn't holding my drink went to grab her knee again. I wanted her lips closer. I wanted *her* closer. I set my drink down and gripped her other knee, pulling her deeper beneath the table, my hands slipping higher up her thighs.

How long would it take to get from this spot to somewhere private enough that I could peel her out of that contraption she was wearing and get my dick wet?

She spoke, and I had to literally shake my head to get back to the issue at hand.

"I only wanted it for emergencies," she said, breathless. My thumbs were rubbing the softest spot up high on her inner thighs. "Not like real emergencies, but if I had a question for you that I wanted answered, for plans or whatever. I just don't want to communicate through Asha anymore." I slid one hand higher, into the leg of her torturous little romper. My fingers teased the lace of her panties.

She gripped the edge of the table, her face flushed.

Our food arrived and I had to take my hands off her and sit up. I didn't look at her again for a time, focusing on my food and willing my raging hard-on to go down. Finally when I had myself somewhat under control, I swallowed my mouthful of prime rib and spoke, "You don't have to have an emergency to call or text me."

She finished swallowing a tiny, sad, sad bite of her greens before responding, "You *want* me to text you?"

I was uncomfortable with the subject, but not uncomfortable enough to stay quiet on it. I had to clear my throat and swallow before I could choke my next words out. "I'd like that."

She just stared at me for a time, food forgotten. I stared steadily back.

Finally she leaned forward, placing the back of her hand to my forehead, brow furrowed, expression thoughtful. It was adorable and it made me smile. "What are you doing?" I asked her.

"Checking for a fever."

"A fever?"

"I'm just trying to find a reasonable excuse for the fact that my husband is suddenly being *nice* to me."

I visibly winced, though her reaction was perfectly understandable. I had no excuse for the way I'd treated her, and no explanation for why I'd had such a sudden change of heart. Certainly nothing I was willing to admit to.

Instead I played it off. "Such a cynical eighteen-year-old," I teased her. Attempted to, anyway.

"Nineteen," she said and went back to eating.

I stared, dumbfounded. *What did that mean?* "Nineteen what?"

She took her time answering, taking another tiny bite of food and a sip of her water. My jaw was clenched impatiently as I waited.

"I'm 'such a cynical' *nineteen*-year-old," she finally said.

"What? When did you turn nineteen?"

She looked thoughtful. She seemed to be calculating something in her head. And she took her fucking time doing it. "About seven hours ago."

"It's your birthday?" You could've picked my jaw up off the floor. "Why didn't you tell me?" I asked her slowly. Perhaps she had a good answer for this.

Unfortunately, she did.

She shrugged. "I didn't even think of it. Why would it concern *you*?"

Why did that make me absolutely livid? I couldn't even understand myself. Who I was I angry with? I wanted to lash out, but who could I blame but myself?

Ah yes. That was who I was angry with.

I wanted to shout. I wanted to rage. Instead I answered her with every ounce of civility I could muster. "It concerns me because *you're my wife*."

Her mouth twisted into an unhappy smile. "Really, Calder. There's no need for you to pretend when it's just the two of us. I don't want you to do anything for *me* out of obligation. I know your father forced you to take me to dinner tonight, so this is all for him, but you really don't need to bother to go out of your way on *my* account. If he asks me, I'll tell him you did everything you were supposed to. I'm not looking to get you in trouble."

Each word was a barb that burrowed under my skin. They'd sting for a while.

And I deserved every one of them.

The worst part was that in her mind she wasn't

even being particularly pointed. This wasn't coming from resentment on her part.

She was just that resigned to my poor behavior. That stung more.

We'd been sitting for a time in awkward, stiff silence when something caught my eye. Two tables away, a couple was being seated.

It was Fatima. She sat in a chair facing me, and her husband took the one opposite, showing me his back. I knew none of it was a coincidence. She'd always had a nerve.

I tipped my glass at her, eyeing her coldly.

She tipped hers back, smiling like the cat that ate the canary. She was enjoying herself, enjoying *all* of this. She liked these sorts of games. I wondered if I'd ever found that appealing about her, or if I'd just been so blind and besotted that I hadn't even spotted it for what it was—petty and conniving.

I glanced back at my wife. She was pushing her sad greens around on her plate and hadn't noticed anything. God, she was beautiful. It wasn't the type of beauty that needed the right angle or lighting. Face painted heavily or not at all, her extraordinary bone structure shone through. It was distracting, really. It was a struggle to look away, to not stare at her constantly.

I must have been careless and let my face

reveal something of my thoughts, for the next time Fatima caught my eye there was something in hers that made me still, dread creeping up.

Of course she was jealous of my wife. She had been from the get-go. She was the type of woman who remained possessive of things, even things she'd tossed carelessly aside.

But seeing us together like this would give her her first real reason to be. Knowing her temper, it was a worrisome development, though I wasn't sure what I could do about it at this point. I'd done all I could.

Eventually Noura caught my eye wandering and turned to follow it. Her face went dead of all expression when she spotted my ex-fiancée. "Is she waiting for us to finish, so you two can go on a real date?" she asked me coldly.

I felt myself flush, though I'd had nothing to do with Fatima's presence there. Just the opposite. I'd wanted to bolt the moment I caught sight of her. "No," I said simply.

"Then why is she here?" my wife asked.

"I have no idea."

"I don't believe you," she said defiantly.

I stared at her. "Excuse me?" I asked, still trying to be polite.

"Is that why you were being nice to me earlier? To make her jealous?"

I stared. "She wasn't even here then. They just sat down. And believe me, the *last* thing I would ever do is try to make her jealous of you."

"Liar."

"Excuse me?" I asked, less polite.

She set her napkin on her plate decisively. "I'm leaving. We've both honored our obligations here. Our handlers will tell your father we both showed up for the date. Goodnight, Calder."

And with that, she left.

I was so caught off guard that I just watched her go. Watched her wind through the crowd and out the door.

I told myself I wouldn't follow her, eyes glued to her parting figure. It was a great view of her perky, perfect two handfuls ass. Mm.

I called for the check, settled the bill, and rang for my car, all the while telling myself that I was just going home. It was only as I heard the words leave my mouth that I realized it was hopeless. "My wife's apartment," I told my driver.

CHAPTER
27

I was at her door when I realized I didn't even have a key to her apartment.

I had to ring the doorbell and I hated it.

Chester answered, and I hated that more.

He squared his huge frame off in the doorway, not letting me in, and raised one bushy ginger brow at me. "Need something?"

I had to force my teeth to stop grinding together before I answered. "My wife."

He just kept staring. "Why?"

"Excuse me?" I gritted out.

"Duchess is busy. It's her birthday, if you didn't know. I'd just as soon you leave her in peace. She should get to enjoy her own birthday in peace, don't you think?"

I opened my mouth, shut it, then opened it again. I wasn't sure what I was about to say, or hell, if I was about to haul off and hit him. I'll never know because that was the moment my wife showed up, quietly telling Chester that she'd handle it.

He sent me one last glare and left, disappearing into her apartment like he lived there, which he practically did.

I hated that most of all.

I'd left the restaurant mere minutes behind her, but Noura had already managed to tie her hair up into a complicated, voluminous topknot and changed out of her torture device romper into an oversized sweatshirt and itty bitty shorts. Spelled across the front of the sweatshirt in large caps was the word DUCHESS.

I stared at it. "Where'd you get that?" I asked tersely. It wasn't where I'd meant to begin, but I couldn't for the life of me ignore it.

She just stared at me, her face carefully, vehemently apathetic. It was impressive, really, how she could school her beautiful, expressive face into the very epitome of impassivity. "Excuse me?"

"The sweatshirt. Where'd you get it, *Duchess*?"

We had a minor stare down before she answered. "It was a birthday present."

"From whom?" I shot back calmly and

instantly. But I knew the answer. Oh yes I knew, and I was livid.

"Why?" she hedged.

"Answer the question," I gritted out, calm gone.

"Chester."

I knew it!

"It's no big deal. You know he calls me Duchess. I don't know why. It's silly." She paused. Shrugged. "I guess it's an inside joke between us."

From her face I could tell that she didn't realize she'd made it ten times worse.

I made myself take deep breaths. I made myself wait until I could at least appear calm before I spoke again. "Are you having some sort of birthday party in there?" I asked. It was quiet now, but I'd heard some definite sounds of revelry when the door had first opened.

She shrugged. "Not a party. They just got me gifts and cake." With the oversized sweatshirt and her sullen attitude, she looked more like teenager than she ever had to me before. It didn't help.

"That sounds a lot like a birthday party, Duchess," I pointed out.

"Please don't call me that," she shot back with automatic speed.

"He calls you Duchess," I said quietly.

She started. "When he says it, he's being . . . affectionate. You're just making fun."

"*Affectionate*? You want his *affection*?"

"That came out wrong. It's just a harmless nickname. It doesn't mean anything."

"See that it doesn't," I gritted out through clenched teeth. "You know, when I assigned a man more than twice your age to be your security, I did so assuming there wouldn't be a problem. I should have known better. No man could be immune to you."

She looked like she wasn't sure whether to be flattered or horrified, and immediately she went on the defensive. "That's ridiculous. We're friends, which is nice since I spend ninety percent of my waking hours with him."

I felt a tick start up in my temple.

"You like him," I observed.

She studied me like I was deranged. "Of course I like him." Her mouth gaped open. "You can't possibly be jealous!"

I didn't bother to deny it. I glared at her, holding up a finger. "If he steps so much as one inch out of line with you, I will know about it, he will be *fired*, and I'll make sure that you *never* see him again."

"He would never step out of line," she defended.

"See that he doesn't, or you lose him. Understood?"

"Understood. It's just a stupid nickname."

"You like it," I accused. "I saw the way you smile at him when he says it."

She didn't bother to deny it. Instead she crossed her arms in front of her chest and stared me down.

"Am I invited to this non-birthday party you're having?" I tried to smile engagingly as I asked the question. I was pretty certain by the widening of her eyes that it came out as more of a grimace.

She sighed, stepped to the side, and waved me in. "Why not? I'm warning you, though, you'll probably be bored."

She was wrong. I didn't find it boring at all. Watching her with her close group of friends—because that's what they were (regardless of the fact that my family paid half of them)—her friends, was unsettling to me, and far from boring.

It was a small group that consisted of Jovie, Chester, Vincent, and one new addition.

It was a rail thin boy who looked all of sixteen, with silver hair, up-tilted eyes, and an impish smile.

"This is Santi," Noura introduced him.

The boy beamed at me. "Nice to meet you,"

he said in a soft, musical voice. "I'm your wife's new roommate."

I blinked at him stupidly. "Excuse me? I think you're going to have to repeat that last bit."

Noura tried her best to do damage control. "He's staying in Chester and Vincent's apartment while he's between places," she said quietly, moving close so only I could hear. "Your father approved it, and Chester did a thorough background check. He's a really nice guy. Please don't be mean to him." She said it all in a furious rush, her eyes on mine beseeching.

I didn't begin to know how to say no to her when she looked at me like that. And that worried me. A lot.

"Can you give us a minute?" I asked the room, but I didn't wait for an answer, pulling her into our bedroom and shutting the door.

I studied her intently. She fidgeted, looking anywhere but at me. I felt something move through me, a new and intense tenderness I was quite afraid I'd never felt anything close to before. It was worrisome. And addictive. "When did this new development occur?" I asked her quietly.

She stopped fidgeting and looked at me. Really looked, like she was trying to find answers as much as I was. "Two days ago."

"How well do you know him?"

"Well enough to know he's a sweet boy who just needs a little help."

I sighed. I couldn't turn the poor kid away, not when she looked at me like that, with a glimmer of hope in her eyes like she'd beg me if I pushed her too hard. "Do you *have to* adopt every misfit you meet?"

She smiled, looking down at her clasped hands. It was a warm smiled, turned both outward and inward.

The sight made me a touch dizzy. The power this girl had over me—if she tried to use it even a little—I shuddered at the thought.

"My mother used to do that too," she remarked quietly.

I stared at her. This was new. She *never* talked about her parents or her family. She never talked about her background at all.

"Your mother used to adopt every misfit she met?" I asked carefully.

She chuckled and I felt myself smiling with her. "They aren't *misfits*. They're just . . . different. And my mom was like a magnet for interesting people. People with different views of the world, different things to say. I always loved that. She wasn't friends with people because they were like her. She brought new things into her life with her friendships, not more of the same. It was one of my favorite things about her."

CHAPTER
28

NOURA

I was surprised at what had just come out of my mouth. I never spoke about my parents. In fact, I tried my best not to think of them.

More surprising than my words though was the way Banks responded to them. He was looking at me with such warmth, with a sort of dazzled, bemused expression in his eyes. Then it changed, his eyes clouding over as some realization dawned. "She *was?*" he asked.

I shook my head and changed the subject quickly. "So you'll let him stay?" I could tell that Banks was baffled by Santi, but he'd covered it better than I could've hoped for. I'd assumed he'd freak out when he heard.

He sighed. "It's not a permanent arrangement, I assume?"

I shook my head, beaming because I knew I had just won. "He just needs to get back on his feet. It won't take long."

"How old is he?"

"Sixteen."

"My God, he's a child."

"Only a few years younger than me."

He flinched. He hated any reminders of my age. Frankly, it was little bit fun to twist that knife.

"How'd you find him?"

I told him the short version of my run-in with Santi a few days previously. It was sadly similar to the way I'd met Jovie. Backstage at a runway show and in a bad way. He was underage, a full-time model, and his much older, fashion designer boyfriend had just kicked him out like last season's fashion trash. All the beautiful, lost kids in New York wouldn't fit into my apartment, of course, but how could one more hurt?

Chester's response to the new addition hadn't been any better than Banks'.

"You're turning me into the worst body guard in the world, Duchess," he'd pointed out. "How can I protect you if you invite every homeless model you meet to live with you?"

I'd smiled at him, knowing from his tone that he wasn't going to fight me on this. "He couldn't be more harmless. Surely you can see that."

Chester had quickly relented with a few reasonable stipulations that involved getting my father-in-law's approval. I'd dreaded my husband's reaction, but hadn't thought I'd have to face it so soon.

Back to the present I was unutterably relieved that he'd taken it better than I could've hoped.

I eyed him as I finished my story. He was chewing on his lower lip, his eyes on the front of my sweatshirt.

"Poor kid," he murmured.

I nodded emphatically. "He had no one to turn to. Nowhere to go. And he's an absolute sweetheart. I couldn't help it. I had to help."

His eyes were on my face now, filled with something that made me ache, made me start to melt, made me look away. His hand chased the motion, cupping my jaw, and turning me back to look at him. "You just can't help yourself, can you?"

"I don't know what you mean."

"You're just too good," he murmured, drawing me close. "I can't take it." With barely leashed ferocity, he kissed me.

Sometime later, his mouth on my neck now, I came back to myself enough to say, "Can we turn on some music or something?"

We were still clothed, but he'd pinned me to

the bed, his weight heavy on top of me as he rubbed himself restlessly against me.

He rasped something unintelligible and bit my earlobe.

I repeated myself.

"What?"

"We have kids in the house," I pointed out reasonably. "I don't want them to hear us."

"Are you telling me I have to be quiet in our *marriage* bed just because you've decided to make this the apartment of misfit models?"

"I'm just asking you to turn on some music. It's a full house tonight."

He pulled away and studied me. "Do you want to go back out and finish your party?"

I looked away. "Do you mind?"

"My dick does, but it won't kill him to wait a few hours."

I smiled and I couldn't help it, I glanced down. He was straining the front of his slacks. "Are you sure?"

"Not if you keep looking at it like that, I'm not." He took my arm in a gentle grasp, tugging me toward the door. "Come on. Let's go hang out with your friends."

My small birthday party wasn't anything exciting, but it was just perfect for me, surrounded by the people I enjoyed the most. We watched

DramaFever and ate cake. I tried to have one tiny bite of it, but Banks cajoled me into more.

He was a bit stiff with my friends, and he didn't say much, but I still appreciated the fact that he was there and no one had forced him to be. And through it all, it felt like something was happening between us, something that had nothing to do with our fake marriage and everything to do with something more authentic than a contract. A budding but genuine affection. And of course desire.

We slipped in and out of the living room a few times to make out like high school kids. The third time we did it, Jovie shouted at our retreating backs, "Figure yourselves out!"

Much, much later we retired for the night. He undressed me slowly and took me to bed.

He rocked into me, eyes on mine. Each jarring thrust moved my whole body, making my breasts bounce with each plunge. His gaze moved down to my chest, then back to my face with each movement.

"Should I call you Duchess while I fuck you? Would you like that?"

The question made me stiffen mid-thrust. He kept jarring into me without pause. I'd forgotten about his jealous fit earlier. He'd been so sedate and agreeable since then, but it had obviously upset him much more than I'd thought. I wasn't sure how to handle him like this, jealous Banks was even more of a stranger to me than normal Banks, so I didn't answer.

Once again, my silence didn't help.

With a growl, he started rutting with a purpose, fucking me harder.

I went mindless for one beat, two, and honestly forgot about his temper for a time.

That is, until his harsh voice sounded in the room, loud enough to be heard over our panting breaths and my pounding heartbeat. "Do you want me to call him in while you're like this? Do you want him to see what I do to you while he's out there *at your beck and call?*"

I couldn't answer. I didn't have the breath to speak. He was ardently fucking it out of me.

Again, it didn't help.

He hissed at me through his teeth. "He's probably fantasizing about you right now. Do you like that? Do you like having that effect on him? Do you get off on the fact that you have that effect on *every* man?"

I squeezed my eyes shut tight, mind too hazy to respond. Frankly, I was closer to coming than answering him, but that didn't seem to occur to him.

Abruptly, he stopped moving. My eyes

snapped open. "Don't stop," I gasped, straining against him.

"Maybe I *should* call him in," he growled from atop me. "Let him see me balls deep inside of you. Let him see that *I* own this." His hand snaked down, fingering my clit, his cock buried to the hilt. "That it's *mine*."

I finally managed to get out a breathy, "No."

Faint as that one word was, it seemed to calm him, or at least it didn't set him off more. He started moving again.

I must have fallen asleep after with him still on top of me because I roused when he moved away.

He was hitching his pants up over his hips when he asked me over his shoulder. "I'm grabbing water from the kitchen. Do you need anything, Duchess?"

"Don't," I said faintly, turning my face away.

"What?"

"Don't call me Duchess, please."

"Why not?"

"Because you're making fun. When he does it, he's just being sweet."

He was in my face again in a heartbeat, body covering mine, madness in his eyes, voice hitched low but *furious*. "He doesn't get to be sweet with you. You need to get that through your head."

Oh this again.

"Are you jealous because I said he was my friend?" I asked carefully. It was actually kind of sweet. "You can be my friend, too. It's not a mutually exclusive thing."

"For the record, I don't want to be your *friend*," he growled. "I want to make you come and watch your eyes roll up into your head. I want to fuck you until you can't walk straight."

I was blushing as I replied stubbornly, "You can do those things *and* be my friend."

"Okay. Fine. That's the kind of friendship I want, but you don't get to have that with *anyone* else."

I just blinked at him. "Well, of course not," I replied simply.

It seemed to mollify him if the way he kissed me was any indication.

"What can I get you for your birthday?" he asked me some time in the night.

My mind shot to one idea immediately. It would make me vulnerable to ask him for something like that, I thought, mind moving furiously. It would *hurt* if he turned me down.

But if he said yes it would be worth it.

If he said yes it might change everything.

"I'd like you to start talking to me directly. No more Asha."

He stared at me for a long time. "You want me to fire her?"

I shrugged. "I just want her out of my apartment. I wouldn't be sad if you fired her, but if she just wasn't in charge of me that'd be enough.

"And you really want to deal with me directly?"

"Yes. I want to deal with you directly."

"Okay. If that's what you prefer, that's what we'll do," he said instantly.

Was it that easy? I wondered.

CHAPTER
29

The next day Asha was gone. She didn't even bother to say goodbye, she just disappeared from my life. I wasn't sad, just the opposite, though I did wonder briefly how I was going to figure out my schedule. I was off today, and I could recall perhaps the next two days' schedule from memory, but after that I'd be in Paris, and I had no clue about my itinerary there.

I didn't have to wonder long as Chester updated me as soon as he walked in the door. "I've taken over your schedule, Duchess. We can go over everything and enter it into your phone so you can keep track of it yourself, as well."

I was good with that. And the pleasant surprises just kept on coming. Jovie just happened to have the day off as well, and Santi was free all morning. We binge-watched Goblin on DramaFever and at about 10 a.m., I received a text. A pleasant one. From my husband.

BANKS: I heard you had the day off. I hired a team to come over to pamper you and your friends. Happy Birthday, Duchess.

I'd no sooner read the text then there was a knock at the door. A small army of spa attendants were let in.

The three of us spent the next five hours getting facials, manis, pedis, and massages in front of the television.

Santi talked us all into watching some strange videos on YouTube that had titles like *Jet Fuel Doesn't Melt Steel, Why the Denver Airport is a Portal to Hell,* and *The Moon Landing was Faked.*

Santi, turned out, was an avid conspiracy theory nut. I was a bit troubled about it, but Jovie thought it was hilarious. She shamelessly egged him on.

Vincent surprised me by agreeing with Santi with more than half of the theories.

At first Chester was adamantly disapproving of our choice of viewing subjects, but as Santi pivoted from the crazier conspiracy videos to the lighter ones, such as one where Shane Dawson focused on a Chuck E. Cheese pizza plot, eventually even he could admit begrudgingly that it was all pretty entertaining.

After much effort I even talked Chester and Vincent into getting scalp massages and wearing avocado sheet masks.

We couldn't stop laughing, and I managed to get some photographic proof, threatening to use it for future blackmailing.

When Santi finally ran out of his conspiracy steam, we switched to watching bad reality TV. Jovie and Santi had a running disagreement about Life of Kylie.

Santi thought it was awful.

Jovie didn't see it the same way.

"I stan her," she said stubbornly.

That comment got Chester involved. "What does that even mean?" he asked her.

"It means she's a big fan of hers," I explained.

"Like obsessed," Santi added. "I don't get it. Kylie's a mile wide and two inches deep. I think Jovie just likes her because they're both shallow."

Jovie was far from offended. "I'm not shallow, I'm *vain*," she shot back, laughing. "And she's a self-made billionaire because of *makeup*." She gave a big sigh. "My dream."

"You can't be self-made when you start out with money!" Santi pointed out.

Chester shook his head, muttering something along the lines of 'kids these days' which made us all laugh.

We were taking turns picking shows to watch, and on one of Jovie's, she chose RuPaul's Drag Race.

"You just like this show because their hair's as big as yours," Santi remarked.

Jovie, as usual not taking offense, patted her hair with a smirk. It was a striking dark blonde that was a trim shade paler than her skin. Her corkscrew curls were particularly voluminous with all the spa treatments adding a warm humidity to the room. "Don't you know my hair is where I keep all the secrets? It's not getting any smaller, honey."

It was impossible to keep secrets from Jovie forever. Even big ones.

The day before I left for Paris, I broke down and told her everything about my marriage. Every little deceitful detail.

"It's all fake," I reiterated after I was completely finished unloading.

"Bullshit," she said succinctly.

I stared. "What? You don't believe me?"

"Oh I believe you about the arranged marriage, the Bride Catalogue, Banks being an asshole, all of that. But calling it fake? Whatever that thing is between you, it's not fake. That man is crazy about you. He loses his mind every time he looks at you."

I mulled that over. She was exaggerating as only a teenager could, of course, but it made me wonder. How *did* he look at me? Did it mean anything? I pushed the thought away. There was nothing so painful as false hope. "It doesn't matter. I don't care."

I knew I was lying to myself. It was a fact that I lied to myself all the time, but at least I never believed me.

From the look she was sending me, Jovie didn't believe me either.

"Now let's go back to that Bride Catalogue," she said, bringing me back to the present. "Tell me *everything*."

I laughed. "Don't even think about it."

"I've got a few years to make up my mind. In the meantime, spill the beans. What is it? How'd you find it?"

"It's not as obscure as you might think. It circulates pretty heavily in the modeling community."

"Why'd you do it?" she asked. There was no

judgement in the question, just probing curiosity.

"I was in a bad place. I'd spent about four years struggling. Don't get me wrong, I had some success, but it never felt like it mattered. My life was not improving. No matter what I did, it felt like I was still drowning."

Our eyes met. "I know the feeling," she stated.

I was sure she did.

"Most models spend all the money they make trying to prove they're worth something on Instagram," she said.

I nodded. "Exactly. The average *successful* modeling career lasts less than four years. I've had more luck at it than most, but I'm well aware that it's temporary. I started at fourteen, that means I'm coasting on borrowed time and, even with some success, this industry will likely still be done with me directly after my teens. I was making decent money, but nowhere near enough to retire at twenty."

"God, that's depressing," Jovie lamented. "And it's all true."

"I wanted to be more," I explained. I wanted her of all people to understand. "To change my *station* in life. To be untouchable."

"And now you're a Castelo. That's about as untouchable as it gets."

I nodded, meeting her eyes squarely. She got

it. "It was a lonely choice to make, but I can't regret it."

Her hand covered mine. "Your life's not lonely anymore. If you have one person, you're never alone, right? You've got me. Always."

CHAPTER
30

Banks followed me to Paris. He came bearing gifts in a wealth of aquamarine jewelry. I didn't recognize it from the family cache. He told me it was a late birthday gift and that it reminded him of my eyes.

And then he stayed with me. I couldn't quite believe it, and I couldn't fathom why or how he was able to take so much time away from all of his business projects, but he did for almost two weeks. He shadowed me everywhere like he had nowhere else he wanted to be. He came to all my shoots and took me out every day after I was done working.

We ate at all the best restaurants, extravagant French food or lavish Italian, and somehow he talked me out of counting most of my calories.

We drank cheap sparkling wine at the foot of

the Eiffel Tower and expensive champagne at the top.

He spent four hours chasing me leisurely through the Louvre, snapping pictures of me only when I wasn't posing for them. At one point, I almost fell into an undoubtedly priceless vase.

He caught me with a warm smile, drawing me close. "We wouldn't want you to fall into anything expensive."

"Except you," I teased.

"Fall into me all you want," he murmured. "As far as you're concerned, I'm free."

I lost my breath. My heart pounded. He had changed so much toward me in such a short time, and I couldn't tell when he was teasing anymore and when he was serious, but I didn't pursue it any further. I was too wary of him still to push my luck.

We spent a day in Versailles, staring at our golden reflections and making out in every decadent, dark corner we could find.

One day we went on a food and wine tour through the R district. I ate some of the cheese and drank all the wine. He ate double all the things I didn't like. The stinky soft cheese, the duck pâté, the caviar, and anything that ended with tartar. My palette for expensive, acquired tastes was underdeveloped, to say the least.

We marveled at every inch of Notre Dame for a full six hours, naming as many gargoyles as we could. We found a pop-up book of the city in the gift shop there and went on a tour to visit every single sight we hadn't already seen. We went over and under the Arc de Triomphe, through the Centre Pompidou, Sacré-Coeur, and Les Invalides.

We took a silly selfie at each one.

Paris was a new chapter for us. I didn't know why it was so, what had shifted, what was growing between the two of us, and we didn't speak of it much, as though afraid we'd talk ourselves out of this spell.

It wasn't my first time in Paris, but it was the first time I saw it through the eyes of a lover.

There was something in the air, a softer filter over the skyline day and night. Rose-colored glasses indeed.

I admitted to him that I loved the French custom of greeting with a kiss on both cheeks. He kissed my cheeks until I giggled and at least twenty times a day after that.

And we talked. He told me about his business interests. The fortune he'd made and lost, the one he was building again. He was passionate about it, which I had a cursory understanding of.

He tried to explain it to me. He bought valuable, calculated pieces of land and built on them, then leased out the buildings and made a steady fortune in the bargain. It sounded a bit boring to me, but it clearly drove him. I gleaned that he was just as driven to surpass his father someday.

It was mid-morning. We were still abed. It was my only full day off on the trip, and we were taking full advantage.

I told him about some of my business ideas, things I'd been working on with his father. My ventures were adding up quickly. What had started out as a small idea to collaborate with Morphe for some signature matte liquid lip colors with my name attached had quickly sprouted into a full-on cosmetics line, brushes included. And I'd gone from modeling for Stuart Weitzman to designing my own shoe line.

As I spoke he watched me intently. His eyes were so soft. All that cold gray had gone melting warm.

Why were they melting at me? Why were they melting *me*?

"Can I ask you something?" he asked me. "I'm not trying to fight, I want to keep this truce. I'm just curious."

"That sounds ominous, but go for it."

"Why'd you do it?"

I couldn't help it, I flinched just the slightest bit. Things were going so well. Why did he want to drag this up? It was bound to happen sooner or later, I supposed.

I chose my words carefully. "I guess I saw the writing on the wall. Models are a dime a dozen. We're throwaway creatures. For most of my career, I've shared a tiny room in a tiny apartment with eight other girls."

"You make good money," he pointed out.

My mouth twisted bitterly. "I make great money *now*. And I did well enough before, I suppose, but most of the money I've made has gone toward my family, in one way or another."

"Tell me about them. Your parents."

Eyeing him warily, I did. "My dad was laid off at his job at GM exactly one week after my mom was diagnosed with bone cancer. I had the opportunity to move to New York for modeling. I did it. I wanted to be with her, but I felt *useless* staying when I could leave and help make ends meet."

"*Jesus*. How old were you?"

"Fourteen."

"Is that even legal?"

I shrugged. "My parents agreed to it, so yes, and my agency helped me get set up in an apartment, like I said, with eight other girls. For that they got a percentage of my jobs, and what

I didn't need for food or transportation, I sent back to my dad. Every spare cent I made went to my mother's bills. None of it saved her. My dad swore it helped, but it clearly didn't help enough. My mom didn't last a year."

"My god. I'm sorry."

I shrugged. "Sometimes I regret leaving her. I was so busy working to help that I didn't see her much in the end. And when she was gone, I still didn't go back home. I wanted to stay busy. Distract myself out of my grief, ya know? So I stayed, kept working, figuring my dad still needed help with his bills anyway."

"You were a good daughter." He had the grace to look sheepish. "I'd heard they passed, but not all the details. Tell me the rest."

"On March 26th." I saw him flinch at the date, the same day as our wedding. "The two year anniversary of my mother's death, my dad's crappy old truck broke down on the side of the road. It was below freezing and his cell didn't have any service. He fell asleep in his truck and never woke up. Strangers found him a full day later. I was saving up to get him a better car. I was too late by two months," I finished bitterly. "After that I became obsessed with planning for a better future. I planned how to never be two months behind surviving again."

He stroked my hair comfortingly and I let him. And I kept sharing.

"Modeling's a volatile industry. We're young, vulnerable, and *for sale.* This business is full of corruption, especially for a single girl without any protection. Not a good scene. When I lost my parents, I felt very alone. And far from safe. I didn't have anyone. I was *so alone.* That's why I'd never had a drink before the wedding. The parties my agency sent me to . . . I was afraid of being drugged. It happened to girls all the time, and they'd just shrug it off, like it was part of the job. I wasn't willing to shrug that off. Modeling's not known for its job security. And say I get a nasty scar or gain fifteen pounds. It's all over. I won't even get into how fast I'll age out of it." I paused. "I wanted security."

"You could have tried to find security *and* love."

I stared at him. "How naive do you think I am?"

"Touché."

"I've seen how it works. Models are treated like commodities to rich men. I decided to make that work in my favor. I wanted to matter," I continued. "People like you matter. People like me and my family suffer and die tragically and *no one cares.* Both of my parents died with only me to mourn them. If I became one of you, I knew the world would care when I died.

Anyway, I heard of the Bride Catalogue somewhere along the way. Models talk about it a lot in certain circles, though none I knew ever admitted if they'd submitted their profiles for it. You know, sometimes when girls disappear into harems for a few years, I always wonder if that was the Catalogue. And of course whenever I see a model in her prime hooking up with an eighty-year-old billionaire, I do wonder if it was the Catalogue that set it up. Regardless of all the rumors, though, I was always reassured that the girls had the final say in the arrangements. By the time I turned eighteen, I'd already made up my mind. It certainly turned out differently than I pictured. No one's ever going to suspect *us*. You're too young and gorgeous for anyone to believe you'd need or want to buy a bride."

"I wasn't the only one who saw your profile," he pointed out. "You know there was a bidding war."

I couldn't hold back the barest flinch. "I'd heard there was some attention, but I'd never heard it worded precisely that way. Do you think someone will talk?"

"No," he said after a time. "No one bidding would be well served by outing the Catalogue. Well? Did it work out how you'd hoped? Does this make you feel safe?"

I couldn't meet his eyes. "In a way, yes." Mostly. That had been the point of it, anyway. And I did feel safe. Every part of me except my heart.

"I wanted a family," I said in small voice, still trying to make him understand. "Dysfunctional. For convenience. But there. Present in my corner when the chips fall, as they *always* do."

"I get it," he said softly.

After a time I spoke again. "What about you? Why'd you do it?"

He took a breath so deep that both of our bodies swayed with the motion. "For all the wrong reasons, if I'm being honest. My parents were pressuring me to get married. Their nagging and . . . other things convinced me it was time."

"Money."

"Yes. Bribery was a big part of it. Getting my inheritance back had its appeal. Now that I see your side of it, I can admit that your reasons were far more admirable than my own."

It was a gratifying concession on his part, to say the least. It was all well and good to say you didn't care whether or not you had someone's approval. It was another thing entirely to mean it. "Why the Bride Catalogue?"

"I didn't want to drag an innocent into this. I

wanted a wife who knew the score. Who knew I could never be a loving husband. Not some insufferable debutante with stars in her eyes."

"Why is that?"

"I gave my heart away once. I'm not about to do that again."

"So you're still in love with Fatima."

"I am not. I hate her for lying to me. For tricking me. I hate that I had no idea she was a fucking fortune hunter, when that's all I've ever wanted to avoid."

It was a dig at her, but of course, I felt it in my own ribs.

"For that matter," he continued brutally, "I'm not even sure love exists, but if it does, I certainly don't want to go through it again."

I kept my face stoic but it was a struggle. "You've had every sweet, tender thing you ever felt about love turn sour," I observed.

"It's not even about that. It's about the fact that you can fall in and out of it. It's the idea that, now that I know it's not a permanent affliction, it doesn't *mean* anything to me. After I realized that, I knew it was all a lie, and that I'd never fall for it again. Once was enough for me. I didn't want to hurt anybody, so I found someone who knew the score."

"And here we are."

He was silent for so long that I didn't think he'd respond. "And here we are," he uttered softly. "We make a strange pair, Goldigger." His tone was rich with affection.

I smirked. "Indeed we do, Spoiled Rich Boy."

Only a few sour notes drifted into our sphere during those brief, golden days, all of them coming from the same direction.

I got a call from an odd number. I should've known better than to answer, but I was on guard with Asha out of the picture and no one yet to replace her, I constantly worried I'd miss a job opportunity if I was too hard to get ahold of.

It was good timing, as I'd just finished a shoot, so I took the call. It was the last person I wanted to hear from, especially with Banks standing a scant few feet away.

"Hello?" I answered, a question in the word.

"Noura," a warm, poisonous voice poured over the voice.

We'd only interacted once, but I knew instantly who it was. I didn't say her name. I couldn't bear to. My eyes were on my husband, who was sending me a questioning look as I said, "Why are you calling me?"

Her delighted laugh was mocking. "A few reasons. But mostly, I didn't want you to forget about me. Your husband hasn't. He never stays away from me for long. And don't take it too personal that he'll never grow fond of you. His heart's just not in it. It's always been occupied elsewhere."

"He's fond enough," I said stiffly. Every word she said was a dagger to the heart. It was little consolation that that was so obviously her intention.

"Don't let him fool you. He can fuck like a prize stallion, but he'll always hate you for the simple reason that his father picked you out."

I was studying my husband's curious face as she spoke, but I was still listening critically, and I caught the fault lines in what she was trying to convey. She believed her own words. She *needed* to believe them. And they were wrong. I smiled. At last I had the upper hand. I didn't hold onto it. Impulsively, I played the hand instantly. "Who told you that? Pasco didn't pick me out."

She sucked in a breath audibly through the phone, a ragged, desperate sound.

I'd shaken her; I knew it in my bones.

"Liar," she hissed back.

I just shook my head. Banks had moved closer and clearly caught some of the gravity of what was happening from my end of the conversation. His brows were drawn together, storm clouds in his storm gray eyes.

"Banks chose me," I said firmly. "His father had nothing to do with *that*. Don't believe me? Ask Banks yourself." I handed him the phone and left to change.

Of course that wasn't the end of it. I wanted it to be. I wanted to pretend I'd never spoken to Fatima, never heard her words, never knew she existed, but Banks just had to bring it up again.

We were being driven back to the hotel in one the family cars, sitting farther apart than we had since our unspoken truce had begun.

"I'm sorry she bothered you," Banks said stiffly, not looking at me. "She shouldn't have done that."

"Me too," I said quietly.

He wasn't finished. "But please don't provoke her like that. In fact don't speak to her at all. If she calls, just hang up or hand the phone to me."

I felt like he'd slapped me in the face but I responded like a pro. "As you wish."

BANKS

It wasn't getting better. I'd thought the reason I was becoming obsessed was that the sporadic, addictive bits of contact we had were leaving me too hungry for more. I'd thought if I took a few concentrated weeks to fuck her out of my system, that would nip it in the bud, but it'd had backfired in a big way. My craving for her was getting much, much worse. Not just for her body, either, which was the most worrisome thing of all.

I craved her company as well. Night and day. Waking and asleep, I wanted her next to me, breathing the same air, responding to my every action.

But back to her body. I was insatiable for it. I went to sleep spent and woke up hard again. I told myself that's why I had to keep her close, but it didn't explain why I had to hold her while we slept, like I was afraid she'd slip away.

Afraid. That was a funny word, but fear filled me with every bit of emotion she woke up inside me. What did I fear, though? Not her, not anymore. Not her intentions or motivations. The fear came from inside, from the fact that the more good I realized she was, the more I knew I didn't deserve her. I'd bought her, but I hadn't earned her.

I was as filthy as she was innocent. The things I'd done in just the first month after our marriage were beyond the pale.

It made the hair rise on the back of my neck just to think about. Had I changed so much since then that I was disgusted by my own behavior now?

In short, yes. Now that I knew her, I regretted everything I'd done to resist her.

And what if she found out? God, the thought was horrifying, because it was altogether feasible. Fatima was just the type of ex to make sure she'd find out at least some of it.

She shifted onto her back in her sleep, but she didn't stir. It was enough. She was naked, nothing but a sheet covering her. I took it off. The shades were open, the city light filtering in enough that I could make out delicious little details of her sleeping form. She shivered at being uncovered, her pert breasts pebbling up. I stroked her, throat to naval, and she curved into my hand. Even then she didn't stir. I rubbed between her legs, watching her sleeping face. Her mouth went slack, eyes still closed. She was wet. I pushed a finger inside her, feeling her. Her body responded, but even that didn't wake her.

I must've really worn her out. The thought didn't bother me. On the contrary, it didn't even slow me down.

I mounted her, shoving in with one smooth, tight glide. That woke her up. She moaned as her beautiful eyes popped open. I kissed her, pumping in and out.

What had I done? How had I allowed myself to get sucked in this deep?

CHAPTER
31

NOURA

It happened on a Thursday. It was a sunny, pleasant day in the city. The sort of day that made you want to walk where you were going instead of sitting in traffic.

I remembered strange little details like that, as though the day were imprinting itself strongly on me before my brain even knew why it should.

I woke up in Banks's arms. He'd stayed the night for no other reason than he'd wanted to. He'd been at my apartment, takeout in hand, when I'd gotten home from a shoot the night before. He'd kissed me like he'd never get enough. We'd had a quiet, intimate meal together that still made me feel warm in my chest just to think about.

For my part, I'd outright admitted to myself

that I was falling *hard*. The man was irresistible when he decided he wanted something, and he wanted *me*.

I was a little sleep deprived after that night. He'd fucked me several times, waking me up at odd points of the night, each one with a tireless desperation that to this day make my whole body clench in memory.

We couldn't resist each other, that much was clear.

And I was starting to feel hopeful about us, about where we were headed, and what we could become.

A cheerful Banks had even taken me to church the previous Sunday. He'd led me in on his arm, seating me in the middle of his family like he did it every week. His brothers had grinned at him, elbowing each other. His parents had gaped. I couldn't keep the blush off my cheeks or the smile off my face for the entire service.

We were starting to build the foundation for something powerful and profound. A real marriage? Perhaps. For the first time I let myself consider it, at least.

The only thing that could hold us back at this was ourselves.

Or so I thought.

Banks had kissed me passionately goodbye on the sidewalk outside my building. He'd gotten into one of his cars, and I'd walked from the apartment to my gym that morning. Chester and I, of course, and even Jovie tagged along. She had a callback at nine, so she'd have to cut it short but she could fit in an hour workout with me beforehand.

I remember that as we were walking, she'd grabbed my hand and beamed at me. "Banks and Noura sittin' in a tree," she'd chanted softly. She was happier than anyone about how things were progressing in my strange marriage. It made her outright giddy. She was painfully young and she'd been through a lot, but she was still an optimistic soul. She was sure that my husband had, against all odds, fallen in love me, and that love would conquer all.

It was a sweet moment, the kind that stays in your mouth for a long time, counteracting some of the bitter flavors that come after.

My trainer pushed Jovie and me through a strenuous and satisfying workout.

"Will you be home in time for dinner tonight?" I asked her on her way out.

"I should be," she replied.

"Well, call if you're not, and don't forget to eat a decent meal. Humans need food to survive," I reminded her. She was like me, constantly monitoring her food.

She rolled her eyes like the teenager she was

but rarely acted like. "Okaaaay, Mooom," she mocked with a smile. She softened it all by kissing me goodbye on both cheeks.

I was still smiling as I walked into the locker room. I changed into a serviceable black two-piece swimsuit and went to do my laps. The gym boasted a good-sized lap pool, but the whole room was rented out for my personal use for this slot of the morning. It was still one of my very favorite perks of becoming a Castelo.

Chester waited just outside the room's only door to the rest of the gym while I swam. There was another door into the cavernous room, but it was Employees Only and locked at all times. Chester still double-checked it every time before he left me to my swim.

It was a nice balance where Chester could do his job, and I could enjoy one of my favorite activities in absolute peace.

It was the time of day I used to clear my head, swimming mindlessly, letting my body and mind float free of care. I didn't count laps. Most of the time I didn't even set a timer for myself. I simply swam until I'd reached my limit.

That day my mind wouldn't go blank, and I didn't mind. It was too full of Banks, and in a good way. I swam with a light, and admittedly, besotted heart.

I remember the heat of the room, the delicious feel of the cool water sliding over my skin. I remember the irritating but familiar smell of chlorine.

And then it all came screeching to a halt.

My hand touched the side of the pool, my body curling, feet purchasing a good grip for the return push. I propelled myself forward.

And stopped with a wrenching pain. What the hell?

At first I thought my long hair had caught on something. And in a way it had, but it was not something. It was someone. Someone's fist.

I'd gone still at the pain, confused but not alarmed, not yet. I was raised from out of the water. For a split second, I caught a glimpse of a man, more his figure than his face, but before I could react, I was thrust down again, not into the water but against the side of the pool, the rounded edge. I had time to turn my head so most of my face was preserved, but that did nothing to protect the side of my head, which made heavy, solid contact with the concrete once. *Pound.* Once. It hurt so much. *Pound.* Twice. I tasted blood. *Pound.* Again. My brain was muddled. *Pound.* Again. I tried to struggle. All I managed to accomplish was a futile squirm mid-water. My feet found no purchase. I was too disoriented to place which way the ground was. *Pound*. Again. I reached up, scratching at the wrist that held my hair. There. The ball of my foot made contact with something, and I pushed with all my might *up*. I gasped in a blessed shock of air. I tried to scream, but it was only a piteous sob before my head was shoved back under. *Pound*. The world went black.

CHAPTER
32

I came to in a wash of unpleasant sensations. The slow scrape in and out of air squeezing through a raw throat. My mind was filled with a wealth of disconnected nightmares that I couldn't remember, but I could still taste like copper at the base of my throat.

My whole body hurt, but nothing throbbed so badly as my head. It was a pulsing agony, and I wanted instantly to be unconscious again.

I was assaulted with beeping, buzzing sounds in my ears, and the astringent smells of a health clinic. I'd never been hospitalized before, but I'd spent more than my fair share in them, and I knew instantly where I was. I hated hospitals. They always made me think of my mother, dying in one while I was hundreds of miles away.

It was a struggle to pry my eyes open, and I

instantly flinched, closing them again. I took a few more breaths and tried again. All I could see once the initial brightness passed were a pair of tormented silver eyes.

"Noura," my husband breathed, squeezing my hand. His gaze was blaring into mine with utmost relief. Like he'd been worried he wouldn't get the chance again.

I squeezed faintly back and let my eyes fall shut again. It was all too much. The pain, the confusion, the rush of powerful emotions that punched through me in a jumble.

"How do you feel?" he asked.

"Like I shouldn't have woken up," I replied truthfully, the words coming out in a croak through my tortured throat. I heard him suck in a sharp breath.

Little details were already floating to the front of my brain. The pool. The struggle. The certainty that I was going to die. *Someone had tried to kill me.*

"How long have I been out?" The words scraped out of me, and I instantly decided it was my last question. Speaking wasn't worth the pain.

"Four days." He said the words with a desperate kind of pain. Like four days was an eternity. It kind of felt like it had been from my end, too.

"Pain meds," I rasped.

"Of course," he replied instantly. "I've rung for the nurse."

There was a rustle of noises. The nurse sweeping in, a murmur of talk, the sounds of buttons being pushed. All the while I felt Banks' stroking my hand comfortingly. Vaguely I mused that it was the only thing I felt that wasn't pure pain. The drugs must have been fast-acting because I felt myself slipping away again shortly.

My relationship with consciousness took quite a dive for a bit after that. It was touch and go. I'd wake up, ask to be drugged, and sleep again. This went on for days. As far as I could tell, Banks never left my side. He was always there for my brief lapses into wakefulness. I'd lost count of how many when I woke up to the sound of my father-in-law's voice. I didn't open my eyes. That still hurt.

"You don't look surprised," he was telling someone in angrily, voice drenched in contempt.

"Of course I'm not surprised," Banks replied, just as angry. "*I'm* the one that told you."

My whole body went cold, almost numbing the pain. *Almost*.

What did *that* mean? I didn't like the sound of it, but I was quickly distracted from exploring the thought.

I must have moved in some kind of way,

something that betrayed my wakefulness because the next thing my father-in-law said was, "I think your wife's awake."

I opened my eyes, directly meeting Pasco's. In spite of his disdainful tone with his son, his expression was soft with concern as he studied me. "How are you, dear?"

I smiled wryly. "I've been better."

"Do you remember what happened?"

I did, mostly. It had all returned to me in blurry patches as I drifted in and out. "Someone tried to drown me," I said softly. My throat sounded better, at least, though it still *felt* like hell. I had a horrifying thought for the first time. "Is Chester okay?" He must have been the one that saved me, but that very fact meant he'd most likely been in direct contact with whoever had tried to drown me.

Banks barked out a laugh that was far from amused.

Pasco's mouth twisted into a rueful smile. "He's been sick with worry for you, but other than that he wasn't hurt too badly. Do you feel up for hearing some of the details?"

"Yes," I answered instantly. I wasn't sure if I was, but I wanted to hear it anyway.

"There were multiple individuals involved in the attack. They were well-coordinated. Two of them attacked Vincent, who was waiting at the front of the building. That drew Chester away from his post, and during the time that was happening, a man came after you in the pool."

I listened with a numb sort of shock. This couldn't be real. What reason could someone have to try to kill me, let alone a whole team of someones? It simply made no sense to me.

Pasco kept shooting looks at Banks that were outright hostile. It was so strange. Banks was visibly upset. And there was obviously nothing he could have done about any of it since he wasn't even there when it happened.

"Is Vincent okay?" I asked.

"A few bumps and bruises. He's old, but they underestimated him. He can still fight, and he held his own just fine until Chester entered the fray, and then it was game over. Chester knocked one of them out cold with one hit, which chased the other one off. The whole thing took about two minutes before he went back to check on you, but it was a very close thing.

We'll be upping your security," Pasco continued, as though it was the most normal thing in the world. "Chester and Vincent did as well as they could, but it clearly wasn't enough. All the guys got away while Chester and Vincent were taking care of you."

"Why?" I asked. "Why would they go to so much trouble to hurt me?"

Pasco and Banks shared a look. "They were hired," Pasco answered.

"By who?"

Pasco's nostrils flared. I darted a look at Banks, who wasn't meeting my eyes.

"We're looking into it," Pasco said tonelessly. It was infuriating, but apparently the only answer I was going to get at the moment.

As soon as it was apparent I was staying awake for longer than two minute stretches, the visits began. A sobbing Jovie almost crushed me with affection while Santi told me cheerfully that I was the sixth most Googled person of the week.

Vincent's bruised eyes teared up at the sight of me, and a gruff Chester patted me on the hand and glared at Banks on my other side.

Pasco and Diana visited frequently. As soon as I voiced my concern about missing so much work, Diana reassured me that it was all being handled.

"I've been interviewing new assistants for you since Asha was let go so . . . unexpectedly," Diana added. "I think I've found a good fit. You'll meet her just as soon as you feel up to it."

That felt promising. An assistant certainly sounded more pleasant than a handler.

I caught some of the bits Pasco had left unsaid on the news from my hospital bed as things developed. No arrests had been made but the men involved had all been identified as professionals. Catching them was unlikely, as they'd undoubtedly left the country or gone underground, but they didn't really matter, did they? The real question was: Who had hired them?

CHAPTER
33

My mother always used to say that bad things come in threes, and as far as I've ever been able to tell, she was right.

The blows just kept coming.

The news broke the day I came home from the hospital. It made a much bigger impact than it would have, I think, because I was already getting so much attention due to the attack.

Turned out, Asha held a grudge. Also turned out, NDAs aren't worth a damn when someone wants to take you down with them badly enough.

It was everywhere. Gossip rags. News sites. Talk shows. Vicious Twitter threads.

My secret was out. And maybe it was a slow week in news, or perhaps it was just that outrageous, but it dominated the headlines internationally.

The Bride Catalogue had been outed to the public, and I was its poster girl.

Everything Asha knew came out in one long, vindictive interview. And she knew plenty.

The arranged marriage. The prenup. The rules and requirements of my lifestyle. Way too many of the sordid details from our awkward wedding night. All of it was now public.

A few other names were thrown around, speculated brides and buyers, but none as often or loudly or with nearly as much detail as mine.

For these reasons and more, I became the focus of the scandal in its entirety.

People put things into patterns they can understand. It's only natural. I had done something that most people couldn't relate to so they put me in that other category people create to separate *them* from *us*.

I was dragged publicly. Deeply and often. The internet went after me with an almost religious fervor. Editorials were written about me that were foaming at the mouth with their own sense of self-righteousness. I was cancelled repeatedly on Twitter. All with endless speculation and a few confirmed facts that kept them going for quite a while.

People who rarely agreed on anything could agree that I was trash.

So much judgement from every direction at once. I was overwhelmed.

Men hated me for what I'd taken in the exchange.

Women hated me for what I'd given up. It was ironic how people would use the fact that you made your own choices to use even feminism against you. I was no expert, but wasn't that missing the point just a bit?

I learned a lot about human nature during that news cycle. How quickly the mob could turn against you. How much it *wanted* to. How effortlessly admiration could turn to antipathy, like that had *always* been the path it was fated to take. How deep and powerful of a hold envy held and how it was *always* poised for the natural evolution into a grudge.

It was so personal, the loathing the horde aimed at me, as though the things I'd done had been done to steal from them rather than to enrich myself.

It would be a lie to say it didn't change the way I viewed my decisions. The way I viewed myself. Those were hard lessons.

But not everything I learned was negative. I also discovered that I had inner stores of strength I hadn't discerned before. I could take these hits. They were hard but they could only knock me down if I let them, so I braced myself and faced it with my head held high, and I didn't have to do it alone. Jovie, Chester, Vincent, and even Santi offered me all the moral support I needed.

Banks was wonderful to me at the hospital while I was recovering. He barely left my side. At home, it was different. My disappearing husband started disappearing again. It stung more than I ever thought it could. I thought perhaps he blamed me for the mud being slung his way, which led to resentment on my part, because it was barely more than a speck on his shoes. I was covered in it.

I wasn't well enough to return to work right away, but more jobs were pouring in than ever. The public might hate me, but the model world loved to model drama above all else, and I was draped in more than my fair share of it.

I met my new assistant, Sara, a few days after I returned home. She was a petite, brown-haired girl in her mid-twenties. She was pleasant but no nonsense and a vast improvement over Asha. She quickly got my schedule in hand. I told her to start booking me again as soon as the bruises and swelling went down enough to be covered by makeup.

Outnumbering the job offers were calls and inquiries for interviews. Everyone wanted firsthand scoop from the mouth of the mail-order bride herself. Pasco set me up with specialized PR coaching before I answered even one question. Part of me just wanted to tell the world, 'Yes, I did everything you've heard, and I don't regret one thing. It's my life and my business. Get over it,' but Pasco talked me down. I was told to categorically deny everything. Rumors were being spread that Asha was just a bitter ex-employee looking for a paycheck. The allegations were so outrageous that it just might work. Why would anyone think that a rich, gorgeous young thing like Banks would ever have to pay for a bride?

I wasn't the only one being questioned and coached. We caught a clip of Banks and one of his brothers being called out by TMZ as they left an uptown office building together.

A mike was thrust into Banks' face as a bored sounding voice called out, "Will you comment on the rumors about your wife? Did you really pay an extra five mil to pop her cherry?"

Banks paused, glared. "That's a ridiculous rumor," he said stiffly.

His brother even stepped in. They made a striking pair, of a height with the same dark coloring and light eyes, though to my besotted gaze Banks was better-looking. "Because young, rich, good-looking men often have to pay for sex," his brother remarked scathingly.

"Who is *that*?" Jovie asked. She was deep in the sofa to my right, eyes glued to the screen.

"Banks' brother, Kingston." I thought for a moment and answered, "He's the second oldest."

"I hate him," she said with rueful smile. She couldn't take her eyes off him. "He's just my type. I can't resist beautiful, sarcastic men. Keep me away from that one, Duchess."

For the first time in days, I laughed. "No problem. He's too old for you."

She sent me sly smile. "I won't be underage forever."

I rolled my eyes.

"How many brothers does he have?" Santi asked. "And are any of them gay or undecided? Or hell, a little bit curious. I can't resist beautiful, sarcastic men either."

I laughed again. It felt good. "He has five and I have no clue. Want me to ask?"

"Yes, please," he said cheerfully.

The next breaking news that rocked my world was perhaps the most predictable and by far the most painful.

The attack didn't kill me, and being dragged by the internet didn't break my spirit, but the third blow nearly did.

New rumors started that Banks had gotten back with his ex. And they came with receipts.

A disheveled, smiling Fatima was photographed on multiple occasions leaving Banks' apartment building. And headlines such as: Fatima Leaves her Husband for Banks Castelo, Two Marriages on the Line as Banks and Fatima Reconcile, Castelo Leaves his Supermodel Wife for His First Love.

Piled onto that was the fact that I hadn't seen him since the hospital.

It all painted a dark picture for the future. A picture I didn't want to see because every time I glimpsed it, it felt like daggers in my heart.

When I entered into this, I was unfeeling. There were things that I wanted that made me willing to put up with the conditions of a marriage of convenience.

But that had changed. Now I felt too many things. I'd have gone back to unfeeling if I could have. Especially as time passed and still he stayed away.

When I finally saw him again, I wished he'd stayed away longer.

CHAPTER
34

He hadn't called or paid a visit for weeks when he suddenly showed up at my door. No one else was home for once. It was a mercy. We needed to have this out in private.

He looked like hell. He was wearing a suit like he'd come directly from work, but it was wrinkled, tie gone, half the buttons undone. His hair was wild like he'd dragged his hands through it. I thought at first that he was drunk, but when he spoke I realized he was instead hungover.

Or perhaps, like me, he'd just been hung out to dry.

His eyes were all over me, hungry, wary and worried all at once. "You look much better," he noted.

"You don't," I shot back, arms folded over my chest. I wanted to ask him a million questions

and slam the door right in his face. The two
instincts were warring manically inside me.

He ran a hand through his hair, looking
absolutely miserable. "Let's go to your room.
We need to talk." It wasn't a request.

When we reached my room, he sat on my
bed. He was looking down at his hands like he
couldn't meet my eyes.

This was going to be bad.

"I have to tell you something, but I really
don't want to," he told his lap after a drawn-out,
frustrating as hell pause.

"You've gotten back with Fatima," I said coldly.
It took a lot to say the words with composure.
They were ripped out of the darkest recesses
of my soul, but at least they came out sounding
matter-of-fact.

His head shot up, his eyes wide with shock.
"What? No. *Fuck* no."

Relief flooded me, but not for long.

"It's worse than that," he continued.

My chest started aching again. "What?"

"She's the one who hired those men to hurt
you."

"To kill me," I corrected before the thought
even fully connected. I wasn't altogether
surprised. The idea had been floating on the
edge of my brain somewhere since I'd woken up

in the hospital bed, especially with the cold way Pasco had been treating his son ever since.

He flinched. "Yes. That. It's highly doubtful we can ever get enough proof together to trace it back to her directly in a legal sense, but I'm certain of it." He took a deep breath. "She's not even bothering to deny it, in fact, she's proud of it."

It took me a long time to respond, and when I did, even I was surprised by what came out of my mouth. "How could you have loved someone like that?"

His face twisted up in anguish. "I didn't know she was capable of—"

"Liar," I said softly, the word filled with venom. "You looked scared every time she and I exchanged words." The words seemed to come together in my mind even as I spoke them. "You *always* suspected she'd try to hurt me."

He still couldn't look at me. "I was worried she'd do *something* malicious, something to fuck with your head, but please believe me when I say that I *never* knew she was capable of *this*." He sounded like he was choking on the words when he added, "My father was always right about her."

I had no reason to trust him or my reactions where he was concerned, but somehow I could taste his sincerity in the pain etched all over him and I *did* believe. It help eased at least some of my pain. Enough that I could catch my breath enough to say, "I guess that's why she's been leaving your place at all hours lately." I paused. "To discuss my attack?"

He looked like he was about to be ill. "In part. Listen, she won't hurt you again. I have a *lot* of dirt on her, things she'd never want to get out. And if there's one thing I know about her, it's that she's self-obsessed enough to keep quiet when her vanity's on the line."

Well, that, coupled with my doubled security, was at least somewhat reassuring. The fact that she'd never face real justice? Less so.

"There's more," he said suddenly in a stricken voice.

I felt the blow coming like a shift in the air. It was heavier with his grief. Even so, I still wasn't braced for what he said next.

"She's pregnant."

"She's *what*?" My mind couldn't deal with what had just come out of his mouth. It took a while for me to grasp it, for my brain to absorb it.

I studied him, feeling a little numb.

As with any fresh, *deep* wound, there was too much blood to see the cut.

He looked so wretched that I almost wanted

to comfort him. Almost. That instinct battled with something building inside of me, something stronger than the urge to nurture.

It was the urge to hurt.

No. I didn't *want to comfort him.*

I wanted to hurt him.

And I never wanted to touch him again.

I took three steps back.

He stood, and took one step forward, but the look on my face stopped him there. He took a very deep breath. "Fatima's pregnant," he said the words like a sickness being purged out of him.

"Is it yours?" I barely choked the question out.

He flinched and shrugged. "We don't know yet. There's a chance that it's mine, and a chance it's her husband's. Either way, he's left her. God, I don't know why she wasn't on the fucking pill. She's *never* wanted kids. It makes no sense."

My hands were tingling, but my body felt a little numb. My mind was following suit. "It makes perfect sense. She did it to *keep* you."

He blinked rapidly, like he wanted to weep.

"How far along?" I asked.

"Three months."

I hadn't realized until just that moment what a fool I was. I'd always been aware that it was very unlikely he was faithful to our sham wedding vows, but right then, I realized that I'd always had some kind of pitiful, ridiculous, hopeless wish that I was wrong. I'd been shooting for the moon with that one.

"How *likely* do you think it is that it's yours?" My voice came out surprisingly composed for that bit of desperation.

"Frankly not very. I *always* used condoms. She claims that one of them broke. I don't remember it, but I was very drunk that time, so it isn't *impossible*."

All my mind snagged on was the fact that it had happened more than once, had happened so often that he'd forgotten the time in question.

I took another step back.

I never wanted look at him again.

Never wanted to breathe the same air.

It's funny how all of your priorities can change in a moment. I wondered, somewhat idly, if they'd been changing for a while and I just hadn't been willing to acknowledge it.

I shook off the thought. None of it mattered.

I'd never agreed to this. This was not in the contracts.

I had sold myself; my body, my face, my time.

But I had never agreed to sell my heart. To

have it ripped from me. To have it stomped into the ground under his heel.

I didn't care about the money anymore. Simply did not give one *single* fuck about it.

This hurt too much. No fucking thing was worth this kind of hurt. Certainly not money.

I didn't just have regrets. I had *every* regret. I regretted every moment I'd ever wasted on my despicable, *faithless* husband.

I regretted it enough to walk away from every single thing I'd been promised.

"Were you sleeping with her the whole time she was married?" I asked him.

He didn't have to say the words, the guilt was painted all over his face.

"Look I was not a good guy for a while there," he said haltingly. "But I can be better. I want to be better. I will be better."

So many years they'd played this disgusting little game with each other. Adultery must get them off. As disgust mixed into my bloodstream, it helped to mitigate some of the pain. "You've been carrying on with her all along," I told him in a hollow voice. "We haven't had one moment together that wasn't tainted by her, have we?"

He shook his head, but his eyes were too desperate to trust anything about to come out of his mouth. "That's not true. I swear—"

"Don't swear to me. Don't swear *anything* to me."

His eyes were wide and wild, and his hands kept reaching toward me. Every time he did it I flinched, but though he kept checking himself, he couldn't seem to stop. "Look, I messed up. I messed up bad. But I thought I hated you then. It was only during that first month after the wedding. I was a mess, and I did all kinds of messed up shit right after, more than I can even remember or name, but I've never lied—"

He was right. He hadn't lied to me. He hadn't needed to. I had done all of that work for him.

As soon as I'd started falling for him, I'd started deluding myself without him ever having to utter one deceit. It was no consolation at all.

"I don't fucking care!" I was mortified that it came out as a rabid snarl. There was so much venom in that it made him gasp. "Lies. Truth. Nothing you could say or have said makes any difference. You fucked another woman after you fucked me. You fucked *her*." That. Right. There. *Her*. That was the part that hurt the most. No. Not quite. *Her* having *his* baby. Them being tied together forever. *That* hurt the most. "Nothing else matters. We're *finished*." I laughed bitterly. "We never started. This was *never* a love story, but whatever it was, I want *out*."

I didn't have anything else to say. I tried to walk out of the room without another word.

He tried to stop me. The second he grabbed me, I screamed bloody murder.

He recoiled. "Don't. Please. Don't let her do this."

My eyes narrowed on him malevolently. It was only as my vision blurred through narrow lids that I realized tears were running out of my eyes, down my cheeks unheeded. "She's not the one who did this," I told him quietly, every syllable vibrating with my hatred. With my pain. "This was always a mistake." The words held as much undiluted ache as they did truth. "All of it. I have so much more to offer than this."

"Please, don't do this," he said. "Can we just talk about it some more?"

I hesitated. Even after everything that had happened, I fucking hesitated. When I realized that, it made me so angry that I didn't bother to answer him. He'd see. "Get out."

CHAPTER 35

L ife is full of giving, taking, borrowing, and moving on.

And balance. For the first time in my life, I meant to find mine.

I filed for divorce as soon as possible. It was ugly and messy. It was as distressing as it was essential to my peace of mind. It was both easier and harder than I could have hoped.

There was also some healing in it all. That I had not anticipated.

I hadn't expected it, but I'd needed it.

His family had always been kind to me, but through the divorce they were the kindest of all.

"We understand why you need to do this," his mother told me. She was crying. It broke my heart. "We don't blame you. But please, never hesitate to ask us for anything at all. We've come to see you as our daughter, marriage or no."

"We still consider you family," his father told me gruffly. "We always will. Nothing will change that. Your security team will stay with you. You're too high profile to even consider going without, and after everything that's happened . . . They're clearly a necessary precaution."

I wasn't sure if I should have protested that co-dependent measure, but I didn't. I needed my team, literally and emotionally.

"And you can say no, it's your choice of course," his mother said, "but we'd like to maintain our weekly Sunday Mass and family dinner with you. We'll dine with Banks on a different day to avoid any discomfort for you both."

"And there will be no fight over any of the financials," his father assured me. "We'll treat you right, I promise."

I didn't know what that meant, but I just nodded. I was the one backing out of the agreement, and even if it was unfair, I knew I had no right to fight them on any of it. Getting weekly business guidance from one of the wealthiest men in the world would be more than enough to keep me afloat.

"And aside from any other issues, you're keeping the apartment." Pasco's firm voice was brooked no argument. "That part is nonnegotiable. You're still a Castelo."

Well hell. I felt tears fill my eyes.

The divorce was supposed to hurt bad, but I was braced for the pain, the swift sting of a Band-Aid ripped off clean.

It was the extra blows I wasn't expecting. The slowly festering wounds. The ones that weren't allowed to heal neatly.

I hadn't expected the added ugliness of divorcing someone who'd never really wanted to be married to me, but also wasn't willing to let me go easy.

At first Banks just refused to sign anything, maintaining that he wasn't agreeing to the divorce.

Eventually it came down to a few strange, arbitrary conditions on his part. They were so unexpected and frankly cruel that at first I outright dismissed them.

Finally, just wanting it finished, I agreed to two of them just to get him to sign.

One was a one hour meeting with him each week, a sort of public check-in. The place and time were completely at my discretion. He didn't care if we met for coffee, a meal, or drinks. He just wanted an hour out of every one of my weeks for an entire year after the divorce.

It was a little thing, small enough to seem almost reasonable and big enough to devastate me.

It was as unfair as it was unexpected and something he *wouldn't* budge on, the spoiled, entitled asshole. Only a rich man would come up with such an outrageous condition.

The second was that I be there when he signed the divorce papers. He wanted to have it out again face-to-face. It was cruel, but I was determined to survive it with grace.

We met at his place. Alone with our paperwork. I hadn't seen him for months by this point. I'd flat out refused to be in the same room with him, because I'd known how it would go down.

It was bad.

That thing between us, the one that had shown itself in barest glimpses of touch, pleasure, addictive sensation, raised its ugly head, and it was worse than even my razor sharp memory's endless replays of it.

And I wanted it. Wanted time to roll back and pause just there, with him heaving over me, his ragged breaths puffing against my face, his flesh gliding into mine. His gruff voice calling my name.

And I wanted it gone. All the hours that had led to this craving.

I wanted it wiped forever from my memory as

if it never happened. Wished he and I had never shared the same air.

He was dressed immaculately, not a hair out of place. I was decked out to the nines.

Both of us in our breakup best. Oh sweet vanity.

"Thank you for everything——" I began, looking unflinchingly into his unbearably handsome face. I'd been rehearsing the words.

"Don't thank me," he interrupted in a terrible voice. He grabbed my shoulders in both of his big hands. His grip was hard. His eyes were desperate.

"Don't fucking thank me." He was shaking as he said it, shaking so hard he shook me with him.

I shrugged him off, stepping back. "Thank you for the opportunities," I continued determinedly. "And for the *lessons*." It came out heavy and thick, like something unholy being dragged out of me.

"Stop it," he said.

"Happily. Now sign the papers, and I'll be out of your life for good."

"Don't do this," he pleaded. "And don't say that. Any of it. Take it back. And don't thank me." He was begging by the end, his voice little more than a whisper. "Don't leave me."

I stared at him. "Is it about the money? Is

that it? Will Pasco pull the rug out from under your business once we're divorced?" It was petty, but I wanted to know.

He glared. "My father already withdrew his initial capital. He did it as soon as you filed for divorce. It didn't matter. I already found other backers. *Fuck* my father's money. This has nothing to do with that. This is about *us*. I don't want a divorce."

It was something. I couldn't even lie to myself about that, but I was still resolute. In a matter of months he'd broken my heart in too many places for me to risk it with him again. Imagine the damage if I stayed longer. "This is all for the best." I was certain of it at that point. I turned to leave.

"What if it's not?" he asked my retreating back. "What if it's for the worst? Will you come back?"

I swiveled back, surprising him. "*Why would I?* Give me *one* good reason."

My lips couldn't shape the words, and his heart could not own them.

I love you.

That might have held some weight, but he'd never lied to me. Why start now?

His silence was just the demolition crew I'd needed to clear out the rest of my heart.

I turned back to leave. My hand was on the doorknob when he spoke again.

"I never lied to you." He seemed to pluck the words right out of my brain, throwing them at me like they should mean something. Like they should matter.

"So what?" I spat back. "You think that outright betrayal is less hurtful than lies? Why the hell does it matter that you didn't lie? Lying would've been a mercy."

"It matters because it means that when I do make promises to you, I'll keep them."

"I won't ask for any promises from you, Calder. You're off the hook. It's just what you wanted from the start."

"It's not what I want now."

I couldn't stand the way his anguished face made me want to believe his tempting words. It made me feel vicious. "How's Fatima, by the way? Are you the father?"

He flinched, taking a step back. "I still don't know yet. She's dragging it out as much as possible. I wish she'd just put me out of my misery."

I swallowed hard. "You're doing the same thing with this divorce, you know. Now put me out of my misery."

CHAPTER 36

Banks didn't quite put me out of my misery, not how I'd hoped, but he did sign the papers.

Our weekly coffee dates were beyond strange.

Beyond strange as in stiltedly civil. Almost friendly but *charged*.

Our first one took place in a crowded coffee shop in Midtown Manhattan. I'd picked it out personally for its lack of intimacy. Chances were we wouldn't even get a table to ourselves.

But either I was unlucky or Banks was the opposite because he was there waiting for me, with a relatively private table in the corner for us. Chester pointed him out right after we walked in, but my eyes had already found him like they couldn't even help themselves.

He stood when he saw me. He was painfully

serious in his suit and tie, dark unruly hair slicked back with a vengeance.

He swallowed a big enough lump in his throat that I watched its progress from across the packed room.

He was wringing his hands. He looked nervous and anxious.

He looked like heartbreak and pain and multiple orgasms.

I wanted nothing more than to say fuck it, grab his arm, and head for the nearest mattress. I wanted him to do absolutely anything he wanted with me. My body. My heart.

I was a pathetic creature. All of our contracts had been voided, but it didn't matter. It was as though he owned me still.

I shook off the urge with an iron will. Nothing had changed. No matter how much his eyes melted with sincerity, he was still the man with the pregnant mistress on the side, the man who'd broken my heart with minimal effort in a few short months.

It was smart to get out while I still had any pieces of it left, I told myself firmly and for the *millionth* time.

My feet had been automatically moving me toward him during that whole masochistic thought process, and before I knew it, I was in arms' reach. He grabbed me by the shoulders drawing me close enough to kiss. I thought he was going to do it, the bold, gorgeous bastard, but he merely gave me two firm cheek kisses before drawing away to stare at me solemnly.

I'd taken a very deep breath when he had me close, drawing in his scent. *God, this was going to be* rough.

I was about five minutes late, so as we sat down across from each other I asked, "How long have you been waiting for me?"

His eyes were steady on mine, glittering with some bittersweet thing I was unable or perhaps unwilling to name. "A thousand years."

"Don't," I warned him, voice steady, heart anything but. "Don't try to charm me. I'm only here because you didn't give me any other choice."

He put his hands up as though surrendering, his face unsmiling. "Consider all the charm off, gone for good. How are you? I miss you."

And so it went. I set a timer and left at one hour on the dot.

One week later, we met at a restaurant instead. I'd decided the coffee was a mistake. At least if we ate I'd have something to do with my hands aside from clenching them hard under the table, tamping down the urge to reach for him.

Again, I'd chosen the place. A noisy deli with a line around the block. A mistake again. Standing next to him, even if it was in a jostling crowd, was worse than sitting across from him. Our arms kept brushing. He took my hand once. I snatched it away, flushing.

He was flushing too. "Sorry," he said, his voice absolutely unapologetic. "Habit."

"We weren't together long enough to develop any *habits*," I reminded him.

"Speak for yourself," he returned in a voice that *ached*.

I was hoping we wouldn't get our food until our hour was up, but once again all the luck was on his side. We had sandwiches in hand in under fifteen minutes. We walked a few blocks to Bryant Park and found a table. Even with Chester trailing us it was downright romantic.

Banks nodded to my food as I unwrapped it. He'd somehow talked me over from a salad sans dressing to a turkey sandwich. "At least I can assure myself that you got one solid meal this week."

I rolled my eyes and ate every bite.

Right before we parted he gathered me to him. Modern day men never did things like this. It was something you'd see in an old movie. "I want you," he breathed into my ear. "Come home with me."

What a bastard, I told myself. Even so, I let myself feel everything for five agonizing beats before I wrenched myself away.

The internet had predictably had a field day with us. The divorce, the pregnant mistress, the public spottings, the ever persistent rumors of the Bride Catalogue, all of it was just too perfectly messy not to gossip about. Even I understood why. We gave good headlines. Our messes were the most succulent fodder for the masses.

We were still coming up regularly, and if someone managed to nab a picture of us together post-divorce, they no doubt got a good paycheck for it, and it would unquestionably go viral. We became a regular segment on TMZ.

That picture of us hurt more than the others. Him gathering me close. The harsh longing on his face. The anguish on mine. I returned to it again and again. I must've spent hours studying it.

We looked so right together. It was hard to look at the image, and remember just why we were so wrong.

"It's not mine," burst from him the second we sat down on our fifth mandatory weekly one hour meeting. He was beaming at me.

"Excuse me?"

"Fatima finally took a paternity test. The baby isn't mine." His expression was asking for a reaction I didn't want to give.

Was I relieved? Yes. God, yes. Did it fix even one single broken thing inside me? Hardly.

"What would you have done if it was yours?" I asked him, wanting to lash out at the relief I felt inside of me. "Would you have stayed together for the baby?"

That got the reaction I wanted. His eyes widened in horror. "*Stayed* together?" He sounded offended. He sounded pissed. "We're *not* together. That was never on the table. And I don't know. I never really believed there was a chance it was mine. I suppose I would have been as much of a father as she'd let me, but me and *her* getting back together, I know that's what she was aiming for, but it was not even in the realm of possibility."

I studied him, wondering if I believed it. Their toxic attachment to each other had survived a lot of obstacles. "So her husband is the father?"

"I have no clue. Frankly, it's none of my business and I'm happy with that. She and I are done for good, Noura. I mean it. Her trying to hurt you . . . It put the nail in the coffin of every good memory I ever had of her. Fatima was a habit for me. An affliction. You're a cure."

"I don't want to be your cure. Don't put that on me."

"I didn't mean it like that. It's just . . . I haven't been living right for a while now. Too much resentment for all the wrong reasons. If some relationships bring out the worst in people, the opposite must be true. And *you're* the opposite. I'm not giving up on us, Noura."

"I miss you," he told me on our eighth weekly meet-up. It was a cheap shot straight to my gut. Not even the words themselves, but the way he said them. Like he couldn't keep them in. Like they'd become the whole sum of him.

I figured he just missed the sex. He was my first and only so far, but even I knew we had something rare between us there. If sex was always like that there'd be less fighting in the world and more cases of people fucking themselves to death. "It'll pass," I assured him.

"I want to see you more often. This isn't enough." He said it with such surety, with such an entitled air, that I found myself bristling with outrage.

"That's not for you to decide. You don't value what you don't earn. And your father may have paid for me, but you never had to earn me."

"So give me a chance to earn you."

"How do you propose to do that?" I couldn't believe I'd even said the words. I wasn't going to entertain this madness.

"Let me show you that I can treat you better. That I can be better. I've been celibate, you know. I'm going to wait for you, as long as it takes."

My breath shuddered in and out. He was too much. What a fool I'd been to think he'd ever fight fair. "I can't ask you to do that," I bit out.

"You didn't ask. You shouldn't have to ask. I didn't make you promises before, and even though you won't listen to them, I've made them now. You're the only one I want. I won't settle for less."

That time, I left before our hour was up.

The next time he showed up with an armful of pink peonies, my favorite, smiling like I hadn't cursed him out and stormed off at our last meet-up.

He was courting me, the subversive bastard.

And so it went. I had to miss a few dates because I was traveling for work.

Once he showed up in Hong Kong just to make sure that he wouldn't miss out on our hour.

I tried hard to convince myself that it wasn't romantic of him.

Once we had a big blowout fight in public when he found out about my nude editorial in Vogue Italia.

"First of all, it's none of your business," I told him after I let him rant about it for a while. He was being loud and unconstrained enough that I knew we were going to dominate the news cycle for at least a solid twenty-four hours. "Second, everything is covered."

"You always say that, I'm not sure you know what it means."

I laughed.

He glared. "Let's negotiate. What can I give you to stop you from showing so much skin?"

"When are you going to get it through your spoiled little rich boy skull? I'm done making deals. This isn't your game anymore. I call *all* the shots in my life now."

That week he was the one that did the cursing out and stormed off before our hour was up.

CHAPTER
37

On week sixteen post-divorce I got a strange phone call from a strange number with a strange man on the other end of it.

Fatima's estranged husband, Antoine Beauchamp, wanted to meet me. I said yes mainly out of curiosity, but I'd be lying if I said there wasn't a heavy peppering of spite factoring somewhere in the decision.

We met for dinner at a swank restaurant uptown. For all intents and purposes, it was a date. It certainly looked like one. Camera flashes clocked me from the moment Chester handed me out of the car until I'd walked into the establishment. Someone had tipped them off. Obviously Antoine. I wasn't the only one here operating out of spite. Both of our exes would likely know about our dinner plans before we even touched a menu.

I'd heard a snippet somewhere that Antoine was French nobility, a Count or something, and the moment I saw him, I could picture it. He was tall, slender, and elegant down to the tips of his toes. His dark hair was slicked back attractively, bringing out his large black eyes. He was quite handsome and reeked of old money.

One would think Fatima was out of her mind unless one had seen just what this man was competing with.

He greeted me with a kiss to both cheeks. Camera flashes told me our paparazzi hadn't been limited to the sidewalk outside. I didn't even comment on it. He'd gone a bit overboard, but I could appreciate more than anyone the extreme degree of Antoine's vindictiveness.

We sat down opposite each other and he shot me an appealing, crooked grin. "Noura. Nice to finally meet you. You're even more beautiful in person. I should have reached out earlier. As I'm sure you've noticed, we have a few interesting things in common."

I laughed. "I heard you were a Count. I didn't hear you were a Diplomat."

His eyes smiled warmly at me. "Our exes are fools, aren't they?" he mused.

I liked him instantly. "They are."

"I have a list of every time I could gather that

they were together while she was married to me," he said, like he was just bursting to get it all out. "It's fairly staggering. Everything is dated, so you can get an idea how many times he was with her when he was married to you. Would you like to see it?"

I was agonizingly tempted, but I reined it in, with effort. "I don't think I need to see that at this point. I'm just trying to move forward."

He was on his phone as I spoke, his fingers moving like a flash. "Well, I've sent it to you, in case you're like me and you sometimes need reminders to hold onto your resolve."

He looked up at me, stashing his phone back in his pocket. "At first I wanted to kill him. A part of me still does. But it was both of them. And frankly she's the one that made vows to me. She's the one that deserves the brunt of my contempt for this betrayal."

Something bitter must've run across my expression because next he remarked, "You probably hate her. I don't blame you. But remember that it was him that betrayed you. Don't make the mistake of vilifying her and giving him a pass.

"Oh trust me, I won't."

"But you're still seeing him."

I didn't question why he thought it was his

business. I didn't really care. I just responded, "Yes, but not because I'm taking him back."

"I thought perhaps you may have been swayed by the news that it wasn't his baby."

"It doesn't matter. I'm done. What about you? What will you do if it's yours?"

"You didn't hear? She got rid of it as soon as she found out that Banks wasn't the father," he said with unmistakable bitterness. "To be honest, I'm not sure she didn't fake the whole thing. But it doesn't matter. Nothing could have kept us together. You two were still newlyweds, and I can't say what your marriage was like, but she's been lying to me for *years*, years that I blindly trusted her. Everything I thought we had has been poisoned by her betrayals. Everything about us was a lie. I'm done."

I didn't really know what to say to him. We were virtual strangers with one painful thing in common. I liked him, but didn't particularly want to share any more of my feelings with him.

"Anyway," he continued, waving a hand in the air. "I have leverage over Fatima. So does Banks. Between the two of us, we can guarantee she won't try to hurt you again. We'll use her pride to rein her in. I just wanted to let you know."

"Thank you," I said simply. For someone who

owed me nothing, he sure had a lot to offer. It was surprising and oddly endearing.

"One more thing about that file I just sent you. I know, I know," he said hurriedly as I began to shake my head. "You don't want to look at it, but just so you know, they were still hooking up for almost a month even *after* your wedding."

His words had the opposite effect he'd intended. I'd already known that. Banks had admitted as much, and while he'd said he never lied to me, some part of me had wondered if it had gone on any longer than that. That first month we'd had only one awkward, mandatory night between us . . . That first month we'd been virtual strangers . . . It was almost forgivable.

Almost.

All of that came out before we'd even ordered. The meal passed pleasantly. Clearing the air between us so quickly seemed to set the mood, which was comfortable and easy.

It wasn't until we were saying our goodbyes that we ran into a snag.

"I'd like to see you again," he said intently after he'd kissed both of my cheeks. His eyes were burning into mine, our faces arrested close together.

I blinked at him. "Why?" I asked.

He laughed, pulling back and shattering the

awkward moment. "Can you possibly doubt that I'm attracted to you? You're gorgeous, sweet, and come with the added benefit of effortless revenge. More than effortless, *enjoyable*. I'd be a fool not to at least ask."

"I'd enjoy seeing you again, but I'm not in the market to date," I told him candidly. "I could, however, use a friend."

He was not put off at all. "I think we have a deal, my dear."

"You went on a date," Banks' voice was a wretched attempt at blandness that landed in an arrow straight bullseye onto accusatory.

We were just sitting down for tea on our weekly meet-up. He said it straight off, before we'd even gone through the usual pleasantries.

"It's none of your business," I said calmly. "Even if it was, you have no room to talk. You were *dating* when you were married to me."

Of course he knew I was absolutely right and he was completely wrong, but he couldn't seem to make himself react appropriately.

"Those weren't dates, and you and I were strangers," he pointed out infuriatingly. "I didn't know it was a real marriage, that I *wanted* it to be a real marriage until I'd fucked up too bad to fix it. You know I regret everything."

I didn't say anything to that. What did his regret matter? Was it real? Questionable. Did it mean anything even if it was? Also questionable.

I let the silence stretch out. It was easier for me than usual. My fake date had somehow given me an edge, though just thinking it made me realize I was enjoying that edge too much, which was a problem in itself. Any pleasure I got from our relationship was counterproductive against my objective, which was supposed to be moving on.

"Please," he said suddenly. He was as wild as I was calm. "Please just tell me. I have no right but I *need* to know. Did you fuck him?"

That surprised a laugh out of me. "I don't have to answer that." I paused. "It's insulting."

Strangely that seemed to soothe him. "So you didn't."

I glared. "Of course I didn't. I'm not *you*."

"I get it, okay? The thought of another man so much as laying a pinky on you makes me ill. I wouldn't wish this feeling on anyone. I can't take back what I've done, but I wish that I could. Why'd you go out with him?"

"He asked."

"Just to mess with me, then."

"Maybe that was an added bonus."

"What did you two talk about?"

"None of your business. Drop it, okay?"

He stewed after that. Went into full-on sullen brat mode until it was time to go. And then he went a little crazy again. "Will you see him again?"

I shrugged. "It's possible."

He swallowed hard, his eyes wide and fierce. "Don't fuck him."

I glared at him. "You have no right—"

"I have every right," he said, voice low and ringing with sincerity. "I can be patient. I'll wait for you however long it takes. I *deserve* to wait. But make no mistake—signing some papers doesn't mean I'm not still yours, and you're not still *mine*."

BANKS

The weekly dates were always sweet torture.

I called them dates, she called them meetings.

I memorized them all. One hour once a week. *Memorized*.

Carved in bloody letters on my heart.

First, to look at her, to see her, my eyes taking her in, *in person*—no photo lens between us. It made my teeth clench so hard they ached.

So many rules—don't touch, don't kiss, don't drag her somewhere private. Don't hold on and refuse to let her go after my hour was up.

So much longing. So much deprivation.

I took it all. I deserved it all.

Her beauty is world class and world renowned, but the most devastating thing about her is her smile, and it stung more than a little that she used it more often now than she ever did when she was with me.

I hated myself for stating my case to her again. I had no fucking right, but seeing her with someone else made me too desperate to try to retain even an ounce of my pride, let alone to respect anything as intangible as fucking *fairness*.

No, I didn't have the right, but I was going there anyway.

I got myself under control. Sort of. Barely. Temporarily.

When it was time to say goodbye, I completely lost my mind. I grabbed her, pulling her to me until our faces were close.

Oh God, to smell her, to *feel* her.

"I *need* you," I rasped into her ear.

She looked away, one lone tear running down her face. "You're so cruel, Banks. Why are you like this?"

I kissed her cheek, licking the tear away. "I

haven't been with anyone else," I whispered. "I haven't so much as looked at another woman. I'm still waiting for you. I'll wait forever. I haven't given up, and I *won't.*"

We were both panting.

Chester got between us.

I grabbed his shirt. I wanted to hit him, but I was trying really hard not to. "What the fuck do you think you're doing?" I snarled at him.

He gave me a look that was hard to decipher, but I could see that his eyes were more sympathetic than anything else.

That sobered me up a bit.

"I'm doing my job, and your stunt back there is going to end up as a headline. How about we quit now before you embarrass her even more?"

I looked at Noura. "Let's go somewhere to talk. Somewhere, anywhere with *privacy*. Please, Noura."

She wasn't looking at me, she seemed completely withdrawn, so it shocked me when she answered with, "Just to talk?"

"Whatever you want," I told her, because I couldn't figure out what her question meant.

Chester craned his head around to give her a look. "Duchess?" The word was chock-full of disbelief.

She wouldn't look at him either, and her voice

was paper thin when she told us both, "We'll take my car."

We went to her apartment. She didn't speak to me on the drive. She stayed plastered against her side of the car, face turned away.

I opened my mouth to speak several times, but made myself stay silent. This was the most I'd gotten from her since the divorce, and I was trying hard not to blow it. Besides that, I preferred not to have an audience even if we were just going to talk.

I was dead wrong. She wasn't interested in talking at all.

We didn't make it to her bed; we didn't make it beyond her entryway. The moment the door closed, she gripped me to her, her hands buried in my hair, lips crushed to mine.

I pressed her to the door, taking handfuls of her everywhere. I couldn't touch her enough, couldn't taste her enough. I was deprived of sex in general, but worse I'd been deprived of *her*. The ache was so complete and familiar by now that it had its own pulse, and its own stark place in my soul. I bit her lower lip. She sucked on my tongue.

I shoved her skirt out of the way, ripped her panties, and hoisted her up. She wrapped her legs around me. I didn't undress myself, just braced her with one arm and pulled my dick out. I grabbed her ass with both hands and shoved hard and deep with one desperate, harrowing thrust.

When I was seated balls deep I paused, but only long enough to jerk her top off her shoulders, baring her tits. I moaned at the sight. I wanted to bury my face there while I fucked her, but it was impossible. I was too far gone, needed to fuck her too hard. I took her there, a hell-bent, stand-up fuck powered by unrequited longing and unprecedented abstinence.

I used to turn her away, to avoid the intimacy of eye contact when I took her. It was the opposite now. I made her look at me. Every time she tried to look away I forced her eyes back, bouncing her on my cock with ruthless precision while our gazes drank each other's souls with desperate adulation. "I miss you," I panted at her.

She flinched, dragging my mouth to hers.

So this was not forgiveness. I'd take it anyway. Drink every drop of attention she deigned to toss my way.

In spite of my efforts, she kicked me out of her apartment exactly thirty seconds after I pulled my dick out of her.

I'd always been stubborn, so I still saw it as progress.

CHAPTER 38

NOURA

I worked on myself. I took a few days off a week, my attempt at having a life outside of modeling. I was sought after enough that I could afford to be more selective. I took some online college courses. I thought I would've been good at school if I wasn't so busy trying to conquer the world.

I even went on a weekend vacation to Mexico with Jovie that had nothing to do with work.

I started eating solid meals, putting my health and nutrition before the next days' photo shoot.

I gained ten pounds and that was hard, but I gradually allowed myself to accept that it was good weight. Most of it went to my boobs and hips, which photographed better than I was expecting. The designers who complained or put me down for it went solidly on my blacklist for the future.

And there were more slip-ups. Of course there were. I'm only human.

I gathered my clothes hastily. I needed to get out of there. It was week twenty-one post-divorce, and I'd impulsively let Banks take me home after drinks at The Plaza.

"This can't happen again," I said without looking at him.

"Why not, Duchess? Quit doing that. Drop your clothes and come back to bed. We'll talk about it in the morning."

I shot him a look. "No. We're not doing this. *This* was a mistake. I can't get over you like this."

"*Good*," he said, standing up. "I don't want you to get over me."

"Then what do you want exactly?"

"You know. I want you to give us another chance."

I went completely still. I thought I was over the bitterness of his betrayal, but there it was, rising in me again. "Do you think you deserve another chance? If the roles were reversed, would you give me one?"

"Yes."

"Easy to say when you'll never be in my position."

He grinned. "Never?"

I rolled my eyes. "I didn't mean it like that."

"I hope you did. I hope you're never with anyone else but me for the rest of your life. And you'll never be in that position again either. That's a promise."

I dressed hastily and got the hell out of dodge. I was in the elevator before I burst into tears.

On week twenty-nine post-divorce, I let him see me up to my apartment. A silent Jovie watched us wide-eyed from the living as we walked by. I made a face at her that meant I'd explain in the morning in best friend language.

She gave me two grinning thumbs up, the incorrigible girl.

Roughly two minutes later he was shirtless, on his knees eating me out in my bedroom when I felt something strange on his shoulder. Like gauze. I worried at it with my fingers for a minute before (reluctantly) pushing him away from his extremely distracting activities.

"What happened to your shoulder?" I asked him.

His eyes were a bit glazed over, his hands flying to undo his belt. He licked his lips. "Hmm?"

"Your shoulder. Is that a bandage?"

He glanced back like he had no notion what was on his own body. "Oh that." His hands dropped from his belt and a he grinned. "Take it off. See for yourself."

Reluctantly I rose, walking around him. Tentatively I touched it. It was definitely a bandage. "What did you do?" I asked him.

"Look," he said.

With more than a little hesitation, I pulled the corner back. Raised angry pink flesh met my eyes. "You removed it," I said, feeling a little lightheaded.

"I decided that I'm not a big fan of tattoos anymore, especially *that* one. It was about damn time."

"You'll have this scar forever."

"It's better than the alternative."

On week thirty-eight post-divorce, I stayed the whole night at his place. We fucked like it was the end of the world. Again and again in every way imaginable. I was his putty and every thrust remade me into his pattern. We were a tapestry, and somewhere along the way, we'd been woven together.

I felt more tender and vulnerable than ever the next morning when he struck.

"You know I'm in love with you, right?" He told my back as I was dressing. He said it with utter rawness, like it hurt him but he wanted the pain.

I turned and faced him head on. He approached me, holding my face in both hands. "I love you," he repeated.

Was his love real? I did not know. I needed to test it, taste it, touch it, see it.

Lay my face in his neck to breathe him in. Love? Still not sure.

Lay my ear against his chest, hear his heart beat. Love?

"I promised myself I'd never let myself fall again." His voice was low and rough and raw. "But I didn't know what that meant. In love there's no free will. That's how I know it's real. I couldn't stop it and I can't deny it. This is it for me."

I couldn't choke a word out. My heart is an organ of excess. It is excessive and unrestrained.

It doesn't give a little. It is an overachiever. When it gives, it gives absolutely everything. Somewhere along the way, I'd given it to him, and no matter how I resisted, I wasn't going to get it back.

I acknowledged for the first time then and there that I wouldn't be moving on. At least, not how

I'd thought, because I knew in my bones that the regret would be worse if I couldn't forgive him.

"I can't settle again," I told him, lips trembling, heart wide open. "I can't settle for less than *everything* from you. From both of us."

"Good." His voice was harsh. His hands were firm on my face. His eyes were a wild storm and they were promising me the world. "I don't want you to. I want to give you everything. I'm ready now. And you better fucking give me everything back."

EPILOGUE

Fatima's father's organization went down two years later. He was assassinated by his number two guy, his place raided in a bloody coup in the middle of the night. After that everything folded, and people within started talking, and Fatima, now glaringly lacking in protection, was an easier target.

They could never pin the attempt on my life on Fatima, but she had gotten some eyes turned her way during the process. Those eyes started watching her, thanks to some Castelo influence, and two years after she tried to have me drowned, she was arrested and charged with conspiracy to commit fraud and a slew of other charges that stuck.

The tabloids caught a much sought after picture of her in a prison yard, looking sullen.

Orange was not her color.

I didn't make an honest man out of Banks again for quite some time, though I did take pity on him and let him get rid of his own sterile apartment and move in with me. I wanted to try the boyfriend/girlfriend thing out for a while.

No contracts and no paperwork.

We were married on my twenty-fifth birthday. Possibly happier about it than us were his parents and his brothers, who'd been pressing us to get remarried since the day they found out he'd moved in with me.

The ceremony couldn't have been more opposite than the first time. We went to Bora Bora with a tiny group of family and friends. We said our vows wearing shades and barefoot on the beach. He wore white linen trousers and a matching shirt that was open at the neck. No jacket, no tie.

I wore a barely there slip of a dress the color of the pale aquamarine waves lapping at our feet.

We'd rented out the entire resort and island for two weeks, which wasn't quite so drastic as it sounded, as the whole place only held fourteen small bungalows. By Castelo standards, it was downright humble.

There was no prenup this time, no payoffs, no

contracts at all, just a wedding license and a full heart.

My lips didn't tremble. My hands were steady in his. We pledged our love and commitment for the right reasons for round number two.

This time I said I do with my head and my heart.

He buried both his hands in my hair and tapped his forehead gently against mine. His eyes were snapped with intensity. "'Bout damn time."

The reception was beautiful, informal, and lasted for days. We danced, we toasted, we argued light-heartedly with his parents about how soon we were going to start making babies. I'd long established that twenty-seven was the right age, but his dad would have preferred five years ago at least. Banks held strong that it was my decision, and he was prepared to do his part whenever I was. Diana good-naturedly complained that she couldn't believe none of her sons had made her a grandma yet. All in good time.

Banks and his father were getting along better these days though there sometimes rose a budding tension between them, as though their natures dictated that they butt heads. They would always be too much alike, I thought, but it was much better now.

We fed each other cake, Jovie caught the bouquet, I danced with every Castelo at least three times, and Banks for all the rest. I wasn't numb for the celebrations this time. I filed every little detail away and treasured it appropriately.

This time it was real. This time it was right.

BOOKS BY R.K. LILLEY

THE LOVE IS WAR DUET
BREAKING HIM
BREAKING HER

THE WILD SIDE SERIES
THE WILD SIDE
IRIS
DAIR

THE OTHER MAN
TYRANT - COMING SOON

THE UP IN THE AIR SERIES
IN FLIGHT
MILE HIGH
GROUNDED
MR. BEAUTIFUL

LANA (AN UP IN THE AIR COMPANION NOVELLA)
AUTHORITY - COMING SOON

THE TRISTAN & DANIKA SERIES
BAD THINGS
ROCK BOTTOM
LOVELY TRIGGER

THE HERETIC DAUGHTERS SERIES
BREATHING FIRE
CROSSING FIRE - COMING SOON

Made in the USA
Monee, IL
11 August 2024

63653734R00243